Writing Baseball
THE SOUTHERN ILLINOIS UNIVERSITY PRESS SERIES

# Man on Spikes

# Man on Spikes

---

ELIOT ASINOF

*New Foreword by Marvin Miller*

Southern Illinois University Press
Carbondale and Edwardsville

Printed in the United States of America

08 07 06 05 6 5 4 3

*Library of Congress Cataloging-in-Publication Data*

Asinof, Eliot, 1919–

Man on spikes / Eliot Asinof ; foreword by Marvin Miller.

p. cm.

I. Title.

PS3551.S54M36 1998

813'.54—dc21

ISBN 0-8093-2200-5 (cloth : alk. paper)

ISBN 0-8093-2190-4 (paper : alk. paper)

97-43204

CIP

The paper used in this publication meets the minimum requirements of American National Standard for Information Sciences—Permanence of Paper for Printed Library Materials, ANSI Z39.48-1984. ∞

**Writing Baseball Series Editor: Richard Peterson**

# Contents

# Foreword

## *Marvin Miller*

There is no scarcity of baseball books. For almost a century publishers have marketed baseball novels, essays, commentary, biographies, "as told to" autobiographies, and much more. With rare but notable exceptions, these works have been less than literary gems for a variety of reasons. Prominent among these reasons is the failure to deal with reality—the tendency to ignore facts and instead to give credence to mythology and management handouts.

Eliot Asinof's *Man on Spikes*, a work of fiction, is infinitely more true than the vast bulk of nonfictional books that have been published. It was written in the mid-1950s when most serious baseball writing consisted of topics combining fact and fiction but presented as fact: analyses of the game played on the field, baseball strategy, the development of the baseball farm system, the imaginary primacy of the office of the commissioner, and the "beneficence" of the owners who, haltingly and reluctantly, followed the success of the Jackie Robinson signing by slowly adding more players of color, based on their ability, to the major leagues.

There was also continued attention to the aftermath of the short-lived Mexican League, which had recruited major leaguers in the late 1940s. The official line was that those who played in the Mexican League should be barred for life from playing professional baseball. Players, who had been exploited by their American owners and who had accepted, after their contracts were completed, offers of double and triple their former salaries from the Mexican League, were almost universally charged with "disloyalty."

Asinof bought none of the balderdash being peddled then (and later). His novel, *Man on Spikes*, relates the story of a talented baseball player who knew everything about the game except the way its finances worked—the problem of almost every professional player before the formation of the players' union in the mid-1960s. A scout discovers him, recognizes his talent, and offers a signing bonus of $2,000—more money than his coal miner father made in a year. Reality sets in when he arrives at the minor league club's training camp. At first he is paid nothing. Then, in the kind of one-sided, take-it-or-leave-it "negotiation" that took place without a union, his $2,000 is whittled down to $250. He loved the game. He took it.

The central character of the novel endures a baseball life that was, and is, all too common when an employee, whether a factory worker, a white-collar employee, or a professional baseball player, confronts an industry allowed to organize and operate as a monopoly. Asinof's player, despite his skills, spends sixteen years in the minors and in the army before his first opportunity (his "cup of coffee") in the major leagues at the age of thirty-five. Those who marvel today at the salary of a modern major leaguer (who, of course, in most cases had to make his way through years in the minors first) would do well to read this work to get some perspective and a reminder of the way it used to be in the "good old days."

Mr. Asinof's sharp eyes and ears seemed to miss little or nothing about the ways and mores of professional baseball, despite the distractions and obfuscations of baseball officialdom and its all too willing collaborators in the media, in the courts, and in Congress. He describes incidents of deliberate lies told to players by general managers and owners to obtain the signature of a disgruntled player on an unsatisfactory contract. It reminded me of a time before players had any knowledge of other players' salaries. For example, a prominent major leaguer was induced to sign a contract after his general manager told him the salary offered was the fourth highest on the club, exceeded only by three acknowledged superstars; anything higher, he was told, would throw the club's salary structure out of whack. Later that year, when the union, the Player's Association, secured all of the salary information for the first time, the player was infuriated to discover that his salary was only the eighth highest on his club. (The year before, he had played in 158 games, led the club in RBI's, and had the second highest batting average on the team.)

In the 1950s, virtually every writer bought the nonsense that the commissioner of baseball was an all-powerful being, a czar he was most frequently called, and that he had total control over everyone in the game, including the owners. His charter supposedly was to represent impartially the interests of the owners, the players, officials of all kinds, umpires, the fans, and the general public! The failure to explain how these obvious conflicts of interest could be resolved seemed to bother few. The discrepancy between such a description of function and power on one hand and the reality on the other was mind-boggling. The commissioner was only an employee of the owners, selected by them, paid by them, given only the limited functions the owners were willing to cede to him temporarily, and when his actions or inaction displeased the owners, fired by them. (Except for Commissioners Kenesaw Mountain Landis and A. Bartlett Giamatti who died in office, every single commissioner has been shown where the real power lies by being discharged during the term of his contract or advised that he would not receive a contract renewal.) Since no commissioner has ever had one cent of his own invested in the game, it should surprise no one that the multimillionaire owners of the major league franchises who hire, pay, and fire commissioners are the real possessors of power. Such facts were virtually unknown to the fans and the public in the 1950s (and are still unknown to some in the 1990s) for the obvious reason that most baseball writers of the era were either ignorant of the facts or chose to play the owners' game and bypass discussion of the true nature of the baseball cartel.

In this context, to read Asinof's 1955 account of the actual role of the commissioner of baseball is refreshing. In one instance, the protagonist of *Man on Spikes* appeals personally to the commissioner concerning his discovery that numerous owners had violated baseball's own unilaterally established rules so that a veteran owner could keep the player under his control in the minors even though major league clubs had agreed to offer him a major league contract. Such an appeal to the owners' handpicked figurehead to thwart the owners' scheme was, of course, futile, but it was consistent with the fairy tales players were told, and largely believed, about the neutrality and authority of the commissioner.

What may bring the reader up short is the realization not only that professional baseball players endured primitive working conditions in 1955 but also that minor leaguers (who outnumber major leaguers by more than five to one) experience essentially the same situation more than forty years later. Although some terms and conditions of employment have been improved, mostly because of circumstances brought about by the Major League Baseball Players Association, in one significant way today's minor league players are worse off than their counterparts in the 1950s. In all the years leading up to 1965, players who contemplated turning professional had the rights of their fellow citizens: they could talk to and deal with as many prospective employers as were interested and could decide which offers they thought were in their best interests. They did not become pieces of property without the basic right to change employers if they wished until they signed their first professional contract. After that, of course, they were without the initiatives taken for granted by other working people.

In 1965, however, the cartelists who ran baseball decided to close the loophole amateur players had been allowed. A draft was established. Baseball arrogated to itself certain of the rights of a sovereign government. Henceforth, an amateur player, usually in his last year of high school, although he had not signed a professional contract or any other similar document, was told that if he wished to play professional baseball he would have to contract with the one baseball organization that had "drafted" him. Failure to agree on whatever terms the drafting organization cared to offer barred him from playing professional baseball anywhere. It was (and is) no different than if potential accountants, plumbers, actors, writers, or teachers were informed that there was only one employer in their respective fields for whom they could work—on whatever terms were offered by that firm—and that they were barred from working in their chosen fields unless they contracted with the drafting employer and accepted its terms.

How this monstrous limitation on players' rights has been allowed to exist for decades is worthy of serious study. It seems certain that this tolerance is not unrelated to the failure to communicate to the public in truthful fashion about the nature of the baseball monopoly cartel. No presidential administration, Democratic or Republican, has lifted a finger. No attorney general or United States Attorney, regardless of political party, has ever taken action. The Supreme Court, whether its composition was "liberal" or "conservative," has not shown a glimmer of understanding of the illegality of the amateur baseball draft (or of other equally illegal practices of the baseball cartel) despite its three opportunities to remedy the situation. No Congress, no matter which major party was in the majority, has done more than hold hearings and issue hot air! Despite the almost unbelievable restrictions imposed by the baseball monopoly in numerous states and cities in this country and in other nations as well, the same members of Congress who profess, for the benefit of their constituents, that they have great concern for the rights of the citizens of Hong Kong or Beijing, apparently could not care less about the rather important right of their own constituents to work and follow careers of their own choosing.

*Man on Spikes*, a 1955 publication, marks Mr. Asinof as one of the few writers who was ahead of his time. His depiction of players' real problems: the nature of the relationships between player, owner, media, club, and league officials; the similarity of the baseball commissioner to the Wizard of Oz; and many other insights was most unusual eleven years before major league players formed the first legitimate union in team sports, seventeen years before the first successful player strike, twenty-one years before the union established free agency rights for major league players, and thirty-nine years before the club owners revealed publicly their belief that a baseball commissioner served no useful purpose.

Mr. Asinof's work demonstrates that he has been a prophet—with honor.

Mickey Rutner, *right,* with Connie Mack.
Photo courtesy of Eliot Asinof, from the author's collection.

# Preface

When I was seven, I lived two blocks from the Alamac Hotel in New York where Babe Ruth was staying. On Saturday mornings, I'd wait for him to come out, eager to get as close to him as I could. One morning, he stopped right in front of me, said "Hi ya kid!" and ran his giant hand through my hair. Transfixed, I ran home as though I'd been touched by God Himself. My father took me to the Yankee Stadium that afternoon and the Babe knocked two out of the park. I would never forget that day.

Twenty years later, in 1947, I went to the Stadium again, this time to see my friend Mickey Rutner play third base for the Philadelphia Athletics. It was an end-of-season game of no consequence to the league standings, but for Mickey, after four years in the minors, plus three in the military, it was special. He was finally in the majors for a twelve-game cup of coffee. It was marvelous to see him knock in two runs off the great relief pitcher, Joe Page, then start a slick late-inning double play to preserve the lead. I would never forget that day either.

We had played ball together in 1940 in a top-rated college league sponsored by big league clubs, and I would have bet my glove he would go all the way. (Even our skipper, Bill Barrett, a hard-ass ex-Red Sox outfielder who called us "Hitler's Hebes" was smart enough to trade me and keep Mickey.) Rutner was no Ruth, but this was definitely where he belonged. The A's, however, had the great Hank Majeski on third, and they loved Mickey in Birmingham, Alabama, where he led the Southern Association in hitting. So they sent him back in 1948, again and again breaking big league promises, refusing to trade him to big league clubs that wanted him, six more seasons in AA and AAA until he quit, thirty-four years old, with a wife and three kids, without ever playing another big league game.

That year, 1953, I published my first short story, "The Rookie," about an aging ballplayer who finally gets his chance in the majors. To my editor, Vance Bourjaily, it was the genesis of a novel. "Baseball fiction seems to be all fluff and fable," he said. "This could be something real. Only *you* can do this!" Heady stuff for a neophyte writer. But it was all I needed to get me started. I met with Mickey and compared notes. Was this to be a story about the plight of a Jewish ballplayer? We talked with Cy Block, who'd been up for a three-season cup of coffee, and Cal Abrams, who had played for the Brooklyn Dodgers, and the great Hank Greenberg, Hall of Famer. Was there anti-Semitism in front office decisions? Did minor league managers and scouts tend toward prejudice? Does a bear dump in the woods? But the real story was much larger than that. To make my hero a Jew would distort the impact that *all* ballplayers were victimized. Too many didn't make it for arbitrary reasons. Like wearing eyeglasses. How could a ballplayer be any good if he wore glasses? Casey Stengel would testify before a congressional committee investigating monopoly practices that Japanese ballplayers were not being excluded; they simply weren't good enough "because they had little fingers!" Ballplayers in those days were held in virtual bondage, owned outright, forced to agree to contractual terms dictated by club owners for as long as they chose to own them. If a player refused to accept such terms, he did not play organized baseball anywhere.

As it was with Mickey Rutner, so it was in *Man on Spikes*, with its hero, Mike Kutner. He was used, victimized by the system that made up its own reasons to exploit his talents. He is, then, like so many of us in all walks of life, an unsung hero who never makes it. Everyone knows that life isn't fair. What remained for me, the writer, was to make sense of it. I had found a theme that dominated most of my work for years to come.

* * *

This new edition, published over forty years since I first wrote *Man on Spikes*, is a special joy. Long since out of print, several times optioned by motion picture companies but never produced, it has become something of a collector's item. Its survival is a wonderment.

I offer one last wrap-up note: in my 1969 edition of *MacMillan's Baseball Encyclopedia*, the stats of George Herman Ruth's record has thirty-three lines. Below, Mickey Rutner's has one single line. But they're on the same page, by God.

This book is dedicated to Mickey.

# Man on Spikes

# 1 *The Scout*

Behind the grandstand the late afternoon sun moved around a big tree and poured its sticky heat into him. He looked up from his hard, backless seat in the rickety bleachers and cursed the big tree for not moving with it. He picked out a shady section and scrambled over the squealing high-school kids who looked at him as if he didn't belong there.

Durkin Fain chewed on his cigar and thought sullenly that maybe he didn't; it always gave him the willies to scout a high-school ball game.

Then he heard the crack of the bat ring out clear and echo off the old brick wall in deep center field. The ball sizzled over the second baseman's head and rose like a plane taking off into the wind. He watched the kid leave home plate in a sudden spurt and start his run around the hard infield as if he were chasing a greyhound. Four hundred feet away, the outfielders converged on the drive as it bounced into the wall. In the stands they screamed at the kid to beat the relay in, knowing that the two runners ahead of him had tied up the game.

The old scout stood now with the rest of them, and his eyes followed this kid as he flew around the bases, hitting each one perfectly with his inside foot without breaking stride, as if he were accustomed to this extra base run. He rounded third and seemed to pick up speed as the throw came in, pulling the catcher a few feet up the line. They had him beat, but the kid suddenly switched his slide and fell adroitly away from the big mitt as his elusive body skidded over the plate in a wild cloud of dust.

There was no doubt about it; he was safe.

Durkin Fain sat back with a broad grin, shaking his head in amazement. In twenty-five years of baseball, from the sand lots to the major leagues, he had never seen a better exhibition of circling the bases. Here, in a stinking coal-town high-school game. For a moment, he even forgot the strong wrists that had clobbered that shot against the wall like a cannon ball. It was the running that amazed him.

Smart . . . this kid Mike Kutner was smart. He played ball like there was a right way and a wrong way. Fain remembered the other day how he pushed a clever two-out bunt past the pitcher to drive in the winning run . . . and later how he trapped a fly ball in short center field to start a difficult double play that saved the game. Kutner did everything the right way. The scout thought, How many punks in the majors even know there's a difference?

As he watched Kutner trot out to center field, working in the pocket of his glove, fondling the leather like it was a dame, he could sense the kid's love for baseball. That was something Durkin Fain always looked for.

Then he looked at the giant, lumbering third baseman they had sent him down from Chicago to sign, and the thought disgusted him. He wrenched the sloppy cigar from his mouth and threw it away. The dumb punks . . . goddamn Jim Mellon and the dumb punks that kiss his butt. They hear about some oversized palooka who swings from the heels and can drive a ball 500 feet against the patsy pitchers, and they itch all over to corner him. For three games Durkin Fain had watched him, a big country clown who played ball like he didn't know three strikes were out. This giant would sit sprawling on the bench, mute and patronizing, while the kids half his size yelled and scrambled and played their hearts out for a few runs. When it was time for him to hit, he'd strut pompously to the plate, swinging four bats with one hand, just to tickle his giggling fans. Then for a brief moment, he'd be alive, digging in with his big feet, shaking the fat bat at the timid pitcher who'd heard of his mighty wallops. The kids in the stands would laugh at the outfielders as they turned and marched back a dozen steps to a new position, ready for what might follow. The chucker would close his eyes, rear back, and stupidly try to throw it by him. The bat would slash viciously around as the big body pivoted for the kill. If the pitch was where he liked it, up and away it went, and it didn't matter where the outfielders waited. The big frame would lumber around the bases, ready to laugh at the kidding of the stingy coach who said he always regretted losing baseballs.

Sure, nothing else matters. If he can belt 'em that far, grab him. Let him belt 'em up in Chicago; that's what the crowd likes. Who knows? He may be another Ruth. If someone else wants him, dangle a check in front of him. But sign him! Sign that big man!

The big man . . . always the big man these days. If he's big enough, take a chance on him. Durkin Fain thought back a half-dozen years, of his losing battle with the front office. He recalled when Jim Mellon had been after some 250-pound ox from Texas who was said to murder them, and the boss had told him to go down and get the giant. The scout had grunted at the meager information they had.

"You're just buying weight," he had growled, ". . . at fifty bucks a pound!"

"We decide that, Durk!" they hollered back at him.

"But you gotta be sure." He repeated their shibboleths. "Suppose he can't field?"

"We'll teach him," they snarled. "As long as he can belt 'em!"

"Suppose he can't run bases . . . or throw?"

"We'll teach him!" Jim Mellon repeated, beginning to lose patience. "You get him, Durk. Get him before anyone else does. Make him put his John Hancock on a contract!"

He couldn't resist a sarcasm: "Suppose he can't write?"

They didn't even smile. "*You* teach him that, Fain!" And they turned from him to the inner recesses where they kept the good booze.

So he had scouted the Texas ox and watched the 250 pounds of sheer stupidity, but it was too taxing on his dignity to sign the monster. Another club had nailed him, publicity and all.

When he came back empty-handed, Mellon was livid.

"Who do ya think you are?" the boss yelled at him. "We said to grab that man. Who are you to say no?"

He protested. "But he's no good. He's a bum!"

"He belts 'em. I heard he belted one for you, Fain—a mile and a half, right before your lousy eyes."

"He's a bum, I tell ya. I'm sure. He'll never make good in the big time. He's too dumb!"

They groaned at his defiance, ridiculing his twenty years of experience. Mellon condescended to reason with him.

"Look, Fain. Baseball has changed since you played it. It's the goddamn long ball they want now. If a man can belt 'em that far, he goes up. The clever boys can only wave at the damn apple as it disappears over the wall. That's baseball today. It just ain't a little man's game!"

Through the years, Durkin Fain stuck to his principle, that it takes a lot to make a ballplayer. He watched the Texas ox belt a few in the majors and then go back to Texas as fast as he came up. But this proved nothing to the front office. Fain continued to look in odd places whenever he could, always for the hustling kids with savvy as part of their talent and he found good prospects cheap. But the big shots wanted the long-ball hitters, and kids had to be six-foot-two to qualify.

Mellon squelched him at every turn, ignoring his telegrams on unknowns. They were too small, it seemed.

So here he was again, with the familiar assignment that insulted his love for the game. Baseball was getting to be big business these days, not like it used to be when he played ball. Gradually, it was moving into the hands of the big-money syndicates, the promoters. Anybody could run a ball club . . . all you needed was a couple of million bucks, and a flare for publicity stunts. Put on a circus with dancing girls, free orchids, motorcycle races. Please the crowd, boys; give 'em what they want most! Everything was big—real big. The front office was decorated like a banker's sanctum, replete with receptionists and secretaries and intercoms. The plush carpets were not for cigar butts, and you couldn't even find a spittoon, except in the can where you didn't need it. The old scout felt a growing antagonism for the new philosophy, the new baseball; and it jarred his relationship with the great game.

Sure, they blamed it all on the public. The public wants the long ball! It recently had its taste of the great Babe Ruth and his sixty home runs in a season. It seemed so easy to win games that way. There was a dramatic finality to it that any child-mind could understand. There it goes, up and out, sailing over the outfielders, miles out of reach, into the bleacher bedlam and that hysterical adulation! It doesn't matter that Babe Ruth could have won more games with a timely, well-placed bunt or a tap through that crazy, unbalanced infield. Fain often argued that the great Babe would execute such a simple maneuver only to show how clever he actually was. Baseball had become less a question of winning games than the way you won them.

Now as he watched the clumsy klutz idling off third base, holding his glove like it was an old rag, waiting for the last inning to start (did he even know the score?), Durkin Fain saw the epitome of the new game. Here he was—the big slugger, the big blast, 500 feet every couple of days. The kids in the stands behind him were like the big-league fans. They squeal at your naked power, big man, and you're the hero. You could probably pick any one of these bright-sweatered tomatoes for a post-game roll in the grass. But for my dough, you stink, buster; and you'll always stink, because you're a one-track ballplayer with a no-track brain. Sooner or later you kick away the game with a boot or a blunder, and that screaming, highly touted shot over the wall is a total waste.

Satisfied with his angry appraisal, Fain lit a fresh cigar. It turned him immediately back to his job, this assignment, and the anxious reality of his dwindling status with the front office. There was no doubt about it; they wanted him less and less each year. Unlike a lot of others he knew in the business, he took his job with a thorough seriousness. Stubbornly, he clung to the standards of judgment in baseball that had made him a first-rate ballplayer in his own day, refusing to adulterate them for the showmen of the present. Too much of him had gone into the baseball world to change those standards. It would have been an insult to all the years he had played and scouted, discovering and developing real talent. His mind was ever ready to list the fine ballplayers who were in the majors as a result of his scouting genius. He was proud of them. They were smart, reliable, aggressive. They had the plus factor that made them invaluable to the club, playing furiously for the win, always ready with some extra piece of business on the diamond that helped the team. Even Jim Mellon thought them valuable. But few of them were sluggers in the big sense of the word. He knew the front office considered this his grave limitation.

One trouble was that the big hitters were everybody's meat. Find any rawboned kid who could blast the apple a mile and you'd wait in line with the other scouts to get to him, dangling the ever-increasing checks before him, promising him the world if he'd come to papa. It was no longer scouting; it was a crazy kind of supersalesmanship. Fain would read the crap in the local gazettes: "Who will capture 'Tiny' Torpe, the sensational high-school home-run king? The scouts are swarming to Austin Oval like flies. . . ."

Like flies . . . it was true. He grunted. Like flies around garbage. Durkin Fain thought, There ain't no flies on this Kutner kid. Watching this boy, he was fascinated by what seemed to him the obvious potential. The kid was young, say nineteen or so, but he looked like he'd been playing scientific baseball all his life.

The scout ached at the ridiculous waste of money and talent involved in his assignment; he felt depressed by his position as agent for such stupidity. But this was his job and he needed it. He determined to swallow his revulsion as cleanly as he could, and get it over with quickly. What the hell, he thought, you got no real choice in the matter. In the front office Jim Mellon tells you to look him over and sign him, so you gotta go sign him. But this "look him over" business is always the big rub. You do the looking, and if you don't like him and let him go, you're in the doghouse. Jim Mellon is the boss and he wants this man, but he wants you to take the blame if he turns out to be a punk. They got you coming and going. Fain, you just gotta learn to do what they pay you for.

So he tried to think maybe he was wrong about the big guy. Maybe he could really bust 'em in the big time. Maybe they could train him to be a passable glove man. The Kutner kid was smart; but did he have everything else needed to make a big leaguer? The scout tried to tell himself he wasn't sure. You don't know, Fain. You don't know, do you? And you're not here for this kid. Watch the big guy. You've been wrong before, Fain. Admit it. So what if the big guy ain't your type of ballplayer? It don't mean he can't make good. Durk, you just gotta learn to be sensible.

Then he watched the last inning and knew what he would have to do. He saw the infielders grow shaky, trying to protect their one-run lead. With the tying run on and two out, he saw the feeble grounder hopping across the diamond at the big hero on third base, and he knew by the look on the slob's face he would bobble it. The routine was familiar enough. This punk, the big slugger, was a million kids climaxing their adolescent dreams of glory in one feverish nine-inning splurge for the big-league scout in the stands. For twenty years, Durkin had heard them in the dingy locker rooms, oiling their unlimited ambitions for a shot at the big time. Every two-bit high-school hero had one foot in Yankee Stadium with 60,000 fans screaming at the mighty blasts he hit in his reverie. Every high-school club had a couple of them, each one a star to his papa or his babe, claiming all he needed was a decent break. As he warmed up before the game, he could smell out the scout in the stands like a bloodhound, trying to believe the old man was there specifically to see him.

But when the chips were down and the going got tight, the old fire would suddenly burn low. Now, Durk watched the crucial ball bouncing like an angry weasel at the big guy, and he knew he'd be wetting his pants, afraid of sudden death. He could almost see him praying for the bad hop that would alibi him. The scout was bored with that look. And then, as he watched him nervously trying to find the handle, exasperated at his fumbling, he would have bet the punk would finally pick it up and throw it wildly away. He saw the ball sail five feet over the first baseman's frantic reach, putting the tying and winning runs in scoring position, and he threw away his fresh cigar in disgust.

Goddammit, you dumb punk, the runner had you beat four steps anyway! Everyone ain't got as much lead in his pants as you! You don't think . . . too damn dumb to think. Get in a tight spot and you don't know whether to piss or go blind.

After all these years, Fain was tired of it. He wanted to see guts out there.

He felt lonely now; the big oaf had deserted him. He should have signed him the last inning when he still looked like he was all there. He thought of telling Jim Mellon he tried to sign this guy, but he didn't want to play ball, wanted to be a coal miner. He had a special bat made with a pick on the end, and he loved to swing it against the black coal and watch it crumble under his great power. That was his distinction. What the hell, everyone was a coal miner in this town. . . .

He remembered he had thrown away a fresh cigar as a tribute to his anger and it made him angrier. He started to jump down under the bleachers to find it, like a kid after a lollipop. But then he heard the resounding crack of the well-tagged baseball, and his mind immediately focused on the long, high drive soaring into deep right center. The base runners took off for the promised land, and the kid, Mike Kutner, out there in the daisies gave chase like a bird.

Durkin Fain watched him turn his back on the ball and set out for the next county, for that blast had extra bases written all over it. He knew what that kid was thinking, for the whole game, win or lose, was riding on that blow. He sensed Mike's assurance as he legged it like a racehorse. It was as if he smiled as he ran, confident that he'd be there when it came down, sure that the ball would drop into the well-oiled leather pocket.

God, how that kid could move!

The ball sailed high into the haze, the thick coal dust of the area making it difficult to see. It headed toward the brick wall, over 350 feet from home plate. Durk strained his eyes, wondering whether it would reach the wall, waiting through the endless seconds of flight, feeling the wonderful exhilaration of suspense. A whole game compressed into a single moment.

Suddenly he stood up with the squealing children in the stands and, in this game-ending crisis, unreasonably swore an oath that he would make this play the crucial test for the kid in center field. Grab it and you're the kid. Grab it, Kutner, and you're the one I want! Not the big guy. You! To hell with the big dumb bastard! What kind of stuff you got in you, kid?

Kutner ran with his back to the diamond, driving his powerful legs hard over the bumpy ground. Leg it, boy, leg it! Durkin watched the ball sinking in the distance, closer now to the imposing brick wall. Turn now, Mike . . . now! Was it going beyond him . . . into that wall? Turn, kid, and pull it in!

Then he saw the chase ending, the fielder's driving, finishing spurt as the ball sped toward the wall. At the last second the boy swerved, reaching over his shoulder with his open glove. The ball fell securely into the leather pocket as the momentum of his body drove him crashing into the solid bricks.

They all gasped as they heard the contact, and saw the boy crumble to the ground. But few doubted that the kid had held on to it. The ball was still in his glove.

For a moment the old scout just sat there as the others rushed out, trying to gauge the full measure of this boy's remarkable qualities. It was a great catch with talent and guts written all over it. The act of a ballplayer playing to win.

Finally he walked out to the wall where the crowd had gathered. The kid had the wind knocked out of him, probably nothing more, but they were rigging up a stretcher to take him home, afraid of other injuries. Fain looked at the boy and reached down to draw the baseball glove from his hand, but the fingers were clasped tightly.

Then he saw the faint smile on the kid's face, for the ball was white and shiny in the pocket.

At once he was confronted by the pledge he had made to himself a moment before the catch. He thought of Jim Mellon in the front office and in his mind he heard the harsh rebukes of a boss who'd been crossed once too often. Durkin winced, knowing full well the possibility of being fired for it. There was no glamour in being fired, even if he was right; this job was everything to him. What the hell would he be without it?

He looked down at the kid and felt the glow rush through him, and he smiled back. It was not in him to resist his instinct, all of his experience.

"Kutner," he said, "I'm going to make you a major leaguer!"

People looked at him curiously. There was silence as the boy struggled to catch his breath. In a moment he looked back at the scout.

"I hope they got softer walls up there," he said. The crowd laughed, relieved, and they put him on the stretcher.

Durkin Fain did not laugh, for the remark scratched at the nagging doubts lying within him. Softer walls? Softer nothing; the higher, the harder, for baseball was a business, a frantic scramble with no holds barred. A fool's fight for the top, and softies ain't good climbers. Sure, there's room for talent. Fain believed that; more, he lived by it. But talent alone was no guarantee, for there were too many dumbheads along the way hunting for lousy reasons to smother it.

"No, kid," he said finally. "Just harder heads."

He watched them cart the boy away, his mind churning with an awareness of the struggle ahead. For Mike Kutner was not the big power hitter they were searching for. You had only to look at him to see he was kind of small. And besides —Fain looked again—this kid wore glasses.

# 2 *The Father*

Old Joe Kutner took his time as he let his tired body off the bus. On the curb, he tucked his lunch box under his arm and fumbled for a cigarette. The late afternoon sun was full and hot in his face, and he kept his eyes shut as he lighted up. Not yet accustomed to the glare, he made for the shade of a few trees along the street and pulled his cap lower to shield his eyes. He remembered something about how his son would come home from playing baseball with deliberate smudges of mud under his eyes. Once Joe had scowled at the boy: "What in hell is that for?"

And the kid had told him that it deadened the glare in the outfield when the sun was low. Joe thought of his own face, a miner's face, black and dirty, scarred with forty years of coal dust ingrained in every crevice of his skin, covered now with a fresh layer of filth. He found it almost amusing that for all his smudges, honestly earned, he could still hardly see through the brightness of the late afternoon.

Crazy . . . crazy goddamn kid, he mumbled sourly. Crazy goddamn game.

He was fully aware that he would be passing, as usual, the brick wall of the baseball field on the street. In the distance he could hear the wild adolescent screams that always grated on his nerves. It was a daily thorn in his side, for the yelling was a constant reminder that his son was amongst them. He used to toy with the thought of going home by a different route, of bypassing the park and the irritating backwash of all his animosities. But Joe Kutner was too proud, too direct a man for detours. The bus stopped at that corner, closest to his home, and this was the shortest route. He would go home this way and only this way.

He started to cross the street and his squinting eyes missed the overhanging hedge that scratched at his face. He felt the sudden sting and gingerly fingered the scratch on his dirty cheek.

"Sonofabitch!" he spat.

And, as if by signal, a sudden burst of high-pitched enthusiasm rose from the ball park, an unseen cheer to punctuate his profanity, and it galled him further. Despite himself, he let this annoyance set off a chain of worn and bitter memories of his son's love for this stupid game.

There had been no games in Joe Kutner's life. He had spent it in the black holes of the earth, clammy and slimy with coal filth, just as his father had done in a mining town in northern Germany. There Joe had seen the old miner shot down by German soldiers during a bitter strike—a helpless sixteen-year-old spectator to the murder of his father. Joe had wandered in the sordid cruelties of that society until he could stand it no longer. Impulsively, a year later, he fled that insane chaos to go to the home of his aunt and uncle—so far as he knew, the only relatives he had left—here in Austin, Kentucky. It had not surprised him to find them as poor as his own family, burdened by the same uncertainties, struggling over the same dried bread and beans. He went down into the mines to earn his keep, the only thing he could do in a mining town. It never occurred to him that there was anything ironic about leaving the old country to come clear across the ocean only to bury himself in the mines again. The language alone was different, and Joe, who knew only enough to be thankful, learned it quickly.

For all the forty years that followed, through his marriage to the steady, taciturn Edna Willis from next door and his growing family of two daughters and a son, he struggled through the turbulence of American life, always on the fringes of poverty. There were good times when he worked steadily and could fill his gut and put a few bucks away—and then the rotten days of depression that took it all away.

He loved his family, but he could never find his way close to them. In his life, he learned only to protect them and that they must be taught how ultimately to protect themselves. This he demanded of them as a necessary concomitant of living; for the children, it was as important as school itself. When they reached high school, he insisted they find jobs after school hours, all of them paying for their own clothes and entertainment after a minimum figure went toward the home itself.

These were the 1930's, and playing was for the rich.

The pressure of their poverty fell most heavily on the two girls, both of them older than the son, for they passed through childhood during the depths of the depression. By the time the boy was ready for high school, the worst was over, and the meat and potatoes were piled high on the dinner table. Though the prospects looked good, to Joe Kutner this was not the millennium, and he rigidly held to his simple demands that they continue to earn their keep. It had become a fundamental part of his philosophy and of their upbringing.

Yet, with the passing of hard times, it was also inevitable that he would feel a desire to relax, for the urgency of the pressures on him dwindled with a taste of the living wage. For too long he had been only a provider; it was time to become a father.

He arose one Saturday morning with the thought of his son full and fresh on his mind from the direction of his dreams.

Where was Mike? Fourteen years he had a son and he hardly knew him. He was shamed by it. He came down the stairs in his heavy robe, padding barefooted into the kitchen toward the smell of the strong coffee. He sat at the table while his wife poured him a large cup, and he stared through the aromatic steam that rose before his eyes.

"Fishing," he said quietly. "We're going fishing." And through the haze he saw Mike and himself wading through the clear fresh streams, pulling out the tasty trout in large numbers for Edna to cook—as he had heard other fathers with sons describe days of fishing.

Edna was cooking his scrambled eggs, not his fish.

"What are you talking about, Joe?" she asked.

"We're going fishing. I'm gonna take Mike fishing today."

He saw her look up from the stove, a little bewildered. By accident their eyes met for a moment; they were both suddenly embarrassed by it, for their own reasons. He turned back to his coffee, she to her stove.

"Sure," he went on. "I take the boy for an outing. We'll go to Burton's Creek and pass the day."

"What are you going to fish with, Joe?" she asked quietly. "You haven't got equipment."

He was ready for her.

"Borrowed some from Len Killian." Joe was embarrassed to recall his request of Len, made so quickly after the man had finished telling them down in the mine what a great time he'd had fishing the week end before. Characteristically, Joe had blurted it out as if he were trying to ask before someone else did.

"Len says his wife can show you how to prepare them trout," he went on, ". . . if we catch any."

He looked up at her now, waiting for her smile of approval. She seemed not to have heard.

"Do you want bacon, Joe?"

Her evasiveness disturbed him.

"No," he said. "Just them eggs."

He studied his coffee for a moment, searching amongst the bubbles for the resolutions of his sudden doubts.

"Where's Mike?" he asked finally.

Edna brought him the steaming skillet and scooped the eggs to his plate. He salted them and buttered the huge roll.

"Where's Mike, Edna?"

"He's playing ball, I guess. He left early this morning with his glove and things."

"Is that where he goes every Saturday?"

"And Sunday, Joe."

He started to feel resentment toward the boy's absence.

"He don't help you at all, Edna? Don't he do chores for you on Saturdays?"

"Oh, sometimes, when I ask him to."

By her tone he knew that was very seldom. Mike left the duties of the house to the women while he played baseball. Joe let his resentment grow; in the quiet of his frustration, his dream of fishing with his son evaporated and anger took its place.

"The boy should help you more," he said, groping for something he didn't quite understand.

Edna shrugged.

"Marian and Cathy help me enough. There's really nothing for him to do."

"Find things, then. It ain't fair to the girls."

She sat with him now, stirring her coffee. Except for the sound of her clinking spoon, it was silent for a while.

"Mike is different," she began. "He's a boy. . . ." Her voice was plaintive and defensive. He realized at once she was going to defend him, and he found it annoying. "He goes out with his friends and plays ball. He is like all the other boys on the street, Joe."

"Next year it will be different. Next year he starts high school and he will work!"

For a moment there was silence again, marred only by the sound of his eating. He wondered what was in Edna's mind. He rarely knew what anyone else, even his own wife, was thinking.

"Mike is a very good ballplayer, Joe," she said quietly.

She spoke this as if it were some kind of a question to him. He shrugged his shoulders and his wife went on, eagerly now.

"The other day he came home with a big proud smile. I said, 'What happened, Mike? Did you hit another home run?' 'No,' he said. 'But the older boys from high school want me to play with them this Saturday. Imagine that . . . me, only fourteen years old, playing with the high-school guys!' And then he said: 'Maybe Pop would come out and watch?' "

Joe was touched. There was something about all this that he did not like; but he was touched.

"He said that?" Joe asked.

Edna smiled at him.

"They're playing at the Oval, Joe. The game starts around ten he said."

He got up from the table to avoid her eyes. He wanted to think. This was not the way he wanted it. The commitment had been made, to himself at any rate, that he would take Mike fishing. Now he was being asked to watch a baseball game instead. He felt tricked; and suddenly he was angry at Edna for the emotion she had touched off within him, for it had made him soft and swayed him.

"You'd better get dressed, Joe, if you're going. It's almost ten now."

She cut into his thoughts at the worst possible moment. He whirled around toward her and made another commitment.

"I ain't going," he said. "Don't care to watch no kids play a crazy baseball game." And he shuffled back to the privacy of his bed.

The incident grew in importance, became a symbol to him. Later, when he told Mike he wanted to take him fishing the following week, he saw the cloud that passed over the boy's face.

"Please, no, Pop," the boy protested, as if it were some kind of punishment he was suggesting. "I've got a big game on Saturday!"

Fishing with the father was out for the summer. It would have to wait for the end of the baseball season. The distance between himself and Mike came home to him; he would have to wait until the son was ready to accept him.

This was not Joe's idea of being a father. He was aware that there were other ways, like going to the ball game as Edna had suggested. But baseball was foreign to him, and he pictured himself a fool in front of the others who had grown up with a thorough knowledge of the game. It was too much to expect him to sit through the long hours, to ask questions of children, to watch his son in activities he neither understood nor cared about.

So over the months, his desire to come closer to his son turned against him and broadened still further the gap between them. He retreated to the black pit of his job and the predictability of his struggle for security. The father remained essentially the provider.

In the fall, young Mike entered high school and with the change went dutifully to work after school hours. Joe was pleased to see how hard he worked, as if driven by some special force in this new direction. The boy contributed his share of money, and Joe never bothered to question how he spent the rest of it. He felt no apprehension even when he came upon Mike pounding and oiling a new baseball glove, so engrossed that he never so much as turned his head. Every night he would patiently knead the leather, folding it carefully around the baseball, binding it with heavy rubber bands, bedding it down with oily rags that smelled up his room with a lingering rancidness. And when he'd come home, he'd rush upstairs to his closet to gently unwrap this foul-smelling leather as if it were a prize diamond.

Joe could laugh at all this foolishness; he fondled the memory of his daughters with their first dolls.

One evening that winter, Joe came home from the mines struggling the last few blocks through a sudden snow storm. The cold winds cut into him, and he let his mind enjoy the prospective warmth of his hearth as he fought his way home. And when he pushed into the parlor, he could not resist a smile as he smelled the burning wood; it was as though Edna had somehow anticipated his desire and built him this fire of welcome. He pulled off his snow-wet clothing and stood before the fireplace, letting the hot glow pour into him.

Later, he sat deep in the huge chair, his feet stretching toward the flames, resting on the battered footrest so old he could not remember ever being without it. His daughters were on the floor with their phonograph machine, their pleasant teen-age voices clear and fresh against the scratchy background of the spinning disks. He listened to the singing and stared at the fire. His slippered foot made clumsy attempts to keep time with the rhythm of the singing.

The girls noticed and they giggled at his ineptness as they turned a record. He heard them whispering something about "pop's favorite song," and he shrugged his shoulders, wondering what song, if any, was even sufficiently known to him to be a favorite. Then he heard their high-pitched voices again, this time singing, "There is a tavern in the town, in the town," and he laughed as he remembered the last clumsy time he had danced with Edna to that record.

He looked up as he heard his wife behind him, and he turned his head to the clinking of cups and saucers.

"Here, Joe," she was saying. "Hot rum toddy."

Joe laughed a quick "Ha!" and sipped gingerly at the large cup. He heard the wind rattling the windows behind him, and he laughed again at the pleasures this room suddenly held for him. This was a good winter, he knew. It was a winter of much ice and snow, but he had kept his family warm and fed. These had been the cruelest months in the hard years of his past. But this winter he had won the battle, and his simple moment of triumph lay in a fire and a hot rum toddy.

Marian and Catherine were on their feet dancing, or at least pretending to, and Joe saw that they were imitating his own gross movements the last time he had tried to steer Edna around in a dance. He laughed at their skill, at the silliness of their fresh young bodies posed in simulated stiffness. He stood up and grabbed Edna's hand, suddenly prompted to try dancing again himself. But the record ended and instead, he brought his arms hard around her and hugged her to him. Edna gasped and the girls squealed with delight.

It was then he thought he was missing someone. Yes. . . . Where was Mike? Even as he asked, the answer was heard pounding through the house, the fist smacking into the still-virgin pocket, heard easily through the thin layers of walls that separated them.

Joe smiled. "Listen to that!" He shook his head, and suddenly he gave in to an impulse to take off his big soft slipper and pound his fist into it, trying to keep time with the boy upstairs. It seemed like a crazy game. Edna began to laugh, her laughter multiplying with the ludicrous repetition of Joe's pounding. She infected them all, and shortly they roared together—pounding cushions, the couch, the floor itself.

"You're out!" Joe shouted, delighted at his own rare giddiness, and he smacked the slipper until tears formed in his eyes.

It was then that they noticed him, the little brother with the curly black hair and the dark-rimmed glasses, holding the brown leather glove. He stood there in the doorway, staring at them, wondering at their laughter and their pounding, and his face showed his knowledge that the merriment was at his expense.

"What's so funny?" he asked finally, looking at them.

Somehow, the serious face was suddenly too serious, or too hurt or too bewildered. They wanted to bring him into the room with them, but he could not share their mood. They began laughing again, without apparent cause.

"Well, what's so funny?" he repeated.

Joe felt responsible, but how could he explain? He looked at his son and chuckled, still shaking with the remnants of their merriment. He saw Mike stare at the position of Joe's fist in the slipper, then back to his own, similarly buried in the pocket of his glove. Their eyes met for a moment, and Joe shrugged his shoulders. Well, that's it, Son. That's what's funny. It's nothing, really . . . but somehow, it's funny.

Mike looked back at him hard; his eyes narrowed in anger, and for a moment Joe thought he would throw that glove at him. Then, just as suddenly, the look changed and the boy's face broke into a fine broad grin. He laid his glove on the table and came in to join them.

Edna put a rum toddy in his hand and the music began once more. It seemed like a party again.

Joe settled back in his chair and watched Marian trying unsuccessfully to teach her kid brother to dance. Joe wished the scene could last all night. He reached out for his wife, seeking her help to somehow or other find expression for his feelings. In all his years he had never really expected that life could work out so well for him.

He turned back to the dwindling fire and poked among the charred logs, stirring them to life. After a while, Mike came over and sat quietly on the arm of his chair. Together (had they ever been so completely together before, Joe wondered) they watched the few tiny spurts of flame that licked at the ashes.

"I'll go get some more logs, Pop," Mike said. "Let's keep the fire going."

"We're all out, Son. . . ." Joe shook his head. "That's all we had."

And in a few minutes, he felt the room grow chilly again.

The winter moved suddenly into spring. The bleak morning chill on the way to work seemed to melt before the early sun. The brightness lit his way into the earth, and greeted him as he rose from it in the late afternoon. It was sweet and fresh and warming to his perpetually tired body, but it made him restless and uneasy. It seemed as though spring was a challenge, as if life must be renewed to live up to the beauty of it. He resisted this feeling as he resisted all change, incapable of adjusting his mood.

Though it did not escape him when young Mike began tapering off his weekly contributions to the house, Joe patiently made no comment, even to himself. And when those payments stopped completely, he merely assumed the boy had had a few unprofitable weeks or incurred some added need for money. They had never talked about his job at the grocery store other than to mention the fact of it, and he did not wish to bring it up now. The father did not permit himself to nurse the possibility that Mike was no longer working, for this was too basic a violation of his deepest beliefs. When such a thought did occur to him, he rejected it, banished it from his mind. He could accept no reason why his son should quit his job.

Yet, one afternoon returning from the mines, he passed the high brick wall of the Oval and heard the staccato shouts of the players. It had been his desire to dismiss the activity on the other side of that wall with derision and disgust, for the whole concept of older boys at play had always been incomprehensible to him. Too often had he heard the bitterness of fathers whose children had wasted themselves in some frivolity. And here, beyond that wall, were the sons of miners he knew, apparently unwilling to lighten their fathers' burdens with a share of daily work. Instead, they ran stupidly around like a bunch of crazy chickens, in movements he had never cared to understand.

Never his son, he had sworn. No . . . never his own!

Before, he had paid little attention to these noises. This time he stopped, thinking he recognized the voice of his boy. With alarm, he turned his head to the wall, tuning his ear to the sounds behind it, and his body froze like a bird dog.

Was that Mike . . . ? Would his son quit work to play baseball? The questions tore holes in him, opening up the floodgates for his doubts to pour through him in a torrent, until he was swamped completely by them. For moments he just stood there, waiting with his swollen suspicion, hearing nothing. It was as if the kids knew he was there and became still.

No . . . not his own . . . never his own. . . .

He wanted to cry out to them. Be still! Be quiet! I don't want to know! I don't want to. . . .

Then suddenly, the clear, piercing yell, just beyond the wall no more than a few feet away:

"I got it! I got it!"

Anger replaced his doubts and rose from his chest to choke him. If he could have grabbed his son at that moment he would have smashed him with all his fury. But he could not even see him. He merely stood there spluttering helplessly in his frustration, spitting at the wall between them.

At the top of his lungs he shouted back, "Yeah . . . you got it? You got it!"—trying to lend some dire meaning to words he did not even understand.

He looked quickly at both ends of the street, vainly trying to locate the entrance to this idiots' arena. He saw only passers-by staring at him, adding to his humiliation, and he could not bring himself to ask the simple question. Instead, he swallowed his fury and carried it burning within him the rest of the way home.

There he waited on the porch for his son, denying himself the pleasure of his daily bath, for he preferred to smolder in righteous paternal anger, crusted with the black filth of his honest day's work. He sat, silent and still, trying not to let his mind wander, yet now knowing what he would do to the boy. Edna saw him from the kitchen, sitting there in his favorite rocker, not even rocking, and she wondered at his mood. Sensing the pending eruption, she stayed away and busied herself in cookery.

An hour Joe waited, until the sun was sinking behind the houses before him and the air grew chilly with spring twilight. The girls had returned and passed him without stopping when he did not acknowledge their greeting. When he finally saw the boy come whistling up the street, he rose from his chair and stood solidly on the steps to wait for him.

He looked heavily into the boy's startled face.

"Hi, Pop," he heard Mike say. The boy was trying hard to hide his anxiety behind a thin smile.

Joe controlled his thick voice.

"Let me have it," he said slowly.

Mike fidgeted under his arm where he held his glove, now partially hidden.

"What, Pop? Let you have what?"

"The goddamn baseball thing . . . that mitt. Give it to me!" And he fastened his stare at the bulk under the boy's arm.

He watched Mike reach for it, slowly, trying to stall before his father's apparent wrath, terribly reluctant to hand over his glove to anyone under any circumstances. Joe noted the boy's fear and had no patience for it. He stepped forward and snatched it from him, turning quickly into the house. Behind him, he heard the sudden, whining voice pursuing him as he made his way down to the cellar.

"Pop! Pop! What're ya gonna do with it? Pop . . . please, Pop!"

Joe rejected the plea without turning. As if by design he walked directly past the coal bin to the furnace and opened the door to the smoldering coals.

"Pop! . . . *No! Pop!*"

The desperate voice infuriated him. He hesitated for a brief moment, torn by the tormented cries behind him. Then he threw the glove, the well-oiled glove, carefully bound in rubber bands with the ball in the pocket no longer virgin, into the furnace and slammed the door. As if by instinct, then, he turned to face his son as the boy charged furiously at him, trying to get by. Joe grabbed him with his powerful hands and for the first time knew Mike's amazing strength as he struggled like an animal. But Joe was ready for him. With a sudden shove, he spun his son off balance and sent him hurtling headlong into the black bin. He watched the boy sprawled there, sobbing convulsively, clawing wildly at the loose coals. The father stood breathing heavily over him for a moment, confused. Then he walked toward the cellar steps.

As he slowly mounted them, he heard Mike scramble to his feet and rush to the furnace. He turned to watch the boy fling open the door and stretch defiantly into the glowing heat for his glove. But he could not reach it. Mike withdrew his arm, shrieking with pain. With the sudden movements of a cat, he grabbed the large poker beside the furnace, and with one, deft move he raked it out. The glove lay charred and smoldering at his feet, its oil sizzling over the cracked leather surface, too hot to handle. He turned slowly to face the cellar steps, licking his burnt hand. He took one step backward, and with all the fury in him, he kicked the ruined glove across the floor at his father.

Joe watched the glove scuttle toward him, like the dying charge of an angry dog. Halfway there, it rolled slowly over and lay still, smoking between them. He looked up to face the bitter hostility of his son, then lowered his eyes, suddenly too tired to feel anything any more, and he turned away.

Through the months that followed, the incident was never mentioned. It festered within him, a malignancy feeding on his guilt. And it changed nothing. The boy got hold of another glove, again brand new, Joe knew not where or how. And he continued to play baseball after school. And on Saturdays and Sundays.

"Let him play," Edna had insisted. "It's important to him. More important than delivering groceries for a few dimes a day."

A few dimes a day! The rage had rushed through him. A few dimes a day becomes a few bucks a week, an hour of digging in the pits. And one night at dinner he turned to the boy with all his hostility, trying to assert himself in the face of his wife's appeasement.

"A few dimes a day! That's food in the gut, you little punk, and you'll work for what you eat! You hear me? In my house you'll work or you don't eat!"

And he watched Mike stare back at him, then calmly push his plate away and get up from the table. The simple truth was that the boy would rather play ball than eat.

It wasn't until the fall of that year that Mike started work again and rejoined the dinner table, quietly, as if nothing had ever happened.

Now, three years later, Joe Kutner was passing the familiar brick wall, the high brick wall that stood as a symbol of the gulf between himself and his son. He knew Mike was behind it at that moment, playing baseball for Austin High School, just as he was on every other afternoon, wasting the years in willful childish irresponsibility. The boy was no good, as alien and worthless as the game he played.

He pulled out his handkerchief and found the cleanest corner. As he walked along, further from the wall, he held it gently against his cheek, for the scratch was stinging him. Behind him, the cheers of the kids resounded through the spring stillness. As if an echo from that fund of restless memories, he thought surely he heard his name called amidst the screaming from behind the wall.

No . . . not *his* name. It was his son's name. Sure, sure . . . cheers for his son. Doesn't that make you proud? They're cheering for your son!

Joe licked his handkerchief, sputtering his contempt, and tested again for blood.

"Goddamn," he grumbled, turning to face the wall for one last parting shot. "Goddamn, Mike."

And he ambled the last few blocks home.

There he drowned his bitterness in the daily luxury of his bath. He sank his tired body in the bright, white, shiny tub and wallowed in the soap and hot water. He scrubbed the filth of the day from him, limb by limb, and occupied his mind in doing so. At length he lolled in fresh water, hotter still, and settled back with the evening paper, skillfully manipulating the pages to keep them dry. At first he read of Europe and the new madman, Hitler. His mind chased over the ocean to the old country and this newest threat of war, and he cringed at the prospects. Then he turned back to the quiet ripple of his bath. He paged quickly to the comics and the Hollywood gossip columns. Conveniently, these two sections faced each other in the newspaper, as if the editor found they complemented each other, and even with the water lapping at his chest, Joe had but to twist his wrist to turn from "Little Orphan Annie" to Hedda Hopper's Hollywood.

Vaguely he heard the commotion downstairs, the babble of male voices not typical of his house at this hour. He caught the anxious tones and he strained his ears for a few key words. In time he heard them, and they destroyed the contentment of his bath: ". . . doctor . . . accident . . . Mike."

When he'd hurriedly dried and dressed and made his way downstairs, he found his son lying peacefully on the couch, still partially dressed in his baseball uniform. The doctor looked up from packing his instruments and smiled his doctor's assurance.

"The boy is O.K., Mr. Kutner . . . just a bad jolt, that's all."

Joe nodded, relieved, and looked at his son. Mike tried to smile up at him.

"Hello, Pop," he said. "I feel O.K."

"What happened, Son?" he asked slowly.

The question hung there for a moment, as though there were no direct answer. The silence was broken by a strange voice behind him.

"He made a great catch, Mr. Kutner. A truly great catch."

Joe turned his head halfway to the stranger and walked over to his son, waiting for an explanation.

The voice behind him went on.

"The kid legged a crucial ninth-inning belt over 100 feet and brought it in, crashing into the wall. It saved the game."

The man spoke nonsense. But the wall . . . that wall. Joe snarled at the words, the only words in that gibberish that made any sense to him. That goddamn brick wall.

"I'll be O.K., Pop. The doc says I'll be up in a coupla days."

"As good as new, Mr. Kutner. As good as new."

"In a few days?" Joe balanced the phrase against the Friday-night-Saturday-night job Mike had promised to start. Four bucks a night, eight bucks a week end, thirty-five to forty bucks a month, a long-awaited concession to the realities of life. Now he would lose the job, even before he had worked a single hour at it. And all because of that goddamn baseball playing. It would never end, never!

The doctor was putting on his coat.

"That'll be four dollars for the visit, Mr. Kutner."

"Four bucks . . . sure." Joe tried to swallow his anger until these strangers left. But he turned to the boy with an unbecoming smirk. "Can you pay the doctor? Can you? You got it, Mike . . . in that . . . that . . . monkey suit?"

He stared at Mike now, waiting for an answer though he knew there was none. He tried to make it feel like some sort of victory.

But the kid rested on his elbows and stared back, and the armor of his defiance was thick, impenetrable. Joe saw Mike's lips part, beginning some crude piece of profanity under his breath, his eyes weirdly hidden by the light reflecting off his glasses. Joe turned away from the bitter silence and fumbled through his bathrobe pockets.

"It's in my room, doc. I'll go get it."

He climbed the stairs slowly, nursing his self-righteousness all the way. Pay for your son, Joe. Shell it out. Four dollars more for running into that wall. What the hell does that goddamn kid think he's doing? What kind of crazy nonsense is this? He kicked open the door of his room and reached for his wallet in his pants. Four dollars . . . your son is seventeen and he ain't even got four dollars. Work hard, Joe . . . back to the mines early tomorrow, cause you gotta make some more four dollars, so your seventeen-year-old son can play more baseball and run into the goddamn brick walls. He threw the wallet into an open drawer and started back. Goddamn baseball. I was right . . . never should let him play . . . never . . . sonofabitch. Never!

When he returned to the living room, the doctor was gone. Edna was serving tea to the stranger.

"Have some tea, Joe," she said to him. "We'll be having dinner late tonight."

"Where's the doc?"

"He left, Joe."

"But the money. . . . Who paid him?"

Again, silence.

"Who paid him, Edna?"

"Joe," she said evasively. "This is Mr. Fain. He's come to see about Mike."

"Did you pay the doctor, mister? Why . . . ? What makes you think you can pay our bills?"

Fain pulled out a cigar and unwrapped it slowly.

"To tell the truth, I felt kinda responsible for the accident. It was easily worth four bucks to see that catch."

"Worth it to you! What about my son? *He* got hurt!"

Joe forced the crumpled bills into Fain's hand. The scout shrugged and lit up.

"The boy's all right, Mr. Kutner. And it'll be worth a lot more than four dollars to him."

Joe saw Mike turn to face him. Edna was quiet behind her tea. There was something in the air.

"What are you saying, Mr. . . . Mr. Fain? What are you here for, anyway?"

"I'm a scout for the Chicago Lions, Mr. Kutner."

The words were spoken with a certain dignity, in a tone that indicated their importance. But to Joe Kutner they meant nothing. He hesitated in his ignorance.

"Pop . . . you see. . . ."

Edna stepped in to close the gap.

"Joe . . . that's a baseball team, in the major leagues. Mr. Fain finds players for them."

Edna was eager to tell him, the shy, retiring Edna; and she spoke as if this was all elementary information.

Joe felt a familiar embarrassment. For years, he had heard the baseball talk amongst the miners, and the constant jabber of Sunday radios tuned to this nonsense. But he had rejected it, finding it strange, and in recent years had hated it as the folly of his son. Now, all of a sudden, he sensed that this had been a mistake. He sensed it in this man Fain, certainly no bum, and in the tone of the conversation.

"I see," he said. He was treading lightly and carefully. "You are interested in Mike, mister?"

"Yeah . . . ," he replied. "I am very much interested."

He half turned to Edna again and spoke with only a little sarcasm.

"And what does *that* mean?"

Fain ignored the tone. "I would like to have yours and your son's signature to a contract which would permit him to play baseball professionally."

Joe watched the thick, white cigar smoke drift closer toward him before it rose to the ceiling.

"For money, that is?" he asked.

"For money, Mr. Kutner."

Joe felt the fresh redness in his face, felt the tingling hotness on the back of his neck. For money, play baseball for money. He had heard of such a thing, of course, but he never suspected that his son . . . never suspected. . . .

Suddenly, the question rose from within him, the question of his doubts.

"How much, mister?" he asked. "How much money?"

The big cigar moved across the mouth, from one corner to the other, moved without help from hands. Fain was leaning back in his chair, jingling the loose change in his pocket.

"Oh . . . seventy-five, eighty bucks. That's just the first year, of course."

"Eighty bucks a week?"

"A month, Mr. Kutner. This is for playing baseball, not . . . not mining coal."

Joe saw the boy's frown. The scout lowered his eyes to his outstretched feet knowing he should not have put it that way. Joe could not see Fain's face as he replied.

"I don't make eighty bucks a week, Mr. Fain. I don't know any coal miners who do."

Fain swallowed heavily behind his cigar. He'd have to try a different tack.

"I'm sorry, Mr. Kutner. I meant no offense."

Edna leaned forward with a teapot and a smile.

"More tea, Mr. Fain?"

"Sure . . . thank you, ma'am." And he turned to Joe, starting again. "Look, Mr. Kutner. Baseball is a big thing in this country. It gets a lot of respect. Schools, churches, our leading citizens. The President himself throws out the first ball on opening day. It's a wonderful game that most everybody loves to play and millions enjoy watching. Your son here happens to be damn good. He's young and inexperienced, but he looks good to me. It's obvious he loves to play ball. I'm offering him a chance to make a career out of it—playing ball."

Joe was demanding:

"At eighty bucks a month . . . for how many months a year, Mr. Fain? How many months? Five? That's only four hundred dollars a year! We are poor people. My son can't afford such a career."

"Look here, Mr. Kutner. How much money did you make when you started going into those mines? And did you enjoy going down in that hole day after day, breaking your back down there? Here's a chance for a kid to be doing something he likes. Sure, it ain't much money at first, but your boy has a chance to get to the top. I've seen a lot of kids in this racket, Mr. Kutner, and I know a good one when I see one. I could tell you about the ballplayers I discovered, but I gather you don't follow baseball. But they're up there, up in the big leagues, making the big dough. I can't promise anything, Mr. Kutner. But your kid has a damn good chance."

The cigar did not need another match, but Durkin Fain struck one to punctuate his words. Joe Kutner sank deep into his own thoughts. When he spoke the words seemed without anger, and the tone of his own voice surprised him.

"I once read in the paper," he said, "where the movie scouts from Hollywood found a girl at a soda fountain, and they made a big star out of her. She was nothing, but she looked good to them and they made her a star and paid her more money, I suppose, than there is in this goddamn world. After that, one of my daughters would hang out at soda fountains every chance she had. Nothing ever happened, but she told me a soda fountain was no longer just a soda fountain."

Fain looked hard at the father, uncertain as to which way the conversation was going.

"What are you telling me, Mr. Kutner?"

"All this 'success' stuff. You make kids dream too much!"

"But this is baseball! A game of skill. You were talking about Hollywood!"

Joe became aware his voice was rising in anger.

"Movies are respectable too, mister! Schools show 'em, church people and leading citizens, as you call 'em, see them. I even read where President Roosevelt likes Greta Garbo or somebody like that."

Durkin Fain got up from his chair and walked to the window. It was too dark to see outside, but he stood there staring out as if he could. Joe watched him for a while, wondering what the hell this argument was all about. He knew now his kid would play baseball, that he couldn't stop him no matter what. Somehow he guessed he was just enjoying himself sounding off like that. Yeah, even coal miners could talk. It must've set that Chicago guy back a peg or two. Yet the whole business disgusted him. Baseball had been the silent word in his house for three years. He was tired of the whole goddamn business; he was tired of his son.

Durkin Fain turned from the window, a paper in his hand. This time he talked to the boy on the couch.

"Mike," he said. "I'm right about you. Dammit, I know I'm right about you! I'll get you two thousand dollars if you sign this . . . two thousand dollars!"

The boy smiled all over, and looked quickly at Joe. The father jumped to his feet, very much alive.

"Two thousand? For doing what?"

"Two grand for signing his name, and reporting to the ball club we assign him to. Two grand. We call it a bonus, Mr. Kutner."

Joe was staggered. Two thousand dollars was as much money as he made in an average year. Two thousand dollars in his hands was the end of his mortgage, the end of his indebtedness, the opportunity to take it easy for a spell. Two thousand dollars was a car, a refrigerator, a lifetime of saving never achieved. His mind raced over the red and black arithmetic of his family finances through the years and all the harsh penny-pinching that was poverty. Work! How hard he had driven himself for a few extra bucks, always nursing the hope of a decent pension against the darker days of his old age. And now here was the kid who had scorned all this, rewarded for his indolence with a pot of gold. He gets two thousand dollars for agreeing to play baseball!

He looked over at Mike, propped on the couch on a load of pillows. At that moment he seemed less like the injured boy recuperating from a bad jolt and more like a big shot taking a siesta, sprawled out luxuriously on the couch to be waited on hand and foot. Suddenly it appeared to Joe that there was something terribly funny about it, and he began to laugh his gruff, throaty laugh. Louder and louder he laughed. At first he was conscious they were looking at him, and he wanted to stop. But he couldn't. He became giddy from it, as if the laughter was a thing apart from himself. You threw away his glove, Joe, right into the furnace. The hot coals sizzled at the leather and destroyed it. Can you beat that? You destroyed it, Joe, the tool of a two-thousand-dollar bonus. In his mind's eye he saw the furnace again and the open door to the burning coals. But the glove was not there; instead, a wad of green bills. They were rolled around a baseball, bound by those heavy rubber bands. They were turning black and charred in the furnace heat. And it was he, not Mike, who was reaching through the fierce red heat, trying to save the bills before they burned to ashes.

Gradually he subsided, exhausted by his emotions. He slumped into his chair rubbing his arm as though he had burned it, his body shaking and hot.

After a moment, Durkin Fain laid the papers on the table and pulled out his pen.

"You'll sign then, Mr. Kutner?"

"Sign? Sign? Sure, I'll sign. Why not?"

He grabbed the pen and scrawled his name hurriedly across the dotted line at the bottom of the page. Fain blew on it and handed the pen to Mike. The boy looked over at Joe before turning to the paper, wanting something the father could not give. Joe looked away, terribly confused. When he looked up again, he saw the boy's wide smile as he wrote his name. The scout put the papers in his pocket.

"You'll hear from me, Mike. Take care of yourself, now. You belong to the Chicago Lions."

There was nothing more to say and he left.

For a moment, their powers of speech went with him. The three of them lingered in silence, sipping the dark, lukewarm remains of the tea, drinking deeply of their own thoughts. It was Edna who smiled and picked up the saucers.

"I'll fix some dinner. The girls won't be home till late." And she started toward the kitchen.

Joe nodded and looked at his hands. He started up to follow her, carrying his teacup as if it were still full. He was stopped by the hard pull of Mike's voice.

"Whattaya say, Pop, am I allowed to eat tonight?"

Joe never turned. He stood in the doorway and nodded, aware only that he was tired and his brain was swirling with his doubts.

"Yes, Mike. You can eat," he said, wanting to go.

Behind him the voice held him again, loud and demanding.

"On the table, there, Pop. You see it? Bring it over, will you?"

Joe turned toward the table by the door and saw it, the wad of brown leather with the white ball barely visible inside it. He reached over for it and walked slowly toward the couch. Mike was looking up at him, his eyes searching. He held the glove out to the boy, but Mike declined to take it, as though there was something more important to see. Joe had to lower his eyes, and they rested on the glove in his hand. It was soft and smooth and pliable and strangely alive, like it was clutching the ball of its own will, clasping its fat fingers around the hard white surface.

He knew what his son was thinking.

"Here, Son," he said. "Here's your glove. Take it."

Mike reached for it and smiled.

"Thanks, Pop." The tone was quiet now. "Thanks very much."

Joe nodded and walked slowly back to the kitchen. He

heard the fist pounding into the glove again and he stopped once more in the doorway.

"Pop," he heard. "I'll pay you back the four bucks. I'll send you the two thousand when I get it. I figure I owe you a little something."

"That'll be fine," he said quietly, for he didn't know what else to say.

# 3 *The Manager*

The hot rain lashed against the locker room window with great bursts of fury. Above, thunder crashed in accompaniment, apparently very close by.

"Goddammit. . . ." Lou Phipps pushed his grizzly face against the steamed-up window and looked at the angry sky. "Goddamn friggen weather for the Fourth of July, ain't it?"

He tried to sound convincingly distressed without being too profane. He did not convince himself, for the vilest profanity was essential for even his slightest moments of rage. Actually, he was relieved by the weather, and he wondered if the other knew it.

"Guess we'll have to call it off," he added.

Christ, yes. Call off the double-header, the stinking six-hour nightmare, the endless afternoon in this Southern furnace with the white-hot sun draining every ounce of yesterday's booze from your feeble friggen pores. Call it off for the easy pleasures of a shady bar with a giant fan blowing soft breezes up your butt.

Behind him, the young man, slick in the clean summer suit, smoked his college pipe. Phipps looked at him. What was he doing here in the stench of this cruddy locker room with his fresh barber's shave and his crew cut?

"Not yet, Lou," the young man said. "It's only ten-thirty. Might be a brief local storm. Sometimes they ride over in no time."

Oh, sure, you sonofabitchin' college punk; you know all about the friggen elements, I suppose. The goddamn club owners with their Fourth-of-July gate receipts. All morning long they get down on their pink knees and pray for the pretty sunshine.

"Well, I hope so, Clark. But the field'll be too damn wet."

"It's a possibility. . . . But we haven't had rain for almost a week. I'm told there's good drainage out there."

"I'm told . . . ," Phipps repeated the phrase to himself. You're told, you college bastard. *I* told you about the drainage. Yeah, goddammit, there *is* good drainage . . . sandy soil . . . and if it stops raining, you'll have your friggen double-header.

He swallowed his contempt for the youth because he knew he had to. His mouth was fuzzy from his hang-over and he needed a cool drink of water. He turned to the sink and let the water run for a while, passing the time regarding himself in the mirror. His beard had grown heavily in the heat of summer, but he hated to shave before a game. The sweat would sting the tender areas of his skin, and his catcher's mask would rub it in; he'd have an ugly rash for a couple of days. He looked at the redness in his watery, bloodshot eyes, recognizing that it went with the stubby, black beard. He sure looked lousy, he thought. Lousy and old. Christ, he looked old! He was forty-three (or was it forty-four?) and not well preserved. Looking down at the reflection of his chest and gut, visible enough under his T-shirt, he tried to contract his tired, overtaxed stomach and hide that aging flabby rim of fat. He felt old at forty-three, especially since there was nothing but kids around, day after day, stripping their young colt bodies, lean and agile and strong. Sometimes, they'd try to kid him about his age, his growing softness . . . the goddamn pipsqueaks; kid *him*, Lou Phipps, eleven years a big-league catcher! He hated it and dressed alone whenever he got the chance. When he didn't, he barked at them savagely. It shut them up. What the hell, he was the manager!

He turned back to the flowing water and laid a finger under the stream to gauge its temperature. It was still warm. He watched the rusty-looking water pour over his ugly hand, broken too many times through his twenty-odd years working behind the plate, receiving that wild assortment of too many pitches, his fingers threatened by too many foul tips. He saw the brackish color of the flow from the single broken faucet into the cracked, stained metal sink, and he thought with disgust that this was Maldeen, Mississippi, and it was strictly class D.

No more than a dozen years before it had been different. Oh Christ, how different! Then he had been riding the plush pullmans through the big-time cities of America, staying in the best hotels (where the water ran cool, even icy, from a special tap), dressing in the clean and spacious locker rooms of the double-tiered stadiums. That was the way to live, he knew. . . . Yeah, that was the way to live. . . . And he thought with bitterness of the passing of his prime, which had made him valueless in the majors. He thought bitterly, and foolishly, Why did I have to get old?—as though this were something peculiar to him.

Finally, he filled the metal cup and tasted the rusty warmth of the water. He settled for a loud gargle to refresh his mouth and spat it sloppily over the sink. At his locker, he reached in for a butt and lit up.

At the window, now, the slick white suit was surveying the newest clouds.

Phipps laughed crudely.

"It's tough on the gate figures when you rain out on the Fourth, eh, Clark?"

"I think it might break. . . ."

"Wishful thought. You're getting to be a regular general

manager already, kid. You wish hard enough for the rain to stop . . . and it always rains harder."

"Suppose the storm does break, Lou; suppose it clears up, say, by noon or half past. Does that give the fans enough time to get out here?"

Phipps scowled at the thought. He could just see that blazing ball of flame work its way through the clouds; in this humidity the area would be a steam box that could melt steel.

"Your uncle shoulda warned you about class D baseball, kid. He's the boss in Chicago and he's used to that high-class steak and potatoes. Down here in Maldeen you're gonna eat crap . . . and more crap. They'll come to see this stinking ball club when they got nothing else to do or when they're feeling ornery and want something to snarl at because they're sick of their fat-assed wives."

Clark laughed for a second.

"This club is supposed to be a success—first division and all that."

"You just got here, kid. Take it easy. Your uncle wrote me he wanted you to learn from the bottom up. You got your job back in the front office sitting there, so just relax and learn. You're here, at the bottom of the garbage pile in this business, the class D bushes. So just keep your eyes open."

"And my trap shut . . . eh, Lou?"

Phipps looked up at the cool, clean white suit and warned himself to be more careful in the future. This is old man Jim Mellon's nephew. Mellon . . . the same name. And it all adds up to old man Phipps's bread and butter.

"They'll come to the game, Clark. The sonsofbitches come on the Fourth . . . always."

He noticed now the rain had subsided. He looked out the window at the shifting clouds, thoroughly annoyed that the kid's prediction might be right. He could just smell that sun coming through.

"Say, Lou, when are you going to use that new kid Durkin Fain picked up?"

Phipps was going to gargle again; he stopped at the question.

"Did Fain talk to you about him?"

"Sure. A lot."

"What'd the old bastard say?"

He noticed the kid raise an eyebrow at that, for there had been no love in the tone he used to refer to the scout. He could've counted to twenty through the silence.

Mellon answered slowly, weighing his words.

"The old bastard, as you chose to call him, believes this boy to be an excellent prospect, sufficiently to stake his reputation on his ability to produce. And sufficiently, as I'm sure you must know, to condition an investment of two thousand dollars hard cash!"

Phipps snarled at the hot-stuff vocabulary and spat into the sink. So, the kid thought highly of Durkin Fain. Well, he could handle that his own way. He knew goddamn well that old Uncle Mellon didn't.

Fain, the wise sonofabitch, always trying to squeeze some little squirt into the system with his so-called "smart baseball." Phipps had managed and played with kids like that, always talking delayed steals, fake bunts, squeeze plays and what have you. They screw up a ball club faster than a fag on a rainy road trip. Fain had hated Phipps in return and once in the old days tried to get rid of him. The feeling had been mutual over the years.

"Durkin Fain can shove his friggen prospects up his butt," he snarled between his teeth. "I don't think much of this kid."

"You haven't used him."

"I played him!"

"A few innings here and there . . . pinch-hitting. . . .

What kind of a test is that? God, Lou, we've put two thousand dollars into him!"

Phipps weighed his answer for a second.

"No, you aint. He ain't got a dime yet."

"What! We sent it down, two thousand dollars along with the regular monthly salary allotments. We had to. It was in his contract!"

"Screw the contract. Fain's contract, not yours."

"My uncle countersigned it. It was an official contract. Fain had the power to do it."

"Yeah, but what'd your uncle say? What'd the boss say when he heard what Fain did? Did he like it? Or did he groan like he used to when he gets mad?"

Phipps was much too aroused. His feeling for Durkin Fain was like a fever.

Clark tried playing carefully around the edges of the sore spot.

"No, he didn't particularly like it, Lou, but he stuck by it. The money, I repeat, was forwarded."

"Was he mad, though? I wanna know. Did he groan?"

Clark turned away.

"Yes . . . he groaned."

Phipps smiled in relief. He looked down at the old metal cup in his hand, wondering what it was doing there. Then he remembered and turned on the faucet again.

Young Mellon watched him, apparently weighing all the jumbled issues. When he finally asked, "Lou, what about the money?" Phipps was gargling again.

"What money?" The words sloshed around in his mouth, hardly audible.

"What about the two thousand dollars for the new kid?" Clark repeated.

Phipps spit it all out. He rubbed his face sloppily with warm water and turned back toward the white suit.

"I'm saving the club two grand. Tell that to your uncle. He'll appreciate it. He spends enough on his bush-league clubs. I'm saving him two grand."

"But how? Fain signed him!"

Phipps wiped his face with a clean towel from a nearby locker, not his own.

"Durkin Fain scouts ballplayers like a blind man with a tin cup. We don't have to pay the kid, I say."

"But—"

"Now look, Clark. You're down here to learn. One of the main deals is to save a buck wherever you can. I can show you plenty, and your uncle knows it. That's why he sent you here, ain't it? So just relax."

Clark smiled, nodding to himself—and keep your trap shut. He fondled his pipe thoughtfully.

"Tell me something, Lou," he said in his most intimate tone. "What's this kid really like?"

Phipps walked over to the window to check again the changing weather. Still raining; some, at any rate.

"Just a little squirt, no more'n 160 pounds or so. No power. I could use another power hitter in the outfield. This kid's probably a goddamn sneaky bunter type. I hate 'em. Always gunning for the batting averages. Besides, he wears specs."

He thought for a second that so did Clark, and it might sound wrong. But then he realized that this was different. The Kutner kid was supposed to be a ballplayer; Mellon wasn't.

"The goddamn specs are a pain in the ass," he went on. "When you're in baseball long enough, you learn to keep shy of the players who ain't got perfect eyes."

"The lenses correct the vision, Lou. With glasses, I see perfectly, as well as anyone."

"Sure, kid. Lotsa people wear glasses." He volunteered a sarcasm now. "Funny though . . . in the majors, you can count 'em on the fingers of your left hand."

Phipps watched Clark refill his pipe and light up, calmly taking his time about it.

"Still and all, Lou, I'd like to see this boy play."

Suddenly the outside screen door slammed shut. He heard the footsteps on the locker floor and glanced at his watch. It was just after eleven, too early for the players, even the eager ones. He looked around into the serious young face of Mike Kutner.

Phipps brought his guard up and smiled.

"Hello, kid, how goes it?"

"O.K., Mr. Phipps."

"Whattaya think of this weather. Helluva thing for the Fourth, eh?"

"Yeah, but it looks like it's gonna break in a while."

"It might, it might at that. I can remember times when the rain had everyone—"

"Mr. Phipps!" The kid actually broke in on him, his face even more demanding than his voice. "I want to talk to you."

Phipps stopped and shrugged. "So, we're talkin'."

"I been here in Maldeen over two weeks, Mr. Phipps, and, well, I haven't played hardly at all. . . ."

It was obvious the kid was embarrassed, especially with the strange white suit standing behind him. Phipps thought he'd been through scenes like this a thousand times: the cocky, disgruntled ballplayer who doesn't like the setup.

"So?"

"Well, I've been wondering why you haven't used me."

This was easy.

"Look, kid. I don't have to have a reason except that I'm satisfied with the outfield as it is, and we're kicking pretty strong up there in the first division."

"But, still—"

"But, still what? You think you should be in there anyway?

You think you've got something on Schroeder in center, or McKann? You're a better ballplayer than them guys?"

He tried to make it sound impossible.

The kid looked down at his hands.

"Yes," he said. "Much better."

In the corner, Phipps heard young Mellon make a noise, something like a chuckle. His own face reddened, half with anger.

"That's your opinion. Not mine."

"But you haven't seen me play, Mr. Phipps. Give me a chance."

"You'll get your chance, kid. Take your time. You're still young."

The kid nodded at the old conversation stopper, and turned slowly to leave. Halfway out he stopped.

"I hate to bring this up, Mr. Phipps, but my contract says I'm supposed to get some money for reporting here. So far I haven't gotten any."

Phipps gave it the light treatment.

"Oh, that. That comes down from Chicago. They musta got your name on this list too late this month. You'll get it next month, Kutner."

The silence covered the room like a dirty blanket.

"O.K.," the kid said, and he left.

He sat there, now, feeling the eyes of young Mellon on him, and he wondered if the guy was hostile.

"Next month," Clark said. "Why do you tell him next month?"

"Next month will take care of itself."

He watched Clark shrug and take off his glasses to wipe them clean.

"As I said before, Lou. I'd like to see that boy play."

Suddenly the sun broke through and flooded the dingy room with its brightness. Phipps turned quickly from the window, squinting harshly. He looked toward young Mellon, but the sunlight on the clean white suit blinded him.

"But you won't, Clark," he said. "You won't."

And he turned suddenly toward his locker to arrange his gear for the goddamn double-header.

It was true, he didn't. With the exception of a few ludicrous pinch-hit assignments (you could count 'em on the fingers of your left hand), Mike Kutner cooled his heels on the bench. The full impact of Phipps's contempt for Mike must have come home to him when Schroeder pulled a muscle out in center and had to be carried from the field. The kid rose out of the dugout like a bird freed from a cage. His glove was already on his hand when Phipps called into the dugout at him:

"Where ya going, kid? Nobody picked you out! Get back in there and relax."

And he sent a big second-string pitcher out there because he took a good cut at the ball. This arrangement continued for six or seven games while Schroeder took his time recovering, knowing his job wasn't being threatened by the big punk who replaced him.

Phipps watched Mike smolder at this patent piece of contempt, especially since the big lunkhead was practically a total zero with the stick and certainly no Tris Speaker with the glove. He rubbed it in further when he used the injured Schroeder, a left-handed batter, against a southpaw for a pinch-hit job when the bench was almost used up, instead of using the kid who always seemed to get wood on it. When he finally did send him up to hit, he figured the kid would've shot his bolt stewing so long in the juices of his rage. He was right. With two out in the ninth, no one on, and three runs behind, Kutner popped feebly to the catcher on the second pitch to end the game . . . and everyone went home.

At the end of the month, the manager sat with Clark Mellon

and paid off the players in the locker room. When the others had left, Kutner approached the table, a big black cigar sticking out of his boyish face.

Phipps smiled and reached for the kid's envelope; they watched him open it to count his money.

"You're short, Mr. Phipps," Mike said, the cigar bouncing with his words.

"Yeah? How much? Fifteen, twenty cents?" He grinned at Clark Mellon at his side.

"No sir. Two thousand dollars."

Despite himself, he reddened.

"Oh, that. . . ."

The kid waited quietly.

"Well, I'm sorry, Mike. But the front office must have made a slip again. Mr. Mellon here will vouch for that. They know you're here because I turned in a regular report on you. Ten days ago."

Mike looked up.

"A report? What kind of report?"

Phipps shrugged. "Just routine. The office likes to know what the rookies are like, how they're doing."

"Look, Mr. Phipps; what've you got against me?"

"Against you? I got nothing against you."

"You must have. Why don't you use me, then?"

"I do, when I need ya; when I ain't got better players on the bench."

And he watched this gross insult burrow deep into the boy.

"Look, Mr. Phipps. I wanta play ball . . . every day. I'm good, I tell ya."

"Sure, kid. All the kids do. But we just ain't got the spot for you on this club."

"Then trade me, or let me go!"

Phipps smiled.

"Now, we can't do that. Chicago has invested two grand in you. They wouldn't want to waste that kind of money."

"Well, I'm not doing them any good now."

"At least you're our property."

"Let me go, Phipps. I can get a good spot on another club. St. Clair needs an outfielder badly."

"How do ya know they'd take you?"

"They already asked me. The skipper told me to try to make a deal with you. He said he can't do nothing unless you let me go."

He nodded.

"That's true, Mike. We own you."

"But you won't use me."

"Maybe, maybe not."

He watched the exasperation mount in Kutner's face. The kid was trapped and knew it. Phipps leaned across the desk at him.

"I'll tell you what, son. I'll try to arrange something for you. You wanna play ball more'n anything, don't you?"

"Yeah . . . ?"

"Well, I'll get you over to St. Clair if I can assure the front office they haven't wasted a pile o' dough on you."

"Whattaya mean? I don't get it."

"Suppose you sign a paper releasing Chicago from that two grand we owe ya; you'll get your freedom."

The cigar was out of the mouth now, leaving the boy's face pale and empty. Phipps watched him wrestle with it.

"I can't. That's . . . that's important money. My father . . . I promised it to my father."

"You wanna play, Kutner?"

"Yeah, but it don't seem fair. It was in the contract. That's supposed to be something."

"The contract will not be broken without your consent."

The kid turned away.

"No." He was almost whining. "I gotta have that money. I've gotta send it to my pop!"

Phipps got up from the table and grabbed a butt from his coat in the locker.

"I'll compromise, kid. I'll get you two hundred and fifty dollars cold cash. You can send it to your pop and he'll be tickled to death. Two hundred and fifty dollars is a lot of money, son. And you'll be playing ball every day. Who knows? Maybe you're better than we think. At least you'll get a crack at it. Sure, I admit it ain't much of a start for you, spending a season sitting on the bench of a class D club."

The words tore into the kid like buckshot. Phipps saw Mike's wet red eyes behind his specs and the tightening muscles of his jaw. Behind him Clark Mellon was lighting his pipe, this time fumbling nervously. They waited.

The kid took off his glasses and played at wiping them on his sleeve.

"O.K.," he said quietly, "I'll sign."

Phipps rubbed a hand across his chin to hide the grin he could not suppress.

"I think you're smart, kid," he said. "Drop in here in the morning and we'll have the papers ready. I'll wire Chicago for consent on the deal. I feel sure they'll O.K. it."

Mike returned his glasses to his face. He nodded and started toward the door. They watched him stop, remembering something. It was the cigar. He picked it up and lit it again, with something strange and distant in the way he handled it.

"Tell me, Mr. Mellon," he asked, "where is Durkin Fain these days?"

"Fain? I don't know where he went. He was released late last month."

"Fired?" The boy seemed suddenly incredulous. "What for?"

The young Mellon fingered at his watch chain.

"Incompetence, I suppose. The front office thought they could no longer respect his judgments."

For a long moment, the kid stood there in silence, contemplating the worn cigar as if all the answers lay somewhere in its crumbling ashes. Phipps kept thinking Mike was about to smile.

"I see," he said under his breath, barely audible. "I see."

Phipps watched the distressed face, the shy, timid manner.

"I'll be here at eleven, Mr. Phipps," Mike said, turning slowly to leave.

"O.K." He was relieved that this crummy piece of business was over.

But Mike stopped short at the door, and when he turned, the timorous look was gone; his face had suddenly grown harsh with rage. He stretched out his arm, pointing the stubby cigar at him like an extra, warning finger.

"And I won't sign a friggen thing"—his voice roared with his fury—"unless you lay the goddamn money on the table!"

Phipps watched the door slam appropriately and grunted his private contempt.

"Goddamn little punk. Some of these little bastards sure think they're hot stuff."

Clark was distant.

"Sure, sure," he muttered.

Phipps ignored the sarcasm. He made himself laugh, a phony laugh at a trumped-up moment of triumph.

"Well, we dumped the kid and saved your uncle a neat little pile of dough!"

His enthusiasm was lost on the other.

"Your concern for my uncle's dough is touching, Lou."

"Like I said, kid, he appreciates it."

Phipps leaned back in his chair, his feet sprawled grossly

over the table. He reached in the drawer for a large envelope and tossed it to Clark.

"When you get a moment," he added. "Sign these reports, will you?"

Clark reached out for it, hoping to get off the subject. He opened the papers and quickly scanned the contents.

"It's a final on Kutner! So soon?"

"Sure. I've had it ready for days."

Clark was a little staggered.

"I'd like to know something, Lou. What made you so certain he'd settle for this deal?"

"The kid wants to play ball. Wants to be a big leaguer."

"Yes, but how did you know he could make a deal for himself elsewhere?"

Phipps laughed, this time for real.

"That's easy. I fixed it up myself!"

"You? With St. Clair?"

"Sure, why not? They needed a kid out there. I told Jocko Mullins to approach him. Jocko tells him he can play regular, hit in the number one slot, and the boy'll give his left eye to move there."

"I must say, Lou, very neat."

"Like I said, kid, your uncle sent you down here to learn how to cut corners. Just keep your eyes open."

"O.K., Lou, O.K.," he broke in. "But it seems like there must be another way."

He turned back to the report and scanned the page. He read at random:

" '. . . The player's attitude is poor and uncooperative. . . . He has no team spirit. . . . His hitting is weak. . . . He has no power. . . . He shows no special ability to warrant further interest or consideration.' " He looked up at Phipps. "You want me to submit this? It isn't exactly true, is it?"

Phipps grinned.

"It's what I believe about the kid."

"You mean it's what they want to read in the front office?"

"Why not? Two grand saved from a class D club ain't peanuts."

"Two grand minus two hundred and fifty dollars, you mean."

"The kid was a dud, a regular Durkin Fain dud. The organization is rid of both and richer by two Gs. O.K., minus two-fifty. It looks to me like good business all around. The report here, with your John Hancock, closes the whole deal."

He watched Clark Mellon finger the rest of the report, his doubts evident in every move. Phipps wondered, What if he wrote another, different report? How would Clark's stack up against his own? Could it, in the end, do him damage with the front office?

Then he thought of old man Mellon and found reassurance in their solid relationship. Damn, that old coot knew how to operate! "Always make the best deal you can for the club; the club comes first, not the player." Phipps smiled. What the hell, everything he knew about the business came from those years with Jim Mellon. The old man had told him more than once he had a future in the organization. "As long as you 'play ball,' I'm a goddamn loyal boss." *There* was a guy to work for, without benefit of a lousy college degree. Jim Mellon could always make a buck even when things were rough all over. This jerk here, after riding twenty years on the back of his uncle's brains and experience, has the friggen gall to say, "It isn't exactly true, is it?" Superior sonofabitch. A goddamn college education and a few talks with Durkin Fain and he questions me! Look at him, readin' and rereadin' the report, playin' with the idea of showing me up. What could he say? That Mike Kutner never was used, never had a chance? That I deliberately sat on him and reported him a waste in order to show up Fain and get him canned? Hell, that don't hold no water. I saw him work out a dozen times, take a turn with the stick every day. I say he's a lemon, a punk goddamn lemon. What the hell does this college kid know about baseball to contest it? Let him write his own. I got nothing to worry about. Let him.

He watched young Mellon lean back from the table, stuffing the barrel of his fancy imported pipe like it was a big thrill of some kind.

Suddenly Phipps reached into his pocket and brazenly tossed his fountain pen on the table in front of the other.

"Sign the report, kid!" he said flatly. "It should be in the mail in time for the evening plane for Chicago!"

Clark looked up slowly, and Phipps saw the tense, troubled face. The young man swallowed heavily and reached for the pen.

He signed his name and pushed the pen and paper back. Phipps folded them into the envelope and sealed it.

"You'll do O.K., Clark," he said. "Yeah, I'll tell your uncle you'll do O.K. He'll be proud to hear it from me."

# 4 *The Old Ballplayer*

It seemed like an awful lot of clowning for a ball club just before a play-off game. They were like a bunch of school kids on a Saturday morning.

"Com' on, Doughnut, get the wood to it!"

"The name is Cruller, you bastard. Herman Cruller."

"It oughta be Doughnut. You got a big-enough hole in your head!"

They were standing around the cage watching Herman take batting practice. The hitter stepped out to holler back.

"You guys who kid about names give me a pain in the ass. If yer goddamn name was Krlinkowizc you'd blow up if I called you Krinkle, or something. A handle is a handle. Mine is Cruller, and you damn well know it. Cruller, you hear?"

They laughed at his trumped-up anger, for Herman was a guy you were supposed to kid.

"O.K., Bagel. Show me something."

Herman shook his head, resigned, and pounded the plate as another pitch passed him.

"I can't see a friggen thing. It's too damn dark!"

They all laughed, knowing it was true. The twilight had settled during their turn at batting practice before the night game, and the lights hadn't been turned on yet. A thick haze made it even tougher.

On the bench, manager Jocko Mullins was yelling at them. "All right, all right. Quit the clowning. You don't wanna hit? Then get outa there."

"Hell, Skipper. Tell 'em to turn on the lights. I can't see a friggen thing."

"That shouldn't bother you, Cruller; you never could."

Herman looked down at the catcher.

"Now there's a funny man. I've hit .300 for twenty years in practically every league from here to Jaypan, and the skipper tells me I'm blind."

The pitcher laughed.

"No, it's true. You are. You been around so long you hit by osmosis."

Herman winced. "Osmosis? What the hell league are they in?"

The catcher spit through his mask.

"Naw, that means you take it in through yer skin."

"Oh yeah? Com' on, you cruddy patsy," he hollered at the pitcher. "Throw the damn ball; and not at no skin, either!"

Herman watched the easy motion, and rode into what he saw of the soft pitch. He drove it through the box, forcing the chucker to dance awkwardly to elude it. The guy ended up on his back across the mound.

Herman laughed but Jocko didn't. He was acting like a manager tonight.

"All right, Cruller. Outa there. Circle the sacks, and make sure you touch all them bases!"

Herman took off grinning. He was happy that everyone seemed to be feeling so loose.

He had seen too many clubs freeze up on the big day, unable to come up with the timely hit or make the right play when they had to. It was a feeling a club had, and it would spread amongst the players like a contagion. No one was fully immune. Even the toughest, the oldest, the most seasoned—if a team had the jitters, they would all be infected. And if the game situation finally got down to it, the pressure would hang heavily on each of them and drag them down just enough to destroy their power to produce.

Herman Cruller didn't understand it. He merely lived through all the years of it. At thirty-eight, he had run the gamut of minor-league clubs, season after season. He had never been a major league player, though his heart had cried out for it. Baseball was all he ever knew, all he ever cared about; and he couldn't leave it. Each year now, he made whatever deal he could, lowering himself down the ladder from his few years up in the International League, AAA, a decade ago to the sewers of the Mississippi Valley League, class D. He knew baseball from the thousands of games he had played, for his memory recorded the smart plays and the boners, the tactics that worked and those that failed. He learned only from the totality of all the hours he had spent on the diamond. He did not think baseball; he merely breathed it. Like the pitcher had said: he played by osmosis.

It was a good sign that the guys felt like kidding around during practice, and he was perfectly willing to be the butt of their gags. If they were loose enough now, they could slip into the game without too much tension. As he jogged around the bases loosening up his aging muscles, he added to their mirth, leaving each infielder in stitches as he passed, for he punctuated the skipper's last order by loudly passing wind as he stepped on each base.

"Tight spikes," he said.

Herman's control was legendary.

He returned to the bench for a drink and stirred the dipper in the water pail. He sipped it slowly, savoring the coolness. He sat on the bench and spat through his teeth, a steady, thin stream like a water pistol. Some of it found the navy-blue pant leg of an umpire and the boys on the bench laughed.

The ump leaned in to face the laughter, wanting to share in it, hunting for the gag.

"Hey, ump," Herman grinned. "You oughta train yer dog better than that."

They laughed again, and the man in the blue suit growled in his anger that the gag was on him.

"You're a scream, Cruller," he snarled. "You'd even be funny in the majors. Too bad you never clowned yer way up!"

Herman smiled at that.

"Tell us about it, Clarence," he baited him. "Tell us about how it was in the big time."

The umpire started to say something, growled, and left.

The kids on the bench looked after him.

"He was a ballplayer once, wasn't he, Herm? Wasn't he up in the big leagues for a while?" They asked the questions solemnly.

"Yeah. He was one of them duds who get up there every once in a while. He wasn't no better than me, but he made it. But all of them come back down the glory road, trying to gloat over their former 'greatness' like they were still worth a million. 'Yeah,' they say, 'I did a stretch with the Cards. I did pretty fair, but they sent me back subject to recall.' But the bastards are never recalled . . . never. They piddle around a few years in the bush leagues, making believe, waiting for that next chance. They play ball with only one eye, using the other to look for the scout in the stands who's gonna tell them to pack their cruddy bags for the high-class Pullman back to the big town." Herm watched Clarence disappear into the clubhouse. "Old Clarence was one of 'em." He laughed. "Lissen to me . . . 'old' Clarence. He ain't so old. We played ball together, him and me, fer Chrissakes."

"How come you never went up to the top, Herm?"

Herman Cruller shrugged his shoulders. They were watching the end of hitting practice in the growing darkness. In the distance they could see the fleet outfielder scurrying after a long drive, his body relaxed as if he were gliding at a great speed. It was almost too dark to follow the ball now, and they watched the chase in silence, wondering how the fielder could see it himself. They saw him reach out for it without breaking stride, turning his back to the diamond to make the catch. On the bench, it was hard to believe he had caught it.

"It's hard to say what makes certain guys go up, Sam. You never know what they'll look for in a ballplayer, whatever they say. Take that kid out there; you see him make that catch? There ain't five guys in the league who could see it, much less bring it in, and that little guy Kutner with his specs on makes it seems like a can of corn."

Jocko Mullins grunted in the corner.

"The kid hit .341, eleven home runs, and stole a coupla dozen bases for us. He plays ball like he owns the game and brought us to the goddamn play-offs. My dough says Kutner will go far. And two months ago that rummy Phipps let him go."

The others watched the skipper chuckle and nodded their heads.

Herman went on.

"You may be right, Skipper, but it's a friggen long way to the top. I don't know. The kid is good, all right. Christ knows he's good enough for any ball club I've ever played with, starting right now. He's fast and clever and plenty good with the stick. Out there in the gardens he's even sensational. But . . . I don't know."

"Ya mean because he ain't big enough," one of the kids asked, "and he wears them glasses?"

"Maybe; and maybe because, like the skipper says, he plays

ball like he owns the game. But he don't. No one does. When you go up the ladder in this game they start taking pot shots at you to knock you down, and you gotta know how to fight back. This kid thinks a pitch at his skull is something you duck for 'ball one' . . . and that the shortstop's spikes are just to keep him from slipping while the kid tries to steal second. He'll get his lumps handed to him twenty different ways. He's the kind of pesky ballplayer they gun for; he's gotta be twice as tough as the big slugger. He's gotta learn how to be mean and rough and just as dirty as the guy who throws a sharp spike into him. He's gotta learn to fight without hating. Some guys never do"—and he spat down the length of his bat—"and they never go up to the top."

They watched Herman's face, for he was spitting out his words with a bitterness they didn't suspect he had. It was almost as if he were talking about himself.

"Besides," he went on, "baseball is a game of personalities, like any other business, I suppose. Some cruddy skipper don't like the way you part your hair and you sit on your ass for a season. You can never tell. Look at this slob Phipps here at Maldeen. The guy's been years in the majors. You'd think he knew something, wouldn't ya? But he sits a kid like this Kutner for over a month, leaving some fat-assed .260 hitter like Schroeder out there in center. By Christ, Schroeder don't belong in the same league with Kutner."

Herman was thinking hard. "Naw . . . there ain't no way of knowin'."

Someone called from the batting cage.

"Your turn to hit next, Cruller!"

Herman grabbed his stick and started out of the dugout. He looked up at the dark sky and sat down again.

"Frig it," he said. "I ain't had my carrots today. What do they think I am, a goddamn owl?"

Jocko nodded his head.

"They should turn on the lights," he said laconically.

"That Phipps. He's a cheap bastard. If he had his way, he'd have them lamps turned off between innings just to save a few pennies."

Sam nudged him with his elbow.

"There he is now," he said.

Herman hollered.

"Hey, Phipps. Tell 'em to throw the switch, or are we playin' the crucial series with phosphorescent balls?"

The Maldeen manager turned and scowled.

"Up yours, bush leaguer, up yours!" And he made the appropriate gesture with his finger.

Herman laughed.

"Up mine, up mine! What a brain that guy's got! For years he's been telling me, 'up yours!' like it was some part of my name. I'll never forget the time we was playing his club, maybe ten, twelve years ago. It was before they had lamps. The game ran fourteen innings into the twilight and it was as dark as this. Up-yours Phipps, here, was the sticker with two men on and a chance to bust up the game, but we screwed him out of it. Our catcher meets the chucker halfway to the mound and secretly takes the ball from him. Then the pitcher winds up as if he has it and makes believe he's throwing to the plate. The catcher slams the ball in his glove like it was right over the heart of the dish. The ump calls 'strike one!' but he never saw a friggen thing. The catcher does the same routine again and it's strike two, and the ball ain't even been thrown! I'm playin' the third sack as usual and I can figure the deal, and I'm laughing my head off. Old Phipps steps out of the box to knock his cleats . . . and rub his eyes . . . and we get set for the same thing to strike him out. Again the pitcher winds up and the catcher bangs the ball in his mitt. The ump is a tired, blind bastard anyway and he calls 'strike three, yer out!' And whattaya think Phipps does? He steps over to the ump with his ugly map and puts on a rhubarb: 'Ya blind bastard,' he hollers, 'that pitch was a foot outside!' "

The guys around him laughed, though they'd heard this old chestnut a dozen times before and knew it had probably never happened to Phipps. Herman was the kind who enjoyed talking, and he talked all the time. When he said something funny, he laughed himself, and the kids laughed with him, respecting his experience, his knowledge, his happy disposition. They were kids, most of them, seventeen, eighteen, maybe nineteen years old, just beginning in organized baseball; and they grasped at advice and anecdotes from a man who had been up, almost to the top, and had come down again. That they listened and appreciated him made Herman happy, for it gave him a purpose out there. And it kept him talking.

St. Clair's batting time was up and the bell rang. The players in the field trotted in to the bench as Maldeen got set for their infield practice.

The lights went on.

"Ha!" Herman yelled. "I can see you now, Phipps, and you look as ugly as ever."

"Up yours," Phipps returned.

Herman reached for his glove and pounded the well-worn pocket. "That Phipps is a moldy bastard. From as far back as I kin remember, guys have hated his guts. Once they dumped a load of itching powder in his jockstrap, his own teammates!"

"What happened, Herm?"

"Nothing. Would you believe it? That Phipps is so cruddy he never even noticed it!"

In the corner, Jocko Mullins was serious as he followed the ball around the infield.

"He's mean, too. Phipps is mean."

Herman nodded. "When he feels like it, he can make it nasty for you."

"He's a pretty smart ballplayer," said Jocko. It was obvious he wanted to end the conversation.

There was silence for a moment, as if they were obeying him. Then they heard a quiet voice, hardly audible. It was Mike Kutner.

"He's not smart. He's not smart at all."

The words came from under his breath, charged with bitterness. Herman spat juice over the bat rack.

"Maybe not, Mike. But he knows a few things that make up for it. They ain't particularly nice, but from what I've seen, they ain't illegal either."

Jocko was reaching for the ball bag. "O.K., O.K., you guys. Quit the yammering. Get out there and warm up."

Herman grabbed a ball. "Com'on, Mike, let's throw some," he said. "Might as well get used to seeing the ball in these cruddy lights." And he stepped out onto the field, feeling that wonderful excitement that always picked him up before a game.

The game was a tense seesaw battle. Both clubs threatened to have a big-scoring inning several times, but something always happened to snuff out the rally. Herman had a feeling about games like this; the tension grew taut and pulled at you. It usually followed that something would snap and the tight game blow up.

Up to the seventh, the lid was still on. Maldeen came to bat in the bottom of the inning trailing 5 to 4. With two out and the tying run on first, Phipps himself got up there to hit.

Herman moved over to third base and kicked it in a bit, considering the possibilities. Phipps would probably try something to edge that runner around. Steal, hit-and-run, or maybe he'll just shoot for that long one to put them ahead. He moved three steps deeper behind the base, aware that Phipps could pull the ball hard down the line. He was ready for almost anything.

The pitcher tried working the corners and missed the first two pitches. Herman thought, Well, here it comes. Something up now. He was behind the hitter and couldn't afford to waste another pitch. He had to come in with it.

Then, out of the corner of his eye, he saw the runner make his move. On the pitch, Phipps shifted his feet quickly to poke the ball toward right, behind the runner. He got good wood on it and lined it over the second baseman's head. Mike raced over from center and got down on one knee to block the ball as he fielded it; it was too late for a play at third. Mike would play it safe and throw to second, holding the possible winning run at first.

But suddenly as the ball reached him, Kutner seemed to bobble it. Fiercely, he turned and started to leg it back toward the outfield fence. Instinctively, Herman straddled third base and made believe the throw was coming in to him, trying to force the runner to slide, hoping to prevent his scoring. In line with his vision he saw Phipps rounding first, taking off for second with a big grin on his face, his bulky body galloping for that extra base that would put him in scoring position.

Then, just as suddenly, Mike stopped running and whirled in his tracks. As if by magic, he had the ball in his hand and threw sharply to second, a perfect throw on one hop. Phipps didn't even slide. He was out by ten feet, and the inning was over.

At once, Herman realized what the kid had done. He had faked the error out there in the lousy lights, teasing Phipps into trying for that extra base. It was the perfect setup for this sand-lot maneuver, and Phipps fell for it. The kid had made a bum out of the old major leaguer with a high-school sucker trick.

In the dugout, Herman slapped Mike on the back as they sat down.

"Great play, kid. Great play!"

Mike smiled back at him.

"Like I said, he ain't so smart."

Herman shrugged, and had a different feeling.

"Maybe not, but we all pull a boner every once in a while. He's a goat now, but he'll figure a way to get square."

"He ain't smart enough."

This was the trouble with Kutner. The kid was right as far as his thinking went, but it didn't go far enough. For even the dumb guys like Phipps knew enough to protect themselves.

Herman wanted to pursue it, but they were moving into the eighth inning and they had a game to win. Besides, this was a lesson the kid would have to learn the hard way.

It was still 5 to 4 in the top of the ninth. St. Clair had runners on first and third with nobody out and it looked like they could put the game on ice. Herman was the hitter and the infield moved in to make a play at the plate and cut off a run. He got in front of a curve ball and laced it savagely down the third base line. But the fielder made a quick stab for it, and it bounced into his glove. Kutner, who was running third base, was trapped ten feet off the bag and had to make a move toward home. As Herman rounded first he could see the kid was caught in a run-down. The runner from first had legged it around second and was heading for third. Herman made for second thinking they'd end up on second and third with one out, even if it left Mike without a chance to make it back to the crowded base. It was up to Mike to remain in that pickle long enough to give them both time to advance.

Herman watched the kid scurry toward home, forcing the throw to Phipps. He would stop in front of Phipps, waiting for the slow, heavily equipped catcher to chase him back to third. Phipps tried to rush it, hoping to make it a twin killing and bust up the threat. But Mike was too tricky with his body. He faked his move first one way then the other, and they had to chase him back and forth three times. Herman settled on second base and Evans easily made third. Kutner could try for home now, hoping to force an error, or give himself up. Herman grinned as he watched the lumbering Phipps, exasperated by the kid's clever running and the screaming of the crowd.

He saw Mike finally make his run for it. The throw went quickly in to Phipps who stood in front of the plate. The burly catcher grabbed the ball and waited there for the kid. Herman watched Mike stop in front of Phipps, as if waiting to be tagged. Phipps moved two steps up the line to make the put-out, and Herman suddenly felt he could call the shot. He saw the tag, the brutal, vindictive slugging into Mike's body, just under the heart. A baseball is harder than a fist, and the kid went down in a heap.

Sure . . . there it is. Herman had seen it coming. This is baseball, and Phipps played it the way he had to play it. If a guy gets troublesome, you figure out a way to get rid of him. It happened a hundred times in every league he ever played in. It was ugly and stupid, but you had to take your lumps when someone felt like handing them to you. The crowd only saw part of it, excusing the roughness in the heat of a tight ball game. What the hell, Phipps was their hero. He ran a winning ball club for the home town. If he tagged a guy too hard, well, that's too bad. The handful of people who booed him would forget it soon enough.

Herman rushed in and looked down at the kid writhing in pain. He could only stand there while they worked over him. This was a baseball reality, however little sense it made. The simple truth was that there was more than one way to win a game. And almost any way was an old way and acceptable.

"See, he ain't so dumb!" he mumbled to himself. "He ain't so goddamn dumb."

They were helping Kutner up now, his arms draped over

their shoulders. Herman saw the pain in his face; the anger stirred within him and he turned to Phipps.

"You bastard. You cruddy bastard."

Phipps looked away from him, and threw the ball to the pitcher. He had nothing to say.

A few days later, Maldeen and St. Clair met for the final, decisive game of the series, this time at St. Clair's ball park. It was a hot Sunday afternoon, with the park thermometer hovering at about 104 degrees.

Pre-game practice was uninspired and torpid. The players were tired and jumpy in the heat and lacked the full measure of drive that had brought them to this high point in the race. Jocko Mullins tried to drive them, prodding at the lethargy of the men. Normally a subdued man, quiet and even ineffectual, the manager became blustering and irritable. Someplace he had heard that a manager could not be a nice guy and win pennants, so he worked at being tough, trying to force his will upon them. They raised their heads to his sudden tirades, as if looking to see who the stranger was, and when they saw, they turned away from him and kept their distance.

Herman Cruller knew they had carried too much anger since the injury to Mike, all of them seeking some form of revenge. Kutner had a cracked rib and would be out for the series, the doctor had told them. It left them with frayed nerves, in a perpetual state of agitation. They had played hard in their anger, but not well; for baseball is not a game of anger, but one of control and precision. Every pop-up with men on base irritated them too much; each misplay added to their frustration, their feeling of helplessness.

And now, before the umpire hollered "Play ball!" for the last time that season, Herman felt deflated. He could not look forward to the tension and excitement of the game. The crowd was there, sweltering even in the shade of the stands behind him, pressuring the players with their boisterous presence. Even the bleachers, where the Negroes sat blistering under the naked sun, were full and demanding. They were all there, defying the heat, for this was the "big one," the game that decided and ended a season of games.

Herman looked up into the stands and watched people fanning themselves with their programs, their throats already parched from rasping calls but soon to be lubricated by long draughts of cold beer. For years he had listened to their routine, opinionated braying during the practice hours, the little pieces of stupidity from the big blaring voices. Sullenly, he watched them hollering their pre-game nonsense: "Lefty Moss stinks. He couldn't even strike out my Aunt Mabel, and she's ninety-one!" "I'll bet ya a ten-spot he goes the route, horse-face; I'll bet ya another ten-spot he wins, too!" "Aah, hell. Gowann." Thinking with their brains in their asses like a bunch of children betting their hard-earned money as if they knew what they were talking about. For all the years he had played professional baseball, for as far back as he could remember, he hated the loud ones in the crowds who had watched him those thousands of innings. He hated them for their fickleness, their blaring derision, their hooting and squawking, the sadistic way they kicked at the guy who was down. He hated the phony effort at what they called sportsmanship, the brief moment of applause that supposedly justified the hours of razzing they had really come to revel in. It was as if the ballplayers were not playing a game they could watch and enjoy, but were caricatures representing objects of love and hate, were either heroes or villains. And if they had love for a player, still they were quick to jeer at him when he booted one or fanned with a crucial run on base. They seldom considered the player a human being, capable of error as well as competence. Their money was their admission to the arena, and it gave them rights unlimited. For half a buck they could scream and jeer and sound off with their cruddy opinions as if they were speaking gospel. When they felt like it, they unleashed their venom against a ballplayer who displeased them until their scorn itself was part of their picture of him. He was a bum in their eyes, and he had to battle against them with as great a power as he did against the legitimate opposition on the field. When the crowd was down on a kid, the odds were you could count him out, for he was hitting with a pair of strikes against him and the rattling of catcalls in his ears.

He had seen the whims of a crowd make a goat out of more than one good ballplayer and then ride him right out of the league.

But it was the crowd who paid him his stinking forty bucks a week, fair weather and foul. If he forgot, the management was right there to remind him. Baseball was a big game, and all kinds of people came to watch it for all kinds of reasons. He was paid to play for them all.

But the afternoon was hot and he was tired, and the game was a chore. It wasn't in him to please this crowd.

You're bitter, Herm, he told himself finally. You're bitter and beat by the heat. You're old and tired and near the end of the stinking line in this game, and you're taking it out on a bunch of people no different from yourself. Give yourself another year or two and you'll be paying your dough to sit up there and guzzle beer with the rest of them.

Below him now in the dugout he heard the excited voices of his teammates, and it stirred him from his gloomy thoughts. He turned into the bench and saw Mike Kutner dressed in his uniform, for the first time since his injury.

The appearance of the kid was a tonic to them all. They had not seen him for three days.

"Where ya been, y'old four-eyed bastard?"

Mike was evasive.

"Aw . . . no place in particular."

"How d'ya feel, kid?" Herman looked him over closely.

"O.K. I'm taped up some."

"Why didn't ya come around? Everyone was wondering about you."

Mike stared at his hands.

"They had me in the hospital. They told me to take it easy, so I listened on the radio."

"Oh yeah? How did it sound?"

Mike smiled.

"You guys sure stank up the joint, didn't you?"

For the first time that day, Herman saw them all laughing.

Jocko Mullins came over and shook Mike's hand.

"What'd the doc say, Kutner? Can you play?"

He rubbed his taped-up side and shrugged his shoulders. "I'm supposed to take it easy, Skipper."

Jocko spit over the bat rack; his face fell to his navel.

"O.K.," he said. "So take it easy."

The game was a tight, fast pitchers' duel. Both pitchers worked smoothly through the steaming hours, catching the corners with their curve balls, overpowering the hitters with a fast ball that seemed to rise with the heat. Seldom were either of them in trouble, and the game rushed hurriedly along without anyone coming close to pay dirt. The crowd, at first excited by the excellence of the pitching, turned their praise to contempt for the hitters, as if they suddenly decided that the whole business was a frame-up by the players to get home early. What appeared to be a dramatic game in process, loaded with the tensions of some pending eruption, became dull and plodding to them and they unleashed a steady vituperative stream of scorn at every hitter who failed to get on base.

Herman tried to ignore it and couldn't. When, later, he went down swinging for the second time—this time with two men on—his feelings were all too sharply aroused. He walked the sickening walk back to the dugout, and the crowd bellowed at him over their beer bottles from no more than twenty feet away.

In the dugout they avoided him, watching the next hitter, leaving him in privacy to nurse his failure. But behind them they could hear the harsh, relentless contempt of the grandstand jockeys.

Herman felt a hand on his arm.

"The wolves are working the jaws, eh, Herm?"

He snickered at Mike now for repeating an old line of his own.

"They love you, Herm. In reality, they love you."

The words were designed to kid him and he shrugged them off.

"I love them too, the sonsofbitches . . . ," he mumbled, and knew he never hated them so much.

In the ending of the sixth, the score was still o–o, and St. Clair came to bat. Jocko suddenly had a brain storm.

"Let's change the luck," he said. "Kutner, go on out and handle the first base traffic. Maybe we can push one across."

"That's his stroke of genius for the day," Herman muttered.

The kid grinned and walked out to the coach's box.

Suddenly, all hell broke loose. The home-town crowd, hungry for something to yell about, saw him for the first time this series, and they stood up to cheer as if some sort of seven-star general was returning from the wars. The kids at the game started their rhythmic, high-pitched chanting: *We want Kutner; we want Kutner.* Louder and stronger it grew, till the stands were jumping with it, as if there were nothing more to the game than the test of an injured ballplayer to show if he could be the hero.

They tried to ignore it on the bench, as they ignored all the rest of the jabber, and concentrate on the scoring of a run.

Jocko prodded them.

"Com'on, let's get a man on and they'll shut up."

But they went down in order, and in their half of the seventh, Jocko kept Mike on the bench, as a defense against another demonstration. But it didn't stop them. They felt cheated by this obvious denial of his presence on the field; they growled at the manager and shouted insults at every batter who failed to get a good piece of the ball. And, on top of it all, they yelled for Mike.

Then, in the top of the ninth, the visiting Maldeen pushed across the first run of the game. A base on balls with two outs, and a two-base hit down the line. It came so late in the game it was something of a surprise, as if it weren't supposed to happen. St. Clair moved in for their last time at bat, suddenly feeling the sharp edge of tension that comes with a ninth-inning climax.

Herman had felt it in his bones that this would be a rotten day. All along he had waited for the ax to fall, knowing inside him that they just didn't have it. And now that it had happened, and they were down to their last three outs, he was exasperated by the knowledge that he wouldn't get another chance to hit. Now, too late, he wanted it. More than anything he wanted to prove he was still a buster and could bang away in the clutch like nobody else. So he sat there torturing himself by recalling his dismal trips to the plate and the languid, helpless feeling within him as he had faced the pitcher. He had been a failure, and his only vindication would be the victory of his team. All at once, this came to him in his anger and frustration. He picked up a bat and pounded it against the dugout steps, his tired husky voice demanding a rally from them.

"Com'on, you cruds! Let's get moving on these guys. Let's pour it on the sonsofbitches!"

His throat was parched and his mouth tasted only the hot,

dry dust of the infield, the same he'd tasted for the past two hours as he'd mouthed the million chatter-words at his pitcher. He turned to the water pail, yelling as he went, his eyes red, both from the concentrated heat of the day and from the emotion of their impending defeat.

On the bench they caught the ragged edges of his mood and were infected by it. For the first time that scorching afternoon, they really jumped on the Maldeen pitcher with their jockeying, chewing away at his poise and the security of his one-run lead.

"Ho, ya big long-legged bean pole. You throw like yer stepping in slop."

"Yeah, what'd ya sit in, Lefty? Lookit that spot on yer ass!"

"Lookit that goddamn dirty spot. Whattaya got in yer pants, Lefty?"

"Keep your foot on that rubber, dammit. Hey, ump, make him keep his foot on that rubber. He's takin' an extra step!"

"Don't slide that big, flat foot off, Lefty, or we'll knock it off. Keep that foot where it belongs!"

"Hey, there's that dirty spot in his pants again. God, that looks awful!"

And, as if in direct response, he walked the first man up.

The crowd responded with a new expectancy. They began stamping feet and clapping hands in a steady thumping rhythm till the grandstand shook with their eagerness. Herman found himself slamming his bat against the steps along with their beat, trying to drive this tying run across with the sheer force of noise.

Jocko had the next batter bunt the potential tying run into scoring position at second base, and the crowd leaned forward in their seats to watch the resolution of this final crisis. It did not escape them that there was little power left in the St. Clair batting order to bring this run to pay dirt. Nor did it escape them that Mike Kutner was sitting in that dugout, dressed in uniform. They started in again, a few of them at first, chanting the magic words: *We want Kutner! We want Kutner!* The game had been dull for them, without the excitement of hits, runs, and action. They were hot and tired and it angered them. It also granted them the right to make demands. They started stamping their feet again, calling with the tempo of the bouncing floor boards: *We want Kutner! We want Kutner!* The sound of it rose to a furious pitch, louder and louder, until they were all swept up into it, even those who were there for the ride, those who knew nothing of Mike Kutner nor really cared which team won.

The pitcher was the scheduled hitter and he never made a move from the bench. He was exhausted beyond measure; his arms hung heavily at his side unwilling to hold a bat. Herman watched Jocko look down the length of the bench, wondering whom he would pick. In class D ball, there are no professional pinch-hitters. Let Carter hit, Herman thought. For a pitcher he does O.K. with the stick. Or even Blaine. Blaine can get wood on it. Behind them and all around, the roar of voices—*We want Kutner*—demanding, demanding. Listen to the crowd, Herman thought; listen to them. He saw Jocko's look, worried and uncertain. Want a coin, Jocko? Herman mused bitterly. Let the goddamn coin decide. Heads it's Carter, tails it's Blaine. What the hell, it's the best you can do. *We want Kutner!*

Finally, the skipper turned to face the kid himself, his eyes at once questioning and demanding and apologizing. Can you get up there? Never mind the cracked rib. Drive in that run. A cracked rib ain't nothing. Go ahead, Kutner, go ahead and hit!

Herman saw the kid feel under his heart, testing the tenderness of the injury. Don't you get up there, kid, he thought. For what? To be a hero for these cruddy class D bastards? You got a whole career ahead of you. Do what the doc says and take it easy. He waited while Jocko waited, wondering what the kid would do.

Jocko looked like a beggar. Herman knew what would happen.

He watched the kid reach for his favorite stick and step slowly out of the dugout. The rhythmic yelling broke into one long wild scream when they saw him. For a few thousand people, they made more noise than anything he had ever heard before, even in the big towns. He saw the kid looking down at him, no longer doubtful, the set, quiet smile behind the glasses.

"Guess you gotta get that blow, Mike."

"I will."

"They'll run you for mayor."

Mike grinned. "Anything's better than Austin, Kentucky."

And he walked slowly to the plate, swinging the bats.

Herman laughed through his tension, an uncontrolled, giddy laugh like a child in a sudden switch from crying to giggling. How could you keep a kid like that down? His own sunk feeling had left him. He knew in his gut that the goddamn little four-eyed wonder-boy would drive in that run.

The kid took his time getting set in the batter's box. From the bench they could hear the growls of Lou Phipps, jockeying through his mask, though the words were lost in the bedlam around them. They saw Mike ignore him, concentrating on his position, loosening the sticky clothing on his shoulders. In a moment, the pitcher checked the runner dancing off second and let go his first pitch. The ball came in high and tight, right at the head, as hard as the guy could throw it. At the last moment, Mike threw himself on the ground to avoid the beaning.

Herman spat through his teeth. Oh you bastard, Phipps. You think of everything, don'tcha! Ten years in the big time and twice as many ways to knock a guy down! You learned the dirty rules of this game and you play them for all they're worth. Maybe the bastards like you made it too rough for the soft punks like me, but you'll lose against this kid. I swear it, you mean sonofabitch; you'll never knock this kid out!

Kutner stood up and grinned. He dusted himself off without even glancing at Phipps. Herman could see him thinking baseball. This was not a kid who wasted words on a crumb like Phipps for whatever angry satisfactions there might be in it. This was a ballplayer, up there only to hit. Look at him; no jerky movements, no wild waving of the bat, almost no preliminary swing. He stood simply, his feet spread wide and his bat cocked high over his shoulder. Herman thought, Kutner probably looked the same playing stick ball behind his grammar school. A natural.

Finally, they were set again. The pitch came off the sensitive fingers and curved around the outside corner. Mike checked his swing and waited for the umpire's call:

"Ball two!"

At once the crowd let loose its fury, for the prospect of walking Mike at this crucial moment would deprive them of the anticipated triumph of their chosen hero. A base on balls here would be a denial of that test, a small piece of nothing, substituted for the supreme moment. Mike would walk to first base with nothing resolved, a bitter disappointment to their dramatic expectations.

Herman mumbled on the bench.

"Listen to 'em. They don't like it. They're afraid Phipps won't pitch to him."

"Sure, they even want Mike to cut at the bad ones. Anything but a base on balls."

The lefty on the mound seemed worried again, and fidgeted with the worn rosin bag behind him. Phipps was yelling at him, shaking his fist as he stepped in front of the plate, his tired concession to a catcher's routine walk to the mound. Herman grinned at the sight of old Phipps's soaked back, knowing how much this rum-chaser hated working the hot afternoons. Through the mask, Herm had seen those red, wet eyes, bleary from the hot, white light and endless concentration behind the plate, from the wracking pressure of this final ball game that had to be won. And, he would have bet, from the fumes of his well-spiked private water bottle.

Herman knew the lefty'd have to come in there with it, for a base on balls would put the winning run on with the top of the order coming up. Phipps knew the dangers; it was better to pitch to the injured kid than risk putting him on. Yet, there was something in the air that defied this logic, some undefinable feeling that Mike would hit, taped side or no. Maybe it came from the combined will of the three thousand fans jammed in there, or maybe from the batter himself.

Herman watched the pitcher go into his motion and he held his breath. The stretch . . . the hands steady to check the runner . . . now the arm up and back and the pitch moving in. In a split second he could see it was coming in there, waist-high and close to the heart of the dish. He saw Mike level off, his body pivoting with his compact power, and watched that wonderful, snapping swing begin. But suddenly, Mike seemed to lose his sharp timing; the bat rode sloppily around, throwing him clumsily off balance, and the ball sliced harmlessly off to the side of the plate and into the dugout.

"Strike one!" the umpire called immediately.

In a second Mike was on him, his face pushed into the umpire's, red as a beet with instant anger. Above the confused shouting of the crowd, Herman could hear him, his voice pitched high and shrill.

"He touched my bat! He touched my bat!"

The ump was momentarily staggered by Mike's rage and did not respond. But from the St. Clair bench they poured out onto the field and closed in on the man with their collective anger.

"Didn't you see that?" Jocko demanded. "Didn't you see that sonofabitch grab Kutner's bat?"

"Yeah . . . he pushed the end of his bat before the swing!"

The ump retreated, aware that he must have missed it.

"I saw nothing. Goddammit, let's play ball."

Jocko was all over him. "You saw nothing? Everybody in this friggen ball park saw it, and you saw nothing. What the hell are you here for? 'I saw nothing' he says!"

"Play ball, I say. Get off the goddamn field and let's play ball!"

"But Phipps grabbed the kid's bat! Don't you know the goddam rules? The kid gets his base! The kid gets his base!"

"I didn't see nobody grabbing his bat. Now get off the field!"

"You're no friggen umpire. You're a blind sonofabitch. 'I didn't see nothing' he says!"

"Get off the field! Get off!"

Herman moved off to the side. He had always hated rhubarbs and he was always in them. He walked over to Mike who had left the argument to tighten his shoelaces. He stood over the kneeling kid and waited until he was through. Then he saw the angry eyes behind the glasses and he knew that Mike was flustered.

"Goddammit, Herm. Whattaya do with a bastard like that Phipps? How do ya play baseball with a guy like that on the goddamn field?"

Herman's voice was low and thick. He was amazed at his own emotion.

"You gotta show the sonofabitch that you're here to stay, that you can't be pushed around! You gotta teach him that yourself, like you gotta teach every sonofabitch in every league you play in. The ump ain't gonna help you, you gotta do it yourself!"

"O.K., O.K. What do I do, club him over the head with the bat?"

"Mike, you do it any way that ain't assault to a cop and ain't illegal to an umpire. You hear me? Any way!"

The kid's voice was tired.

"But that's crazy. He'll just start in on me again. . . ."

"No!" Herman snapped at him. "He'll quit. Just like the rest of them do; he'll quit! Cause nobody likes to get their lumps handed to them, not more than once from the same guy, anyway. It ain't only Phipps, Mike. It'll be a thousand Phippses to come."

He watched the kid rub rosin over his bat handle and wondered what was in his head.

Behind them the ump hollered:

"All right, Kutner. Batter up!"

Herman slapped him on the back and walked back to the bench.

They were doubly tense now, none of them sitting, but rather hanging on the lip of the dugout as far out as they were legally allowed to be. They were beating on the ump and Phipps and the pitcher, barking through the steaming heat till the air itself became so charged a man could almost see the sparks. The crowd became a part of the electric tension, noisy and bitter, too agitated to continue their united, rhythmic jockeying. Behind his own hoarse shouting Herman thought, A game ain't the same after a big rhubarb.

The pitcher pounded the ball into his glove a dozen times, waiting for Phipps and his sign. Mike dug himself back in the batter's box and they were ready to go. Two balls and one strike, the ump signaled with his raised fingers. "Play ball!" he shouted.

Com'on, Mike. Lay into it. This guy ain't got nothing he can get by you. Pick out the one you like and give it a ride. Com'on, Mike . . . com'on, you sweetheart.

The ball wobbled at half-speed toward the plate, a fluttering junk-pitch designed to keep the anxious hitter off balance. Mike stepped, and snapped at it with his powerful wrists. The ball sizzled past the third baseman like a rifle shot and bounded into left field almost before the crowd had time to react. The runner on second took off with the sound of the contact and drove toward the plate with everything he had left. The fielder moved quickly in front of the ball and tried for the desperate throw home to cut off the tying run. Mike rounded first at full speed, watching the ball out of the corner of his eye. He never stopped running as the throw came in, too late to nail the runner at home, too late to make a play at second on him. He slowed up as he pulled into second base, and the crowd shook the grandstands till they rattled.

God, how they yelled! It was wild and piercing and frantic. Herman saw them throwing up their straw hats, their score cards, their newspapers. He saw elderly ladies scream halle-lujas and children jump up and down like it was Christmas morning. He saw his teammates, sitting back now, shaking their smiling heads in admiration for this kid who was a winner for them.

But the score was 1–1, only tied, and the game had still to be won. The bedlam subsided for the next hitter, for no one could sustain that high pitch of perpetual climax. It was as if the crisis had been reached and the hero had passed the test. What was to follow was of lesser importance to them.

Herman saw the kid edging off second and he knew in an instant that he was far from through. Would he try to steal? With his side taped up, would he try it? Stealing third was a risky piece of business and not often tried, for the short throw from the catcher was just a quick snap and usually accurate. But with only one out, there was much to be gained. On third he could score on a long fly ball or an infield grounder, as well as on a base hit.

The pitcher took his time getting set, trying to settle him-self in the din to confront this sudden threat to his victory. His pitch was high and hard, motivated too much by his anger to be in the strike zone, and he growled at himself as the umpire called it a ball.

Herman saw that Mike was standing relaxed off second as Phipps threw back to the pitcher. He drifted back slowly to the base to await the next pitch. It came in hard again, and a foot outside. The crowd felt the edge on the lefty's nerves and started getting on him again. Phipps stood up from his tired crouch and hollered his own form of encouragement to him. He threw the ball back and turned to his position.

At the moment Phipps began his throw, Mike made his move. He put his head down and broke for third in a sudden sprint. He needed a second or two, the brief moment of time when a team is too startled, too off balance to react to this surprise move. The crowd had raised a protective curtain of noise over the infield. The pitcher was smoldering in his own anxieties, unaware of the kid's delayed steal. He did not hear the warning of the infielders behind him until that critical moment had dissipated itself. Then he whirled and threw to third, a sudden awkward movement, too high and too late. Mike slid in under a cloud of dust. He was safe.

Phipps came out toward the mound shaking with rage. With one sweep of his arm he banished the lefty from the game and called to the bullpen for relief.

It was minutes before the new pitcher was ready to work. It gave the crowd a breather and they turned again to their beer bottles, long since stale and flat. But they cared little. This was something new, and they recognized it for what it was: sheer drama, raw and exciting, thick with doubts and hopes. The winning run stood on third base, ninety little feet from victory, and there were two outs left to bring him in. It seemed so simple: a squeeze play, a long fly ball, a base hit.

Herman Cruller kneeled on the step of the dugout, waiting for the next pitch. He remembered there were two balls on the hitter, and he knew they'd walk him for the chance at a double play on a ground ball. They did, and it brought Evans to the plate. The guy had two hits under his belt already for the crowd to chew on; they greeted him with a new wave of noise, begging him to drive in that run.

Herman watched Evans move into the box and toss his extra stick to the bat boy. It wasn't until the pitcher was getting his sign that Herman realized there was no one in the batter's circle waiting his turn. It hit him in the gut like a fist: *He* was supposed to be there.

What in the hell's the matter, Herm? Don't you wanna hit? You never thought you'd get a crack at it this inning, did you? Oh, how you itched for it then. And now that it looks like you might, you got butterflies!

He grabbed a couple of bats and knelt in the batter's circle, cursing himself for his nervousness.

It's a ball game, nothing but a stinking class D ball game. If Evans finks out, it's up to you. All you gotta do is stand up there and poke out a base hit. One more base hit added to the thousands you've belted over the years. It's a cinch. Against a chucker like this guy, it's a lead-pipe cinch.

But deep within him he knew that it was no cinch at all, but rather the toughest base hit he'd ever beg for after twenty years in baseball. What was it, Herm? What was it that made guys play these goddamn games with their nerves? Why wasn't he relaxed like he used to be and ready for anything? Sure, it was true he hadn't had too good a year. He was down to .276 and lots of times that season he'd moved too slowly at third for those ground balls that hugged the line. But, what the hell, he couldn't be great every season! What the hell did they want from him?

He didn't know any more. He had a feeling through all the years of his struggling that he never really knew.

He had to admit it if only to himself. More than anything he wanted Evans to drive in that run. Old Herman Cruller did not want to be tested again. He leaned against his bats to ease the agony of the butterflies in his gut.

Evans took a strike to get the feel of the new pitcher, and then worked the count to a full three-and-two. The pitcher stepped off the rubber to ponder the crucial pitch coming up.

Herman thought, no, it didn't have to happen now. The guy could strike out, or pop one up, and there still would be one more out and he would be it. Then there could be any number of innings. He'd played games where moments like this were a dime a dozen; they stretched on through an extra hour or two, inning after inning, with men on the bases itching for pay dirt, the big bats stabbing at the crucial pitches, the fielders chasing their asses for the big catch to save the crucial run, till your heart was beating like a cannon.

When it goes down to the wire like that, you just can't shake it off. You forget about your wife and kids and your next year's job, and you sweat for the sudden run to clinch it—or lose it. Deep down inside you know you're gonna lose, that some unconscious .240 hitter on the other club is gonna bleed one by you, trying to stop his swing at a curve ball. You hate him even as he walks up there, swinging two sticks like he's a real buster. You think back that he's fanned twice that day and dribbled one fair ball onto the infield grass. "He's due!" they yell from the other damn bench, and you get that sinking feeling that this is the jerk who'll piss in the pie. You hold your breath and your heart climbs the ladder to your throat, trying to watch the game through your open mouth.

The thrillers. . . . All of a sudden, he hated the goddamn thrillers.

Then he saw Evans hitching up his pants and setting his cap, a regular ritual with him. He knew the guy was good enough with the stick to break up the game if he kept loose up there. Do it, for Chrissakes; do it. Get a good chunk of that apple and bring the kid in. For old Herman Cruller is a tired bastard.

The pitch came in, a low curve ball intended to make Evans hit down on the ground for that double play. He lunged at it with only a part of his power, and sliced it into short right field. The outfielders had been playing shallow, for a deep drive would beat them even if they caught it. Herman watched the guy in right move in to settle under it, and he wondered if Mike would make a try for the plate after the catch.

Quickly he turned to see him tag up at third, his body crouching and tense like a dash man waiting for the starting gun. The kid was following the flight of the ball as it completed its arc into the fielder's hands. Behind him, the crowd rose quickly to their feet, for here was the play that might end it. The throw versus the runner, both beginning at almost the same second. The runner springs ninety feet, trying to beat the speed of the ball from little over twice the distance. It seemed improbable that Mike would win.

Herman stood like the rest of them, aware that there would be more to this play than a question of who gets home first, Mike or the ball, for Phipps would be there waiting for him.

Then he saw the kid take off like a demon, his head thrust forward and his legs digging down that white line like a bull after a red rag. This was no fake to draw the throw; he was going all the way! Phipps squatted over the plate to receive the throw and block the entrance. Then Herman saw him move up the line a foot or two, for the throw was on the third base side, still ready to dive on the kid as he slid in, stabbing with his foot for a piece of the plate with one of his fine fall-away slides.

The ball bounced into the big mitt and Phipps turned up the line to make the tag. Mike was coming in hard, leaning his body as if to begin to slide. Then, suddenly he straightened up and charged into the crouching Phipps with all the momentum of his driving sprint, his knees high, pumping savagely.

Even above the screaming crowd they could hear that crashing contact. Mike's legs seemed to keep going for seconds after his body sprawled in the dirt ten feet past home plate. Phipps lay groaning on his back, spitting out a tooth, with his mitt and the ball halfway to the dugout.

The umpire spread his arms out wide, palms down.

"Safe!" he hollered.

And the game was over.

Herman kneeled at Mike's side. The kid slowly raised himself to his knees and then struggled to his feet. He turned toward Phipps now, still tense and ready. He saw the big limp body and the bleeding mouth and his face sagged. He shook his head and turned away, walking slowly and holding his side.

Phipps saw him and mumbled through his pain:

"Kutner, you sonofabitch. . . ."

But the words were tired and meaningless, an empty gesture of defiance from a beaten man without anger or conviction, and Mike shrugged them off.

Herman answered for him. "Up yours, Phipps," he said. "Up yours."

In the clubhouse they laid him on the table and waited for the doctor.

"How ya feeling, kid?"

"O.K.," he said.

But they held down the jubilation over their first championship because he obviously wasn't feeling O.K.

Herman saw him looking up at him.

"That's what you meant, eh, Herm?" he said.

"Yeah. You creamed him, Mike." There was little emotion in Mike's drawn face. Herman went on with a rush of enthusiasm. "God, you hit him like a locomotive. He'll never forget it, Mike; not so long as he lives."

But then he realized the words were wasted, for the kid had passed out cold.

Behind him the doctor, pudgy and bald, worked his way through the crowded locker room, boisterous with his greetings to the ballplayers he admired.

"Great game, fellows. You sure pulled it out of the fire. Yes sir . . . and how's the hero over here? You know, I just left Phipps. He's not in very good shape. No sirree. I'm sorry for him, but you know, I guess he had it coming to him. Yes sir . . . he had it coming to him all right."

Somebody handed Herman a bottle of cold beer. He tipped it back and took a long swallow. The tingling flavor relaxed him and he sat down to nurse the rest of it. His head was spinning, dizzy and tired from too much of everything, and he felt as if he'd never be able to get up.

It came to him that he was getting old at last.

# 5 *The Clown*

Charlie looked up suddenly from his Scotch-on-the-rocks and saw her giggling into her glass.

"Let me see . . . ," he said, leaning over. "What's so funny in there?"

She laughed harder at this piece of nonsense.

"No. I'm laughing at you from this afternoon. Out there in the ball park. . . ." Gradually she started to let go, losing more and more control, until her whole body was shaking with laughter. She was consumed by her recollection of his crazy antics on the diamond.

"What . . . ?" he asked, starting to chuckle himself, for her laughter was contagious.

By now she could hardly talk, and when she tried to tell him, she almost choked. "When you hit to the pitcher . . . ," she spluttered, "and ran the wrong way!"

He got a big bang out of her laughter. He had gotten even greater pleasure from the reaction of the crowd at the game. With two out and a man on first, he had slashed one hard at the pitcher, on one hop. The pitcher had the ball in his glove before Charlie could even leave the batter's box. In a sudden moment of wild frustration—for the thought of racing to first base to beat such an impossible play infuriated him—Charlie had pulled a crazy stunt: He'd started scurrying to third. The pitcher got so confused he threw over there, forgetting the play was simply to first to end the inning. The third baseman didn't know what to do with the ball. He waited to touch Charlie for the out, but the runner stopped and legged it back toward home. To the delight of the crowd, he got caught in a run-down, neither the catcher nor the infielder remembering to throw to first. Finally, Charlie sat down halfway to home, laughing at their stupidity, pointing at the first baseman who was frantically screaming for the ball to make the put-out. The mad maneuver had fractured the crowd; they'd talk about that one for a long time.

Finally, now, her laughter subsided to convulsive spasms, and she wiped her eyes and smeared her mascara a little.

"God, you're a riot, Charlie!" But in a minute, she started in again, too exhausted to control herself.

"Oh, come now, Aimie . . . ," he said, trying to settle her, though actually he was enjoying the demonstration. He finally relaxed in his chair to wait, and his eyes rested on her beautiful, bouncing breasts in the low-cut dress. Up and down, up and down, more and more rapidly. She had so completely given herself to hysterics he began to conjure up wonderful possibilities. Fascinated, he toyed with the thought of one of them flipping out, balancing the prospects of the left against the right. Which would be first? In a weird sort of game he decided that if it was the left one he would. . . . But then instinct came to her rescue or she must have read his mind, for she raised a hand to the deep V on her bosom for the support she so desperately needed. Her movements were still attractive to him, and while she laughed he embarked on a chain of erotic pipe dreams that ended with a speculation on what it would be like to lay a girl while she was laughing like that. It tickled him. He thought it was about the only way he hadn't. He stored it away in the fertile closets of his memory, an act to be tried. In any event, he would use it on the guys in the locker room. Whether a fact or a product of his unlimited imagination made little difference. He brought the glass to his lips and drank heavily of the cool, amber liquid, already preparing the adjectives for tomorrow's inspired storytelling.

He looked over again at the blonde named Aimie, and savored her beauty. For all the laughs, it always baffled him that he should be sitting here with such a good-looking doll. That was it, he knew; the laughs did it. God knows he was no Tyrone Power. His round face was pleasant enough, but hardly romantic. It was an open, agile face, and he used its muscles as if it were a rubber mask. What he lacked in beauty he made up for by comedy. But he had always believed that guys like him never got the beautiful girls. The fact that he always got them consistently amazed him.

What the hell, he told himself. It's your charm. You're a charmer, boy. You got that certain thing. You don't struggle through life, you glide.

Finally, she stopped laughing. He toyed with the idea of making her begin again but thought better of it. For a moment, she sipped her drink, avoiding his eyes for fear of his humor, and she groped for something to say.

"I sure do like baseball," she said philosophically, as though she was summing up.

The fullest implication of this remark was not lost on Charlie. She was no fan, he knew. She knew little about the game. She would come because there was supposed to be a crazy nut out there who did funny things. She and a load of others.

This was Charles L. Caulfield Jr.'s claim to fame. He knew he wasn't a great ballplayer, and he modestly doubted that he was even a good one or belonged in AA ball at all. Yet here he was, one year out of college, a regular right fielder with a first division AA club. With a certain amount of assurance he told himself he seldom held the team back. He played his position passably, largely, he knew, because of the brilliance of the kid next to him in center. With the stick, he was on his own, and he had all kinds of trouble with AA pitching. The picture was obvious enough: they were carrying him. But nobody seemed to mind. The fans loved him for the crazy laughs he gave them; the management loved him for the increased gate; and the players loved him, well, because he was lovable. If they put a better ballplayer out there (there were about four of them on the bench, he mused) they might or might not win a few more games. Charlie remembered a day a few weeks before. They had loaded up the bases with two out in a late inning. He stepped up to hit with Houston one run behind. The skipper thought it would be best to substitute the best sticker he had in this crucial spot and sent a man from the bench out there to hit for Charlie. The crowd rose to its feet and bellowed defiantly against this routine attempt to win a ball game, for they preferred the clown to the slugger. Charlie merely waved his hand and limped grotesquely back to the dugout as if he had suddenly incurred some ghastly injury to his leg and the manager was being kind enough to spare him. It was enough for the crowd. They laughed affectionately and rooted for the pinch hitter. And the manager loved him for it.

But, from the bench, he recalled his secret amusement that the guy had fanned on three straight pitches to end the rally.

The whole business of being a ballplayer was easy enough for Charlie Caulfield. He seemed to feel none of the strains typical of the other players. They were out there every day driving themselves through the hot summer afternoons, sweating for that extra-base blow that would secure their spot on the club for a while longer, pushing their tired bodies through the late innings of the scorching double-headers in a nervous show for the big-league scout behind the dugout, hoping against hope that they might scramble another notch up the ladder to the great, big, glorious top.

Charlie was apart from it, enjoying baseball as a free ride.

It wasn't as if he didn't like the game for itself. He did. In fact, he loved it. But he was without their driving ambition. He didn't need it for the simple reason that he didn't need this job. He had contacts enough for a dozen positions in business, all of them solid and secure with promise of a good future. But, at the moment, they held no real attraction for him; he hated the stuffy confinement of an office and the artifice demanded in salesmanship, even though he knew he'd be good at it. Let it wait, he told himself. He'd be ready enough in a few years.

For a lark, he had accepted an offer, the year before, to play minor-league ball in a class B league near the university town. It was no surprise, for he had played good ball in college. In that first year of pro ball, he divided his time and interests equally between the pretty young thing he had known at school and the equally serious affairs of the diamond. And when she left him for a suitor of more serious intentions, he shifted his ardor to the local, well-stocked brothel. He decided it was easier for him to buy a bed partner than a base hit and, he tried to believe, a lot more pleasurable.

Yet, through it all, he had a decent enough season. He batted a respectable .289—largely because he was a clever bunter—and booted no more than his share. But most of all, he enjoyed frolicking for his admiring fans.

The class B club had a working agreement with Houston, and when they came up from Texas to check on players, they saw him on one of his better days. While the others tightened up under the pressure of this scrutiny, Charlie was as relaxed as an old pro. The truth was he had come late to the ball park and missed the agitated chatter about the scouts. He hadn't known they were there. In the winter, they located him by phone while he was vacationing in Florida, and they learned his draft status: deferred for a punctured eardrum. This was in 1941 when a punctured eardrum enhanced a man's value considerably.

So they moved him up to Houston, having lost a number of players to the Army. They tried him out at the start of the season, half expecting to toss him back to the lower echelons. But the club went well and Charlie's antics got excellent publicity. Before long, the fans made a star out of him, and he learned to give them what they wanted. He gave up even trying to be a real ballplayer; he was getting paid for being a freak.

He looked over at Aimie now and wondered what she really thought of him. Probably just laughs, he thought. Good-time Charlie for laughs. He tried not to consider his feeling for her. That sort of thing frightened him. Sooner or later, he would take her to bed, he hoped; their relationship would begin and end on the horizontal. Well, that's O.K. too, he rationalized, as he ran his eyes over her soft blond hair, her prettiness. The time to worry is when they don't.

Then he remembered something important. He looked at his watch and groaned.

"Hey!" he said. "Where's that girl friend of yours? It seems to me she's a bit late. Say, two hours!"

"She'll be here. She wanted to come."

"I gather that. Desperately."

"She'll be here. She likes your roommate."

"She likes him? She doesn't even know him!"

"What difference does that make, silly? Their eyes met. That's enough!"

Charlie grinned. "The hot look, eh? Well, it's a good beginning. This guy could use a . . . a girl friend."

He downed the last few melted drops of Scotch-flavored ice and squinted into the glass.

"Damn the bottom," he said. "Always hated glass bottoms."

"Gee, Charlie . . . haven't you had enough? You got a ball game tomorrow."

"Nah. I heard on the radio it's gonna rain. No game."

"Suppose the radio's wrong. Suppose it's sunny. Then what? I always thought ballplayers went to bed at ten and drank nothing but milk or grape juice."

"Some of 'em do. My roomie, for example. But don't you worry about old Charlie, baby. He'll get his base knocks out there." He was happy no ballplayer heard that one, and he looked around for a waiter.

"But you might not know which way to run."

He looked back at her seriously. "I'll ask; the ump'll probably know."

She giggled again, trying to finish her drink to catch up with him. Charlie signaled a distant waiter. "Damn. Where'n hell are all the waiters?"

"They're around," she said. "Take another double Scotch and you'll see a mess of them."

"I wish I could, but I need a waiter to get one. Miserable paradox," he mumbled.

When the waiter finally came with the drinks, they went at them quickly. Charlie downed his like it was his first drink of water after a hot afternoon ball game. He had reached the point in his drinking where he could really feel the buzz. It made him glow all over and he loved it. It was time to stop. His mind was clear enough, he knew, yet the words he spoke would take him wandering. What the devil . . . it made her laugh.

A few minutes later, the girl arrived.

"Wow!" he said. "You're beautiful!"

He meant it. She was the kind of girl you looked at and never got beyond the face. It was radiant and flushed from hurrying. "And late," he said, trying to clear his head and get her in focus. "At least a pint late." And then he added, mumbling to himself, "It damn well better rain."

She sat down. "Hello, Charlie," she said. "I'm Laura. Is Mike here?"

"Two hours ago he was upstairs in his room. He doesn't care

for bars. He said he'd wait up there. He squeezes his hand-grip to make his hand stronger. He's got the strongest hands in the United States and he wants to make 'em stronger. That's my roommate. Yes sir. He doesn't like bars because he can't squeeze 'em down here."

"Maybe he just doesn't like to drink," Laura offered.

Charlie looked up at her. "Yeah, maybe that's it." He had to admit it.

"I'm terribly sorry I'm so late. I couldn't get away sooner." She fidgeted in her seat. "Couldn't we call him and tell him to come down?"

"Call Mike? He's probably sleeping. We'll go up and get him. He wants to meet you, Laura. He'll appreciate that."

His voice was thick and the words sounded funny, even to himself. "It's all right, Laura. Let's all go up. Com' on."

She was reluctant, he noticed, but it did not alter his plans. He carelessly stuck his name on a bar check and led her graciously to the elevator. Aimie was laughing and held onto his other arm.

"Yes sirree. Gotta wake up old Mike. Do him good to lose some sleep. He's gotta stop squeezin' that damn thing and squeeze something worthwhile for a change." He grinned insipidly in Laura's direction. He saw her blush and it made him laugh. Aimie couldn't stop laughing. She was drunk.

All the way up he fought the growing feeling that this was not going to work out. He knew he was acting like an idiot; he would have liked someone to stop him. You just don't bring two people together this way. Not two like these. Mike would never accept it even if the girl did, which was most unlikely. He looked sidewise at her in the elevator. No college degree, maybe, like you've got, Charles m'boy. But class, plenty of it.

But what the hell. The die was cast. Mike was his roomie and his friend, and this is what the kid needed: a dame. Now that he had gone to all the trouble of arranging this, he wasn't going to back down for some tripe about propriety. (Nice you can remember those long words, Charles.) The kid lived nothing but baseball, day after day. Seven days a week he played his heart out. He drove himself through the season as if that was all there was to life. He never even went to movies for fear of straining his eyes. His diet was strict and measured, and he trained for every game. When he talked of the future, it was only the big leagues, like the world ended there and paradise was the goddamn Yankee Stadium. Crazy, Charlie thought. The kid is crazy. Look what the kid is missing! God knows if he's ever been laid . . . even once! Good ol' Mike. That's the least he would do for him . . . sure . . . the very least.

He took out his key and drove it hard into the lock, as though it would prove he was still sober. He turned to face the girls with a broad smile, trying to infect Laura with a gaiety she could not feel. He thought sourly it would be a slow night for laughs.

"He's gonna be a big leaguer next year, you watch." He opened the door to the darkened room and stepped in, letting the chilly blackness cover his shifting mood. "Sure," he added bitterly now, "big goddamn leaguer in the U. S. Army!"

Aimie giggled behind him as he fumbled for the light switch. He knew what Laura would say.

"Oh, don't wake him up. This is silly." She was whispering, holding back.

"Nonsense," he blurted out in his loudest voice. "He's gotta learn to stay awake with beautiful women in the room. Come on, Laura. Lemme interdooce ya."

The stark ceiling light cut away the darkness and bared the large sloppy room before them. Mike was buried in his pillow, fast asleep, and did not respond to their presence. Charlie moved toward the bed, dragging the girl by the hand. He sat on the edge, listening for a moment to the mild, steady snoring.

"Laura," he said, "this is Mike. Mike, meet Laura."

Aimie sat on the other bed and listened to the uninterrupted snoring. "Oh, Charlie, you're a riot!" She giggled.

Laura turned away.

"This is silly. I'd better go."

"What for? The night is young!" His tone was demanding.

"Some other time, Charlie. Thanks anyway." She tried to placate him. "It's all my fault; I was so late."

"Com'ere! Where d'ya think yer goin'? I'll wake the guy. He sleeps too damn much anyway."

"No, don't. . . ."

Charlie moved toward Mike's ear.

"Wake up, Mike. Wake up! It's yer turn to hit!"

He stirred now, his head rising slowly from the pillow. Laura stood watching helplessly. Charlie turned to her with a grin.

"That gets him; that always gets him. Tell him he can get up there to hit and he'll stop doin' anything. Bet my last bottle he'll rise right up out of the goddamn pine box if someone tells him that. Com' on, Mike! The pitcher's waitin'!"

Mike squinted into the glare and rubbed his eyes.

"What . . . what's the matter?" he asked, groping for his glasses on the bedside table.

"Wha's the matter? Nothing's the matter, you thick idiot. I brought ya a beautiful babe. Put yer goddamn specs on if ya don't believe me."

Mike turned toward Laura and stared hard, suddenly remembering. He blushed through his grogginess and tried to swallow a rising humiliation. He didn't know what to do. He looked at her stupidly.

Charlie laughed at him. "Well, fer Chrissakes, Mike. The least you could do is move over for her."

The words came out loaded with all the gross harshness of drunken lasciviousness. He saw their disgusted reactions and wondered what he had said, for he had meant nothing more than a giddy verbal pass at this clumsy situation.

But it was enough for Laura. He was too far gone to analyze the regret and indignation on her face. He merely heard her muffled "Good night!" and the slamming of the door behind her.

On his bed, Aimie had sprawled out awkwardly, oblivious to the exposure of her rising hemline. "Now, whassa matter with her?" she mumbled.

He followed the line of her pretty legs. "Wish I knew," he said. "Sure do wish I knew."

But the sober vehemence of his roommate upset him. "Get the hell outa here, you two! Get out, will ya? Goddamn you, Caulfield! You and your funny stuff! Get out!"

His anger dominated the room, and they were suddenly helpless before it. Aimie pushed her way up from the bed and studied the whirling room for the direction of the door. In a moment, her watery eyes shut and she giggled again in her waning strength. Charlie watched her fall back on the bed, out for the duration of the night. And he watched, fascinated, as the inevitable finally happened: her left breast abandoned the discipline of the flimsy brassière.

"Ha!" he said, remembering his speculation in the bar.

It was like an omen for him, and he rose from his seat on Mike's bed and staggered over to the door for the magic of a light switch.

Behind him, Mike sounded incredulous. "What the hell do you think this is, Charlie, a whorehouse?"

"Not a bad idea, kid, not bad at all."

"Dammit, Charlie, it's late. You gotta play ball tomorrow!"

Out went the light, and Charlie laughed through the sudden darkness.

"Take it easy, Mike. Someday you'll learn to take it easy."

And he felt over the body on the bed for the silken shoulder strap he had made a note of an hour before.

When Charlie woke up it was raining. Without opening his eyes, he knew this was so. He heard the Texas rain smashing against the windows and he chuckled despite the ache in his heavy head. No game today. Sure. God saved me. And he rolled over to reach for the girl who had shared his bed. She was not there. Then, from the bathroom, he heard the water beating against the shower curtain, and he sat up quickly, frightened lest that was the sound he had assumed to be rain. Through the anguish of his hang-over, he rushed to the window and pulled up the shade. He breathed easily again. It was raining, the good solid rain he had hoped for. It made him feel better . . . almost normal. He sat on the edge of his bed and rubbed his temples, pleased with himself at the way things had turned out.

Coffee, he thought. It would be good to have some coffee.

He reached for the phone and made his request to the clerk, a gangling redheaded kid he enjoyed kidding.

"Do me a favor, Red; run out and get me some coffee and toast . . . for two." The least he could do for Aimie would be to give her breakfast, and he began to wonder how she was feeling. He looked over at Mike's big clock on the dresser. It was almost eleven. Aimie would be too late to go to work this morning. He figured she would wait until after lunch.

The sound of the shower began to excite him as he waited for her. He thought of her in there, her fresh young body splashing under the sharp spray, and he toyed with the idea of going in to join her. No, he thought. Take it easy. You don't know her well enough. The thought amused him and he laughed out loud. He began to consider a sober, morning seduction, calm and tender over coffee and toast. She would come out of the bathroom neatly wrapped in a towel, brushing her hair with his amber brush. He would sit near her, in his bathrobe, and get her laughing again, just a little. He'd be gentle and affectionate and charming, and then, when the time was right, he'd strip the towel from her lovely body.

But when the shower stopped, Aimie didn't come out. Mike did.

"What the hell!" Charlie sat up suddenly. "Where's the babe?"

Mike stared at him. "She got up and went to work," he said coldly.

"By herself? That early? She could do that?" Charlie was shattered.

"She needed some help. She was O.K., though."

The disappointing shock wore off and Charlie lay back, chuckling. He looked over at Mike's rugged, square body and began to laugh at this all-too-visible contrast that made ridiculous the twist in his plans.

Mike looked up at him. "And what's the big joke, funnyman?"

"Nothing," he spluttered. "Nothing at all."

He rolled over on his side and watched Mike dress. There was a special kind of sadness in Mike's face that stopped his laughter. Charlie knew this kid well enough to recognize the signs. He swallowed his mirth and sat up.

"O.K., Mike," he said. "What's eating you?"

Kutner answered the question with one of his own. "What's it to you?" he said between his teeth.

Charlie tried to clear his head. He remembered the bedroom scene of last night and something of his foolish introduction of Laura. But what was so terrible? Aimie knew a babe who wanted to meet Mike. Mike had seen her around and agreed. So maybe it didn't happen just right. He was only trying to be a good guy.

"You're dirty, Caulfield," Mike was saying under his breath. "Everything you touch gets dirty."

Charlie lit a cigarette, suddenly wishing that the clerk would hurry with his coffee. He stared at the messy bed and the sloppy corner of his room. There were too many clothes piled on his chair. He thought of taking his shower now, but the desire for coffee overruled it. It would arrive while he was in there and he hated to let hot coffee sit.

He saw the long ash drooping on the end of his cigarette and he hurried to reach for an ash tray. There was none handy and it fell to the floor. Well, if you smoke, that's bound to happen. And if you drink, you're bound to get drunk at least sometime. And if you like girls enough, you're bound to have a few messed-up nights. It isn't dirty, he thought. No, none of this was dirty.

Yet something about Mike's attitude made Charlie uncomfortable. Though he was ready to swear up and down that he'd done nothing dirty last night, here was another little piece of the truth about playboy Charlie Caulfield. He chose to avoid it. He sat there smoking, listening to Mike clipping his toe nails; he looked down at his own, wondering when he had cut them last. Damn this kid anyway! There was such a thing as being too clean-cut. Let him go to the top in this crazy business; once he gets there he won't be able to enjoy it!

Meanwhile, what would happen to little old Charlie? He shrugged. He'd enjoy himself. He'd play. He'd go wherever his fun, his charm, his laughs took him. Wherever that was, he'd enjoy getting there. What the hell! He could always quit.

So what was wrong? Nothing, really. At least it had never seemed wrong until he met Mike Kutner.

The knock on the door jarred him. Coffee, he thought. He fumbled for some change in his pocket and went to open it.

"Hello, Charlie!" The kid burst into the room. "Rumor has

it you had a ball here last night!" He put the bag of food on the table and slapped his hero on the back.

"Here, Red," Charlie said quietly. "Keep the change."

"I heard she was a beauty . . . a blond doll." Red kept at him. "You're sure a killer, Charlie. You sure are."

"O.K., Red. Thanks a lot." And he steered him toward the door.

But Red ignored the pressure; after all, Charlie was his buddy, and buddies have certain rights in these matters.

"What was she like, Charlie? No kidding."

"Some other time, Red. I'm not feeling so good."

"I guess not," he laughed. "I guess not. Ha! O.K., Charlie. I can take a hint. So long, Mike."

The door slammed behind him and Charlie turned to the coffee. He looked furtively at Mike, relieved he was at the window, staring at the rain. He fed his coffee cream and sugar and sipped uneasily from the feeble paper container. Almost immediately he felt better.

"Coffee, Mike?" he asked.

There was no answer.

"Com' on. Have some coffee."

From the window, Mike sighed. "You drink it," he said finally.

"No. There's plenty. I . . . I bought some for you, too. And toast. Com'on. You can't go out in this rain."

After a moment Mike turned from the window and took the other container. Then he went back.

"Thanks," he said without feeling.

Charlie shrugged his shoulders. He nibbled at his toast, contemplating his own depression. He stretched his tired body and considered the welcome relief of a hot shower.

"Why in hell did you do it, Caulfield?" Mike spoke quietly from the window.

Charlie looked up. "Do what?" he asked.

Mike was sitting on the sill, staring at his coffee.

"Bring her up here like that, so damn late."

His words lodged somewhere in his throat, as though he were on the brink of tears. Charlie caught the emotion and was suddenly embarrassed. Well, you never know. This kid was serious. So serious. About everything.

"What the hell, Mike," he protested foolishly. "What's it matter?"

And even as he said it he knew it was wrong. Mike whirled, splashing coffee on the floor.

"Goddammit, it matters!" he roared. He started to say more, but could not. He put the coffee down and turned from him, back to the window and the splattering rain.

Charlie just sat there, waiting for the silence to end. Finally, he made his way to the bathroom.

He saw Aimie again a few nights later; but it took Mike over a week to summon the courage to make his own date. Apparently the evening was more successful this time. From the distance that Mike kept between them, Charlie watched the relationship begin. It would be good for Mike, he thought, just what the kid needed. He began to wonder what kind of a girl Laura was. The whole affair became teasing to him, for Mike maintained an irritating silence.

It was not till late one night weeks later, toward the end of a road trip, that Charlie sensed the timing was right to pry. Mike lay back on his bed, his hands folded behind his head, staring wistfully at the ceiling.

"All right, Junior, what's on your mind. You're hitting .330, so it must be a dame named Laura."

He saw Mike hesitate, and he knew he had grooved one.

"You go for her, eh, Junior?"

Mike nodded, and Charlie pursued it.

"Well, what about *her?*"

"I think so," he said.

"So?"

Mike took a deep breath and began talking. "Back in Houston . . . the night before we left for the road. She was sitting there in back of third. I got up to hit in the seventh with two men on, and all of a sudden, I felt her eyes burning into the back of my neck. I had to step out." He swallowed. "And then today, out there in the field. I was thinking about getting back home and seeing her, and for God knows how long I wasn't even watching the game! When I came to, I started sweating hot and cold. Suppose a guy had tagged one out my way!"

Charlie hid his smile. By God, this kid is almost human!

"Well, Michael," he said. "It looks to me like you've been bitten. It doesn't really hurt, just enjoy it. From the start I figured that gal should be a gem between the sheets."

Mike took off his glasses and reached for the light switch. "Sure," he snarled. "I gathered you were thinking along those lines."

Charlie slapped his own face in the sudden darkness. Wrong thought, buddy. Boy, you sure can think them wrong. But hell, how're you going to find out unless you ask?

It seemed like minutes later when the phone rang. Charlie reached for it, suddenly aware that it was daylight. Mike was apparently still sleeping.

"Short night," he mumbled, then remembered he had played a night game and hadn't turned in until after two.

"Hello," said a voice. He perked up; it was female.

Charlie said the first thing that came into his head. "Come on up!"

"Honey!" he heard. "How'd you know it's me?"

"Aimie!" he shouted. He wondered what she was doing

phoning so early. Quickly, through his waking fuzziness, he shivered at the prospect of bad news. Let's face it, he told himself. Why should a broad like Aimie call long distance at this hour?

"Aimie!" he repeated. "How nice of you to call."

"Call? I'm here, stupid. I'm downstairs."

It took time for this to register. Downstairs? Wasn't this Beaumont?

"You are? Well, like I said, honey, come on up!"

She laughed. "Are you up? Is Mike up?"

"Well, no . . . not quite. But what's the diff?"

"Laura's with me, silly. We drove all the way to see you guys."

"Laura too?"

The quiet body in the adjacent bed sat up, tense and rigid.

"She's here?" Mike asked. "Laura's here?"

Charlie laughed at the sudden transformation. "Take it easy, Junior. You gotta put your pants on first."

They ate brunch together, and their good spirits rode over Charlie's apprehension at the sudden visit. Laughing, they piled into Aimie's car, anxious to get away from the hot streets and into the country.

"Go out past the ball park," Charlie suggested. "Take the road west. It's nice out that way."

"Do we have much time?" Aimie asked.

Charlie looked at his watch. It was almost two-thirty.

"Well, we've got to be back reasonably early. Game tonight. After all, Mike's the leadoff man."

They laughed, as much at Aimie's driving as at Charlie, and then they grew quiet. The wind rushed by and made it difficult to be heard in the open car. In the back, Mike and Laura communicated with their hands, playing with each other's fingers. Charlie looked back quickly at Laura and shook his head at the clear beauty of her face. There was something about her that made him uneasy, even dissatisfied with himself. At first, he'd been unable to resist the natural impulse to lump her with Aimie. They were close friends, or so it seemed. Didn't it follow that they would share a common attitude toward life? And when he found he'd been wrong, that Laura was beauty all the way through, that she had qualities way beyond the girls he was accustomed to, he found he was strangely moved. Through the early weeks of summer, he watched Mike become more and more involved. Charlie was fascinated, and he thought of Mike with wonder and admiration, unable to figure how such a somber square could catch a wonderful dame like her.

They found a shaded stream about an hour out of town. Quickly they shed their shoes and followed its rocky course away from the road. In time, they split up as a foursome and casually moved to privacy. Charlie led Aimie into a soft green glen and stretched out luxuriously in the grass, only briefly speculating on the prospects for his roommate. Aimie knelt beside him and tickled his ear gently with a leaf. By God, he thought, how far away is a baseball field!

He awakened, later, only to the soft kisses on his neck and the gentle trilling of his name:

"Charlie. Charlie. I think your watch stopped."

"So what," he purred. "Just as long as you don't."

"No, honey, it's getting late. I'm sure it's late."

He glanced at his watch. Three-fifty. He listened for the tick, and looked up through the trees at the dropping sun. He groaned.

"And I had to have the only watch. Well, I'll go get the others. Wait here, honey. I'll make better time alone."

He scrambled down the edge of the stream, calling Mike's name. It was ten minutes before he heard their voices, laughing in the distance. He waded upstream toward the sound, beginning to tire of the heavy foliage that barred his way. Too suddenly, he saw them, out in the middle of a deeper pool, splashing around in water that covered their knees, laughing like a couple of kids. It occurred to him that he had never seen Mike this way, nor even imagined him so. But what held his attention was the sight of Laura, her summer slip wet and clinging to her body. He ran his eyes over her soft, glistening lines and then back to her face. For the first time in his life, it was a woman's face that held him. He couldn't have called to them if he'd wished to.

He watched Mike throw his body into the water and crawl along the bottom to her feet. He grabbed her leg until she fell squealing into the water beside him, and lifted her to him with his powerful arms. Laura circled his neck, less for support than for love, and Charlie swallowed his envy as he watched them kiss. (Take it easy, man. A kiss always looks sexier when someone else is doing the kissing!) Then, Mike released her and backed away, shy and confused. It was nothing, nothing at all. Yet Charlie felt somehow indecent.

"Mike! Laura!" he called from behind the bush concealing him.

"Here!" Mike answered. Laura scampered away to put on her dress as he made his way toward them.

"Have fun?" he asked Mike.

The other grinned. His face, without his glasses on and relaxed in a smile, was hard to fathom. Charlie wondered what the expression would be when he learned how late it was.

"I guess it's time to get moving back," he said.

Mike answered easily. "O.K. As soon as Laura's ready."

They were singing when they reached the car again, and laughing at Charlie's special set of lyrics. At that moment, Charlie was at his best. He was master of ribaldry with a repertoire as long as his string of conquests; he was sprightly and gay, warm and charming. In the fading sunlight, he was glowing with the special joy of this magnificent and unexpected afternoon. Whatever his weaknesses, this was his moment of greatest charm.

But he couldn't turn back the clock.

He drove the car like a man in a hurry, a fact which became apparent to them all. From behind him, finally, out of the warmth of the back-seat silence, came the inevitable question:

"What time is it, Charlie?"

Charlie managed a long yawn before he answered.

"Don't know, Mike. Watch stopped."

He heard Mike sit forward with a start, to look at the clock on the dashboard. Charlie glanced over at it. It read 6:35. They were supposed to be at the ball park no later than 6:15—at least twenty-five miles away.

Mike cried out: "Aimie! Does that clock work?"

Charlie put his hand on her leg.

"It's a car clock, Junior," he answered for her. "They never work. Get on back to your business and save your breath."

But Mike persisted. "It's late! I can tell it's late. Dammit, Charlie, why the hell did you let it get so late?"

"Sorry. I wanted it to stop, but it wouldn't listen to me. Ha!"

Aimie laughed gently beside him, and he squeezed her hand.

"You're a riot," Mike was saying. "I got a feeling you planned this. You're just the type. Christ, Duckie's gonna blast us."

Charlie was annoyed by this childish hammering at him. "It ain't the blast that bothers me. It's the fine."

"Turn on the radio. Find out what time it is!"

"Sorry, Mike," Aimie said. "The radio's broken."

Mike sank back in his seat, groaning.

"Christ!" he said bitterly.

The afternoon, Charlie thought, has officially ended.

They rode the rest of the way in silence. The highway ran straight before them into the early evening traffic from the city. Charlie pulled up at the stadium in the growing twilight, and Mike jumped out of the car, darting toward the locker room. Charlie lingered in the car for a few moments, if only to defy the need to be on time. Anyway, Mike's haste to get dressed would only serve to concentrate the brunt of Duckie's rage upon *him*. Charlie would conveniently follow after he thought the storm had spent itself. He kissed Aimie once again, leisurely, unhappily conscious of Laura in the back. Some guys, he thought, just don't know how to live.

The locker room was empty as he entered, except for Mike who was almost through dressing. Charlie moved over to his locker with a nonchalance he knew would be irritating. He smoked as he unlaced his shoes.

"You see what time it is, funnyman?" Mike nodded toward the big clock on the wall.

Charlie turned to look. "Sure," he grinned. "Ten after seven."

"What's so damn funny? We've missed batting practice!"

Missed batting practice, Charlie thought. Big tragedy. It was too easy to get angry with a kid like this, and he became conscious of his desire to duck it. He turned on him quietly, but so seriously that Charlie hardly recognized the tone of his own voice.

" 'Missed batting practice!' " he repeated with sarcasm. "Don't you realize what else you missed? . . . what *pleasure?*"

Mike winced. "I enjoyed this afternoon," he said.

"You ruined it!" Charlie went on. "You ruined it because you don't know how to live. You let a stinking watch-spring louse up an afternoon for four people. And why? Tell me why? Because you think somebody else is gonna take your place out here? Look! You're still an hour before game time!

If you would open those stupid eyes of yours you'd see they're gonna be goddamn glad you got here at all. But no! Michael Big-Time Kutner's gotta be early. Number-one man dressed, like it was the mark of a pro or something."

He threw away his butt and heaved a big sigh. He jerked his dirty uniform from his locker and spread the pieces on the floor in front of him as was his custom. He sat down on the bench to put them on.

"You know what I'm wondering?" Mike began finally. "I'm wondering how the hell I ended up rooming with a guy like you. You're nothing but a clown. Everything you do is for laughs. You clown your way through life and you think you're getting somewhere. Or maybe you don't give a damn for all I know." He jerked savagely at a shoelace. "But *I* care! Goddammit, I care a lot. I've always thought you had to sweat for what you want, and if you're good enough, and you sweat hard enough, you get it!"

Charlie watched the top of his head, for Mike was talking to his shoes. What he was saying began to sound like an apology, and Charlie felt sorry for him.

"Sure, I'm good," Mike went on. "I'm plenty good, but I intend to keep on sweating until I get to the top." And after a moment, in a tone almost inaudible, he added: "And then I guess I'll have time for the rest."

Charlie shook his head. "The trouble with you, Mike, is that you never let up. Never. You're nuts. You gotta learn to get loose. People'll like you more. It helps to be liked, I tell you. Get the skipper patting your back and swapping a few gags and it goes a long way—longer than all your sweat. You're good, Mike. Sure. But you're not that good!"

He kept his eyes away from the kid now. He heard him get up finally, the spikes clattering on the cement floor as they moved toward the door. For a moment, they stopped; then the door opened, and they moved quickly out to the field.

After a while, Charlie finished dressing. He tightened his belt around him, and as he contracted his stomach muscles, he thought how feeble he felt this evening. He laughed as he thought of the reason. It had been a strenuous afternoon. But his laughter was brief. His legs felt shaky, completely without spring. He knew he didn't have it tonight, that he'd probably damage the club out there on the diamond. He considered the possibility of taking off for a game; he hadn't tried it since the beginning of the season. Hell, it would be easy. He'd get back into street clothes and go to the hotel, have a few drinks, and knock off a steak for dinner. That's what he needed; a good feed. He'd call in with a message he was sick. Terribly sick to his stomach. Ptomaine poisoning or something. Sure, a guy can get sick every once in a while.

Quickly, impetuously, he began to carry out his plan. He pulled off his baseball pants, his sweat shirt, his sliding pads. But as he did so, the door opened behind him, and he heard heavy, leathered footsteps move into the locker room. Just around the bend in the row of lockers, he saw who it was—the coach, Duckie Mays, appropriately named after the low-slung bird he walked like, his fat old body shaking in clumsy haste under the glittering maroon-and-gold Houston jacket he wore both on and off the field.

Just as quickly, his plans changed. Calmly, he fastened his sliding pads and returned his pants and sweat shirt to his body. The fact that he fully dressed himself before Duckie even discovered his presence served only to irritate him, for he figured he could have gotten away with it. Half in anger and half to startle Duckie, he slammed the door of his locker, pretending not to have seen the arrival of the coach. It worked. Duckie jumped at this intrusion, revealing his embarrassment at being discovered late himself.

Charlie frowned in simulated rage.

"You're late, Duckie!" he growled in imitation. "Dammit!

You're late, and don't try to tell me why!" He stalked out of the room, feigning indignation, but not without hearing the amused chuckling of the coach.

That was easy, lad, easy as falling off a bar stool. And he climbed the last few steps into the late twilight clatter of the diamond.

The night would be a chore on his tired body, and he knew at once he had dissipated too much of himself. There was a limit to the strength of even his fully developed youth beyond which he functioned only in part. This he recognized as he sat in the dugout, holding his bat as if it were weighted with lead. He waited apprehensively for his turn to hit, watching the hitters smash into pitches with a kind of savage power Charlie knew he could not muster. And this especially when he watched his roommate. He studied the kid's face as he lashed at the ball, saw the driving intensity of his coordinated strength as the bat rang out with the sharpness of a clean base hit. This was not in him, he knew. Not tonight or any other night, and the cruel comparison of their abilities left him even more depressed. He sensed that he had barely enough in him to tighten his fist, and he generated an artificial kind of fury to run the adrenaline through his blood stream, hoping to bring his muscles to life. When he stepped up to hit, his bat seemed like a sodden, useless stick. He protected himself by bunting.

Like most games, this was a demanding one, and Charlie regretted, as he sensed the growing tension, that it wasn't a lopsided-score affair in which he might relax. The best he could bargain for was a minimum of demands on his own depleted talents, and he found himself hoping in the field that the ball would come nowhere near him. Foolishly, he allowed this hope to build up in his mind as he idled through the early innings, a nonentity to the progress of the game. He rejoiced on the extent of his luck as batters hit to other fields, as each inning passed him by, until at last in the fifth, a feeble fly ball sliced out his way. The shock of the ball's approach temporarily paralyzed him. He finally made a move for it, desperately stabbing at it as it sank a few feet in front of him. By some miracle, he got his glove under it and rolled over in a prolonged somersault. His sense of the dramatic and the ridiculous rose to the occasion and he lay prone with his face in the soft turf, holding his glove in the air like a wounded Hollywood soldier trying to keep the U. S. flag unsullied. It was the last out of the inning and the frustrated Beaumont crowd yelled at his spectacular save, for there were two men running the bases at the time. Magnanimously, they cheered him, trying to believe the ball must have taken a sudden dip in the wind or gotten lost in the glaring lights. Charlie ate it up. He knew they were watching him as he trotted in from the field, and it was not in him to resist exploiting the attention. With characteristic simpleness, he stumbled headlong over first base into the white line of the base path, and again lay prone with his face in the dirt, this time holding his cap in the air as though he were doffing it. When he arose, his face was white with lime. He kicked at the bag in mock anger and walked back to the dugout, his hands outstretched in front of him as though he had been blinded by the stuff.

It was an adolescent brand of corn, but Charlie was master of pantomime. It took a clown to carry it off. They laughed at him on the bench. He had taken a simple fly ball and made it into a big act, almost as if the guy who hit it was his straightman. No one even bothered to wonder why he had misjudged it so badly, as if that was part of the act as well.

Only Mike was hard on him. As they made their way out to their adjacent positions, Charlie heard him mumble.

"Get with it, funnyman. Get in the ball game!"

And when Charlie failed to get to a long drive into deep right center in the seventh, Mike desperately crossed behind him to make a difficult catch though Charlie should have been sitting under it. He heard the kid growl furiously at him.

"You short-legged that drive, funnyman. If you don't feel like running, tell the skipper you got an ingrown toenail or something. Or gowan back to your blonde."

Charlie grinned at the kid's anger.

"Jealous?"

"Screw you, Caulfield."

The crowd was applauding Mike's catch.

"Fer Chrissakes, kid. I just made you look good!"

Mike trotted back to his position in center. "Get in the goddamn game!" he barked.

It was true, what Mike said. He knew it. He didn't have the drive to leg it under that last fly ball. It would have gone for three bases if Mike had not hustled like the madman he is. Well, only a coupla more innings to sweat out, only a coupla more. . . .

But they moved into the first half of the ninth inning with the score tied. Charlie led off for Houston and worked the pitcher for a base on balls. The catcher squawked at two of the calls. The last one brought the pitcher storming in from the mound. In the dugout they saw Charlie smile as he trotted down to first base, and they laughed through the growing tension.

"He probably kidded the ump into calling them balls."

They moved him down to second with a sacrifice bunt—he had to slide and it strained every muscle in his body—and over to third on a long fly ball to deep center. There were two men out and Mike stepped up to hit.

The crowd was buzzing again, for Kutner was having a good night at the plate. The catcher called for time out and walked out to the mound. Charlie sat down on the base and turned to Duckie Mays who was coaching third.

"Do ya think they'll pass him, Duckie?"

"Mebbe. You're the winning run, there's two sacks open, and the chucker's his cousin tonight. What would you do?"

"If I was him? I'd take a drink of seven-year-old Scotch and crawl in the sack with my wife. Man . . . have you seen her?"

Duckie laughed. He indicated over his shoulder. "Yeah, she's right behind us in the front box."

Charlie sneaked another look.

"Some doll. No wonder he throws a few clinkers at times. He's got her to worry about, too."

Charlie looked up at the maroon-and-gold jacket on Duckie. The bright lights glittered off the gold stripes and sparkled brilliantly. It was an eye-catcher. He had never seen a more colorful jacket than Houston's. For a moment he stared at the stripes, fascinated, for they looked like rings of fire. Duckie used those stripes on the sleeves to give the signals. He was always reaching across his fat chest to touch them, trying to cross up the opposition, for they all knew where the signs came from. The old guy was clever enough at disguising them, and at the same time he made them simple enough for the dumbheads on his club to catch.

"Why the hell do you wear that jacket, Duckie? Are you cold at night; or just to give signs?"

"I been with this club for twelve years, Caulfield. Always wore the jacket coaching, 'cept on the real hot days. Does me good to get up a little sweat every day."

Charlie grinned. "I think you just like the flashy clothes, Duckie."

The catcher had returned to his position and was getting set. Duckie tensed.

"All right, boy. On your feet. Let's see if we can push you across with the big one."

Charlie nodded and stood up. He could see at once they were going to pitch to Mike and work the corners. Pitch to him but give him nothing good to hit at. There were two bases open and they could risk a base on balls. Behind him Duckie was alive.

"Look 'em over, Mike! Look 'em over! Pick out one you like! Make sure it's in there!"

Charlie took an easy lead and watched. He was the possible winning run and it excited him. It would be great to score it on his own. To cut loose if the catcher let one get away from him a few feet, or even to steal! For the first time that night his body grew almost sharp and alive, his legs taut with expectancy. He felt the quickened throbbing of his pulse. Take it easy, he told himself. You're not going anyplace yet. And he held his lead off third as the first pitch sped toward the outside corner of the plate.

"Ball one!" The catcher slammed the ball in his big mitt and turned to holler over his shoulder. It was a quick protest at the call indicating it might have been in there. Charlie spat through his teeth, impatient for the next pitch.

This one the ump called a strike and Mike took his turn at making his beef. Routine tactics, Charlie mused. Pressure the umps. Don't make it easy for them to call 'em against you. Not one ump in twenty who isn't susceptible to pressure, however much they deny it. It's human nature. Now the ump was caught between them, the hitter and the catcher both on his neck. He'd hate to be the ump, Charlie thought. That's no spot for laughs.

Charlie felt the tension grow through the next two pitches. Another ball, another strike. From his spot on third, he could see the pitcher trying to beat back the edge of his nervous fatigue, wiping the never-ending scare-sweat from his pitching hand. He saw the guy finally get set on the mound for the two-and-two pitch, his face wearing grim concentration just as his tired body wore the sweated uniform. He flailed his arms like a windmill while the tight corner of his brain sent frantic messages to his fingers to release the ball in a certain way, at a certain split second, so that it would spin delicately across a corner of the plate at a certain precise height on the batter's body. Charlie danced weirdly down the line as he watched him, swinging his own arms in a grotesque, erratic movement, squawking like an angry parrot. Somewhere in that aroused crowd behind him, someone may have laughed at his fantastic gyrations. But for those few seconds, there was none of the clown in Charlie Caulfield's wild attempt to rattle the pitcher.

For a suspended instant of time, the ball sailed toward the plate. Charlie watched Mike draw his bat back to begin his swing and step into the pitch down and away toward the outside corner. Then he held back, having somehow determined through a myriad of his own delicate sensitivities that it was not going to be in there.

The ball slammed into the catcher's mitt, and the eyes in the blue suit behind him took measure of its flight. Unfortunately, Charlie noted, he paused, ever so slightly, before the call. An ump can't pause.

"Ball three!"

A different call could have ended the threat—and the inning. The catcher whirled on him in a sudden violence, the equipment on his body shaking with his rage. Charlie watched him fling his mask and mitt to the ground as if he never would use them again. He shoved his face against the umpire's mask, blasting him abusively as the pitcher charged in from the hill to add his own. Charlie went back to the bag, prepared to relax, for their entire ball club had left their positions and the bench to gather around the umpire.

"The goddamn rhubarbs . . . ," he mumbled to Duckie Mays. He knew them for what they were, the accumulated frustrations of a ball game surging up inside a man, erupting like a volcano when the ump calls a clinker against you. You stand there in all your righteousness, bellowing like a bull without horns at the straw man in the dark blue suit. You haven't a chance of changing the decision and all the time you know it. But you don't give a damn. You're tied to your rage and you stay until he kicks you out or exhausts you. Finally the blue-serged sonofabitch orders you to play ball. So you put on your glove, pretending you're gonna lose the game because of that blind bastard's stupidity, trying to make it seem his fault and not your own. In the end you feel worse for it all, not better, and you're back where you started except you've got an agonizing drumming in the gut.

It was stupid, he thought. He watched them crowding around the ump, steam pouring out of their red faces. There was the pitcher, spilling his guts all over the plate trying to sell a dead horse to a deaf man. A moment ago Charlie had studied this same guy; his face had been stern and controlled, his entire being tuned only for the pitch. But now, how could he spin that fine thread of concentration with an anger-hangover? How the hell could he even think?

Inside his head, the idea burst like a wonderful rocket. He whirled on Duckie with the full force of sudden inspiration.

"Duckie!" he demanded. "Quick! Take off your jacket!"

The fat man was too startled not to react. He fumbled at the buttons before he asked:

"What's eatin' you? Whattaya want it for?"

Charlie was on fire. "Hurry! Get it off!"

He saw they were reaching the end of their rage; he had only a few seconds more. He took the glittering jacket from the coach and put it on, pulling his shirt from his pants and stuffing it into the jacket in front of his stomach. He set the back of his cap high on his head and pulled the peak low over his eyes. Then he reached down and lowered the bottom of his pant-legs almost to his ankles.

It was just the way Duckie's uniform sagged on him.

"Stand over by the bag, Duckie!" he ordered.

"What in hell are you up to?"

"Just stand there, and don't look up. I'm gonna steal home and do it walkin'!"

The ump had broken the back of the rhubarb and the players were drifting back to their positions. Home plate was finally cleared for action. The pitcher set himself in back of the mound and the catcher sullenly put his mask back over his sweaty face. The umpire squared his aching shoulders and hollered the magic words:

"Play ball!"

Charlie raised his head enough to see Mike moving back into the batter's box. The pitcher was fumbling with the rosin bag and the catcher squatted to give the sign. It was time.

Charlie stuck his hands in his back pockets and hunched over his shoulders, lowering his body to a stoop. He turned his feet outward and began waddling down the outside of the base path, his head down with chin on his chest, as if in thought. He went slowly enough, as though he was ambling toward the dugout, hoping the walk was a good mimic job. God knows he had done it often enough for the guys. Waddle, you bastard, he told himself. Waddle! You're a duck with a flaming maroon-and-gold jacket.

Halfway there now. He heard no action. So far so good. Keep your head down, Charlie. (Christ, I hope they don't look back for me at third.) Twenty, thirty feet more. Should he make a break for it? No, not yet. Not yet. What the hell were they doing? Probably waiting for him to get out of the way! He wished to Christ he could see.

Waddle . . . waddle across that dish for the big goddamn run! Fifteen feet . . . ten. He could see Mike's legs now.

Then, out of somewhere, he heard it:

"*Hey!*"

It was all he needed. He took a running dive for it, between

Mike's legs, toppling the batter over his shoulders as he reached for the plate with his hand. He kissed the rubber dish and looked up at the dumbfounded umpire. The guy was having a rough night.

"Well, call me safe, you blind bastard. Don't you wanna go home?"

The ump immediately spread his arms out wide, hollering "*Safe!*" He had to. The runner was home and hadn't been tagged, though it was apparent the ump didn't know exactly what had happened.

The pitcher knew, and flung his glove toward the dugout, fuming at his own stupidity, for he had watched the winning run waddle toward the plate. A helluva way to blow a ball game.

From their distance and perspective, the crowd finally saw and understood, for Duckie himself started waddling in, nude without his jacket on. They began a weird, broken yell, too amazed for the big reaction.

As Charlie pulled himself off the ground, Mike scrambled to his feet from under him, gripping his bat as if it were a weapon.

"What in hell is going on?"

Charlie grinned at him. "Put down the stick, roomie. It's your old uncle Charlie!"

"How'd you get here?" Mike sounded incredulous.

"I waddled, dammit. Ninety friggen feet. They thought I was Duckie!"

The kid growled as Charlie dusted himself off. "What a way to play baseball, Caulfield!" he muttered.

"What's the matter? I scored, didn't I?"

Then Mike saw the jacket, the low-slung pants, the whole getup, and he shook his head.

"Oh, you're a brain. The clown with a big brain! They must have taught you that trick in college."

Charlie was annoyed at this show of bitterness. "You're jealous, Kutner," he said, knowing it wasn't so. "You gotta be the hero, so this burns you up!"

"Sure. That's it," Mike mumbled.

Charlie shook his head and turned toward the dugout, ready to face the accolades of his teammates who were screaming at him like kids at a circus.

"Well," he grinned, "at least they love me in old Dugoutville." And, just for laughs, he waddled the rest of the way in.

When he turned from the hilarious backslapping to watch Mike at the plate, he saw the kid was laughing as he waved his stick at the pitcher, actually laughing. The sight of the kid's face made Charlie Caulfield happier than all the dugout laughter and backslapping.

# 6 *The Sergeant*

The sergeant, red-faced and bulky in all his clothes, pushed into the quonset hut and moved quickly to the oil stove in the center of the floor. He shed his fur-lined parka and shook the icy rain from it. He leaned over the concentrated heat and let the hot air thaw his wind-blown face. Outside the wind whistled over the rounded roof, splattering a stinging mixture of sand and rain against it. The hut rumbled in the sudden gusts, creaking painfully at the pressure of one side against another.

"The ass end of the world," he mumbled.

Suddenly, he realized he had an urgent need to urinate, and that involved dressing again and a trip to the latrine.

"Jesus H. Christ! I just came in!" he roared. He let the weather be a clamp on his kidneys, determined to hold on as long as he could.

Behind him he heard the radio tuned low to the pre-game jabbering of a world-series game, some 6,000 miles away. He looked over at the pfc. lying on the bed, peering at the drab ceiling, his hands folded behind his head.

In a moment, the sergeant sensed his control would not be adequate to defy nature indefinitely. "Storm or no storm," he said to nobody in particular, "my back teeth are floating!" He moved sullenly to the door again, unbuttoning as he went. He decided to defy a recent Hq order prohibiting this, and opened the door only wide enough to perform the job. The freezing winds nipped him, and he tried to hurry. Despite the discomfort, the whole thing began to amuse him; he wondered what it looked like from the outside and he chuckled. He finished and went quickly back to the stove.

"Hey, Mike . . . ya know what some jerk said about the Aleutians?" The man on the bed barely turned his head. "He said that when God made Alaska, He shook the damn mud off His hands into the sea, like this . . ." and he made the gesture of flicking mud from his fingers. "Them's the Aleutian Islands!" He grunted at the picture of it in his mind, thinking he could use that in a letter to his girl. But his companion registered no reaction.

The stove threw off too much heat under him, and he turned his face from it. It was time to warm his rear. He put his hands behind his buttocks and backed into it, rocking on his heels to avoid a constant contact.

He looked toward the pfc. again, as though he were expecting some kind of an answer. But the pfc. only reached up for the dial on his radio and turned up the volume. The static-filled sound of "The Star-Spangled Banner" poured through the dreary hut.

"Game time, eh, Mike!" The sergeant was a master exponent of the obvious. He turned from the stove in silence, perhaps out of deference to the national anthem, and walked slowly to the window. It did seem screwy, though, listening to the world series at eight in the morning with a freezing blizzard outside. He tried to think of himself back in the States, driving up to the ball park in a black Caddy convertible so damn long he'd need a chauffeur in the back seat to steer the rear wheels. He'd be sunning himself in a choice box seat on the edge of the field, with a babe in one hand, a hot frank in the other, and a couple of cans of cold beer at his feet. Aah . . . them people back home don't know how good they have it. It did not concern him that this was hardly an accurate picture of the average baseball fan. Nor, in any way, of himself.

"And here we go with the 1944 annual world-series classic. It's a beautiful, warm, sunny October day out here, and to you GIs all over the world, we hope you enjoy. . . ."

"Aah. Listen to the States-side bastard."

"A quick review of the starting line-ups for you late tuners-in. For the St. Louis Cardinals. . . ."

The sergeant reached into his shirt pocket, remembering the cigar nestled there. He removed the cellophane wrapper and tossed it on the floor, twisting the cigar under his nose. Then he lit it, took a deep drag, blew out a cloud of blue smoke, took the cigar from his mouth and inspected it, and generally went through the motions that suggested he was a connoisseur enjoying a special treat.

"Great!" he remarked. "Got it from George Casey. Did you know? Old Casey is a pop. He passed out stogies in the mess hall."

He noticed now that he had failed to remove the band around its girth. He tore it off clumsily. "Yeah, that's great, ain't it?" He seemed to be leering at the man on the bed.

The pfc. turned with a slight show of interest. "Didn't know Casey'd been back to the States. Twenty months we been here." His arm, hanging over the side of the bed, slid along the edge until his fingers rested on a bottle. He drew it to his lips and swallowed.

"He ain't been back at all," the sergeant said triumphantly. He flicked the first ashes off the tip of his cigar. Then he broke out laughing, a silly laugh at first, forced and childish, like a kid trying to share a dirty joke with his elders. He looked over at the bed for answering laughter but received only a dead stare in return. The pfc. turned back to the game. The sergeant let his humor subside. It was no damn fun laughing alone.

"Jesus!" he said, shifting his approach. "It's no wonder guys go nuts up here. You live like a stinking animal and your wife's back home screwin' around on your allotments. It ain't right. It ain't right at all."

Kutner grunted. The inning was over and there was a moment of dead air. The sergeant saw him glance quickly at the picture of his wife above him on the wall. The sergeant had seen that picture, of course, even secretly examined and admired it. That girl was beautiful all right. Not a sexy face, maybe, but sure good to look at. All the more reason, he figured, why she'd be playing around. Christ knows there'd be a load of guys buzzing around *her*.

"Did you say something?" The sergeant was digging.

There was no answer.

"Well . . . it'll be a messy business when the guys come home again. A difficult adjustment." He'd picked up the phrase in a pamphlet somewhere and enjoyed the sound of it. "Yes sir," he repeated, "a difficult adjustment."

They listened to the game in silence for a while. There was no scoring through four or five innings, and the sergeant grew tired of it, for all the hyperthyroid jabbering of the announcer. In the background, he could hear the excitement of the crowd whenever a man got on, but there wasn't enough real action to keep him interested. He would have preferred turning the radio off, just for a half hour or so until near the end of the game, and maybe playing a few hands of rummy or something. But he knew better than to suggest it to the man on the bed.

He watched the bottle move up from the floor again and tilt to Kutner's lips. He recognized it as his own, a partly filled leftover from a recent party. He didn't much care about it, though even those three inches remaining might be worth a few bucks on a dry week end. Besides, he knew Kutner would pay for it. What baffled him was that Mike was drinking at all.

First time he had seen him drink, come to think of it. He couldn't figure it.

"Ain't it a little early in the morning for that rotgut, Mike? That stuff can drill holes in you if you ain't careful."

There was no answer from the bed, nor even acknowledgement. The game was moving rapidly a few inches from his ear.

The sergeant shrugged his shoulders. So he wants to get crocked in the early morning. None of my business. He ain't no kid any more. Oughta know what he's doing. He regarded the cigar again. It needed another light. Damn stogies, he thought. Never stay lit.

When he looked back at the bed, Kutner was staring at him—or seemed to be. It was hard to tell with Kutner.

The sergeant quickly framed a question:

"I guess this is one helluva place to send a ballplayer, eh? Winter twelve months a year. . . ."

They used to talk baseball a lot in the early days. A professional ballplayer in the hut was an exciting thing, especially one who had moved so far up the ladder as Kutner. Mike was looked on as something of a celebrity. The sergeant had heard that if it weren't for the war, Kutner'd be up in the major leagues. That was something, and for a long time, the sergeant paid homage to the pfc.

But gradually, time wore memories thin, and values changed. A quonset hut on a barren island seemed worlds removed from the Polo Grounds. After a while it mattered less what a man had been in civilian life. For all of them planned big changes *after* the war; what counted was what they would be when they returned. The sergeant, who always prided himself on being "smart," had learned months ago that there were many lucrative flimflams at which he could profitably occupy himself for the duration. With a minimum of ingenuity, he had succeeded in amassing a respectable nest egg, merely by setting up a mainland contact for the acquisition of wrist watches, fountain pens, and various other small properties rare in the Aleutians. Then all he had to do was hang around the crap games at pay day; a big winner was usually interested in such items if approached right. The profits were substantial. It made sense.

Of course he wasn't a pro at it like some. Take this young guy Stanton, for instance, Warrant Officer Petey Stanton. He was a smiling, affable, quiet Joe, and the sergeant held him in awe. At first it had been hard to believe everything he'd heard about Stanton's black-market whisky operations. But the rumors had persisted and then the sergeant had actually seen the whisky and the money change hands at twenty-five or thirty-five dollars for a fifth. Stanton was a supply officer and the pilots that flew the cargo ships from the mainland of Alaska were his special friends, for a price. And the price that Stanton got from the enlisted men (it was the only genuine booze available to them on the island) was supposed to be filling a footlocker full of bills.

But Stanton was taking chances. Too many people knew about him. The sergeant would stick with a few innocent watches and fountain pens, settle for a smaller wad and not worry himself to death. In the beginning he'd tried to interest Kutner. The ballplayer was popular, looked up to. He'd have been a big help, and then after the war maybe the sergeant would've had a major leaguer for a buddy. But Kutner hadn't even understood what the sergeant was getting at. He'd stood by his bunk, slamming his fist into the pocket of that damn baseball glove, shaking his head and peering through those glasses. The sergeant quickly gave up the idea of his partnership.

So his early respect for the professional ballplayer had turned into disinterest and then a kind of mild pity. Hunched over his footlocker he would count his roll of bills and consider schemes for doubling it. And every once in a while, he'd watch the ex-ballplayer take out that useless glove and pound it wistfully through the freezing summers of his prime. The sergeant would stack his loot against Kutner's dreams any day, and after a while he got to changing the subject if anyone even started talking baseball.

Then one day, many months ago, Mike had wrapped his glove, cradled it in a box, and mailed it home. The sergeant had stood over him, watching; and when he had finished, Mike had looked up at him, apparently embarrassed at the great care he had taken. He had smiled sheepishly. "I guess my wife'll get more use out of it than me," he had said. With the glove gone Mike never mentioned baseball, and so far as the sergeant could gather, the man shed his identity as a ballplayer, even to himself. Kutner was just another dogface, a 208 classification, a cook feeding the night shift from the hangar and repair shops.

The cigar had gone out again, and this time he threw it away. He pulled out a deck of cards and shuffled them on his footlocker. He looked over at Mike, hoping to draw him into one of their card games.

"Rummy, Mike?"

The answer was silence, so he dealt himself a hand of solitaire to kill his boredom. A moment later he heard the bed squeak, and he looked toward the sudden sound, anticipating Mike's change of heart. Mike was up from the bed, moving past him to the door. He opened it enough to let in a dog, an overactive Siberian Husky they called Herman. The dog yipped in greeting and shook the rain from his powerful body.

How the hell did he know the dog was out there? The sergeant was closer to the door and farther from the blaring radio but he had heard nothing. There was something queer about it, for it had happened several times before. This had always amused the pfc.—not an easy guy to amuse—and he'd smile, shrugging his shoulders: "I heard him, that's all. You can hear dice shaking three huts away. Me . . . I hear Herman."

Mike moved down the hut to his sack with Herman jumping on him, ready for roughhouse. But the master lay back on the bed, resting his hand gently on the dog's head. The dog sank to the floor and lay quietly at Mike's side, pacified at least for the moment by the touch of his hand. It was as though a part of the man's mood ran through his fingers and into that dog.

The sergeant shook his head and began a new game of solitaire. He was conscious of Herman looking up at him, steady and searching, and he wished the dog would turn away. The two big eyes distracted him. So he cheated a little in solitaire! So what? It was only a game. Suddenly he thought that Herman, in repose, looked something like his master. Without his glasses, of course. Quiet, steady, a little brooding.

The cards turned against him again, and he let them lie. The game was moving into the last inning, and he became suddenly interested in its climax. The radio announcer with that professional breathlessness, was setting the scene:

"Well, folks, here we go into the ninth inning. The Cardinals lead 2–1. If they can goose-egg the Browns in this half of the inning, the first world-series game is theirs. Three little outs. That's all that stands between the Cardinals and. . . ."

The sergeant wanted the Cardinals to win, though he didn't remember why. He sat on his bed now and turned his concentration to the radio, ready to dramatize the ending. The Browns got two men on with two out, and the announcer made the most of it.

"This could be it, folks. This is the man who can do it! Big Bill Mazil is stepping up there, swinging two bats. He throws one away to the bat boy and here he comes, up to the plate. Mazil has two solid blows already, but this is the big one. Can he do it? Can he do it?"

The sergeant got up from the bed, suddenly too tense to remain seated. Drop dead, Mazil, he thought nervously. Then he noticed Mike staring at the floor, as though the game somehow no longer interested him.

"And here comes the stretch, the pitch. . . . It's a fly ball into short right field! The runners are moving. Caulfield is coming in for it, slowly, he's under it." Then suddenly, the voice six thousand miles away broke, and shrieked. "No! No! He dove for it! He had to dive for it! The ball took a sudden dip in the wind. He got it, though. He made the catch and the game is over! Charlie Caulfield had to dive to the ground to come up with that ball! He rolled over and came up with it. Look at him dancing and laughing out there like a little kid! It was a great save. Yes sir, a great catch to end a great ball game!"

In those few seconds, the sergeant lived through a whole game, generating enough excitement for a momentary rush of goose flesh. He laughed at the victory as if it were his own.

"Well, we did it!" he shouted. "Yes sir, we did it. That Caulfield is a great ballplayer. You watch, Mike. He's gonna be the hero of the series. I feel it in my bones."

Then, suddenly, he remembered to whom he was speaking and he shut up. He was fully aware he didn't know what the hell he was talking about. Embarrassed, he looked over toward the bed. There he saw Mike shaking with laughter, a crazy silent laughter that jarred his whole body. His hand hung over the side, gripped tightly around the scruff of Herman's neck. As he laughed, he tugged at the fur almost brutally until the dog let out a yip of pain. At once Mike let go and brought his hands to his head as though he had a sudden pain. It was all confusing for the sergeant. He watched Mike struggle to his feet and wipe his eyes with his sleeve. On the floor, the bottle fell over, empty, and Mike let it roll under the bed. Still laughing, he made his way over to the sergeant and put his big hand on his shoulder.

"Ken," he said. "Get out another bottle. Com'on! Whattaya say we get a little party going. About time we had a party. On me, Ken."

The sergeant sat down by his footlocker again. He didn't know what to make of it.

"Sit down, Mike. Let's play some rummy."

"Nah. Let's get the guys and have a party! Come on, Ken . . . where's a bottle?"

The sergeant shook his head. "You can't have a party now, Mike. Fer Chrissakes, it's only ten in the morning. The guys are all working!"

Mike wiped his eyes again, his laughter dwindling. Finally, he sat down across his footlocker.

"O.K., Ken," he said. "I guess you're right. A little rummy, but double the stakes this time. I owe you too damn much. Gotta win it back."

The sergeant reached for a pencil and paper and shuffled the cards. He heard Mike's sudden laughter again and he shook his head.

Now what the hell's eating him? he thought.

# 7 *The Reporter*

Orville Jenkins pulled the sheet out of the typewriter and assembled the pages of the day's article. For a long time he leaned back in his high swivel chair and watched the rain splash against the huge window, waiting for it to stop. And when it didn't, it surprised and angered him, as if he were victim of some broken agreement.

"Rain, rain, rain," he mumbled. "Enough!"

The weather had cut into him. He found it difficult to write about baseball when there was no activity. He knew his column had been dull and lifeless these past few days. There had been critical comments from his readers and they disturbed him. He couldn't blame them any more than he believed they should blame him. It had rained. He had to write accordingly. But for all the logic, he felt he owed them something, as though the weather itself was his responsibility. He had determined to give them a column that would arouse their interest, some provocative story that would really rock them.

He looked down at the finished article in his hand and began to read it, as if for the first time, he tried to believe, just like any of his readers.

ORVILLE SAYS . . .

There's one kind of athlete I've always disliked: the guy who sets himself above the rest of the club, the guy who puts his own interests ahead of the well-being of the team as a whole. A baseball club has to be a friendly, tightly knit, smooth-running unit to be a winner. You can have the greatest aggregation of stars in the league; but if they're pulling against each other, if there's dissatisfaction, if there's someone who thinks he's better than the others—then you're apt to be a second division ball club by the Fourth of July.

We're expecting big things this year. A great baseball town like Houston deserves it. We've been out of the money for too long. As everyone knows, there have been big changes over the winter with the purchase of the club by the Major League Chicago Lions. There will be new blood in the Houston Steers in the 1946 season.

The fans of Houston are excited by it. They are eager for baseball to begin. I have spoken with hundreds of them. And I was there when the players reported into the shiny new locker room the other day, and their eyes popped out of their heads. It was big time, they said. They, too, are excited for baseball to begin.

All except one man. He, alone, arrived late. He, alone, had no smile, no cheer, no enthusiasm, it seemed. He, alone, had not signed his 1946 contract.

He is center-fielder Mike Kutner.

Now, it's not in my province to discuss salary disputes between a player and the management. I don't even know any details in this particular case. But it always seems strange to me when only one man chooses to hold out. It indicates the owners have not been stingy when the contracts went out in February.

However, it should be noted here as a matter of record that Kutner is in no way entitled to any increase on the basis of his 1945 performance. He was no star last year. He hit a weak .271 and slowed down considerably from the flashy speedster he was in the prewar days of his prime. I have all the respect in the world for Kutner's war service to his country, but he must not be allowed to jeopardize the harmony of the club with demands for special considerations. After all, there are other veterans, some who faced active combat, working for a spot on this ball club.

So this reporter suggests: Get off your high-horse, Mike Kutner! Get in with the spirit of the new season! Let's all

> pitch in with our new manager and work together for a pennant. Put your name on that contract, Mike! Put a smile on your face! After all, baseball is great fun, and not such a bad job, is it? Remember what the great Babe Ruth said when they came to discuss salary terms with him: "What! You're gonna *pay* me to play ball?"

Orville Jenkins nodded his head in appreciation; he enjoyed reading it. It was alive and kicking. It would stimulate his readers. And coincidentally, it would be well received in the new, plush offices of the ball club. He liked the ending especially, for it charged his imagination with a dazzling picture of the great Babe waving aside some big wad of money to step up to hit. The Babe was his first hero. He liked the majesty of the man, the fabulous stories, the Herculean home runs, the grandiose gestures. He liked the giant stature, the two hundred and thirty pounds, the wielding of the huge forty-inch bat. Nobody did things in the grand manner like the Babe.

Orville Jenkins had great respect for this kind of bigness. It was synonymous with power. It was insurmountable. He looked up to it with his flaccid face, conscious only of his own smallness. He'd never had the courage to compete with bigness nor the wisdom to avoid it. He found it most opportune to stand there until it bid him follow. This was his basic motivation.

It was easy for him. He was strictly a little man.

There was a cool, fresh-paint smell in the locker room that was strange to him. It didn't smell like a locker room at all. It was still clean, still virgin. That summery tang of sweated uniforms and bodies, of oiled leather and liniment, of victory and defeat, hadn't yet combined into another more durable flavor.

A faint haze of cigarette smoke rose from the far end of the room where a group of ballplayers sat around playing five-and-ten-cent poker, waiting for some word about practice.

The rain had finally stopped during the late morning, but the field was still wet. The coach and groundskeeper were out examining the diamond to see if a brief workout was feasible.

Orville made his way toward the table, nodding affectionately to the youngsters pounding and oiling their gloves. His keen eye was quick to see a copy of the early edition of the *Houston Evening Post.* It was open to the sports page, and he saw his picture upside down on the floor. He knew they read his column every day; he knew they discussed it amongst themselves. But seldom did they mention it to him, as though his position in the fourth estate was a lofty one and above comment. This amused him, and tickled his ego more than he was ready to admit. He liked to believe that they even tried to butter him up a little. He was sure they liked his little word-pictures of them, for his column was usually flattering enough. He had seen them cut it from the paper and send it home, point it out to the wife to put in the scrap book. And when it happened that he was critical of them, or one in particular, they'd regard him furtively, with a quiet, hurt look, like kids who'd been unjustly punished.

He saw them as a bunch of colorful children without intelligence or individual personalities. In the locker rooms, they were innocent and playful and incredibly simple, happy for their victories and depressed by defeats. For all he knew, their lives began and ended there every day.

But when they put on their spikes, they changed. Their bodies were covered with a uniform of professional anonymity. He would marvel at their intensity; their faces, almost hidden under the long, lowered peaks, were serious and confident. They'd stand up there at the plate with admirable concentration, zeroing-in a full measure of coordination and power into a single, savage stroke of the bat. Suddenly, they were men, determined and competent, capable of great performance. Then Orville would remember them shower-room-nude and childlike, and he'd be amazed again at the transformation.

He came to the table and stood by them. He was the little roly-poly man, scarcely taller standing than the big boys sitting. Ostensibly, he would watch them play; but actually, he wanted to listen to their talk, for the conversation of ballplayers was mostly baseball, even in poker games. His column was his life, and here was the material from which it was fashioned.

It did not escape him, however, that this time they discreetly discontinued their talk as he approached. He pretended not to have noticed.

They dealt a hand in silence, confining their subsequent remarks to the cards and their bets, acknowledging his presence with only a polite nod in his direction. He moved quietly behind them, peering over their shoulders at the make-up of their hands and the manner of their betting. Unwittingly, he settled behind Mike Kutner to watch.

The silence began to eat away at him, wearing his patience thin. He waited for a convenient moment in the game to volunteer a comment:

"Well, boys, looks like the rain's stopped, eh?"

One of them nodded to him.

" 'Bout time, I'd say." And they left it at that.

He tried again a minute later, tossing another bone to be picked at.

"Let's hope the new skipper will bring the sunshine with him today. He's due in from Chicago late this afternoon."

From across the room he heard a grunt, but no comments from the table; they were quiet again with a new hand.

In front of him, Kutner threw in his cards, muttering at his luck. Orville watched him slowly flex his fingers as though he were crushing an imaginary ball to nothing in his fist. Then the fingers opened again, and repeated the exercise. He had never seen such a powerful hand; it almost vibrated with strength. It so fascinated him that he almost missed hearing Kutner's words.

"Tell me, Orville. How much money do you make?"

He looked from the hand to the top of the head.

"What's that again?"

"I said, how much dough do you make?"

The question knocked him off balance for a moment. He noticed a few of their glances and he answered haltingly.

"I make a living . . . ," he said evasively. "Why?"

He saw the shoulders shrug in front of him, ever so slightly.

"Just wondered what kind of money a sports writer makes for his talents."

The words were not lightly spoken. He could not see Kutner's face and he tried to guess its expression. He looked down at him, at the thinning hair on his head, suddenly glad and uneasy at the same time to be behind him; and he waited for what would follow.

"Orville says . . . ," he heard now, as if the man were rolling the words around in his mouth, weighing the sound of it. "Orville, do you know how much money Babe Ruth made in a typical year of his prime?"

It was strange, Orville thought. Before the war this boy called him Mr. Jenkins.

"Sure. The records show his top salary was around seventy-five thousand dollars."

Kutner anteed a nickel and picked up his hand.

"That's a pretty fair salary for a man who didn't expect to be paid for playing baseball, wouldn't you say?"

There was a chuckle again. Orville didn't look over to pin it down, nor did he answer. He merely watched Kutner draw to a four-card flush in diamonds.

"Orville says . . . ," the voice in front of him droned on distantly, as though his concentration were on his cards. "But what does Orville know? Does Orville know that the great Chicago Lions saw to it that I got a contract with a *de*crease this year?"

A voice from across the table was aroused, almost incredulous.

"No crap! They lowered you, Mike?"

Orville saw Kutner shake his head slowly behind his fifth diamond. The flush was king-high.

"No. They're just trying to." Kutner raised the bet a dime. "But they ain't gonna be able to. . . ." His voice trailed off as he watched the pot raised again by two others. He raised them back, although they, too, drew only one card. There was silence until the betting stopped. Across the table, a man turned up a full house. Orville watched Kutner throw in his hand, face down, almost as if he had expected to lose.

"Since you brought it up, Orville," the ballplayer went on, "I'll tell you some news. I don't ever play ball for less money. I play only for more. And since you wrote about last year, you oughta be reminded that I'd just gotten out of the Army, and despite what a lot of you civilians liked to think, the war ain't always good for a man's condition. I hadn't played ball in four years, not an inning. I wasn't ready when they stuck me in the line-up. You were there when I told the old skipper that. Seems like you're always there, Orville, come to think of it. Sure, I had a bum year. Charley horse for three weeks, sore arm, and what not. A man don't like to play ball when he ain't just right."

The voice across the room followed it up.

"No more'n a reporter likes to write with a busted ass, eh, Mike?"

They all laughed now, embarrassed at the nature of the joke. The reporter tried to laugh with them. In his mind, however, he made a note of the man who'd said it.

The laughter subsided as quickly as it began. The silence that followed only added to a curious tension that suddenly filled the room.

Kutner seemed bent on continuing, his voice a little more

sharp and biting now. Still it seemed almost as if he was talking to himself.

"It ain't fun to be a holdout; but money is money, and the size of your check is a way of measuring what people think of you. So you sweat it out every year. It's always the same goddamn deal. All winter long you dream over your best games from the summer, and you're guessing how much more dough you're gonna get. Pretty soon February rolls around and the contracts go out. Yours reads, say, three hundred and fifty dollars a month—same as last year—and you know right away that ain't enough. For one thing, how the hell's a man gonna make out on less than two grand a year?"

"A man can do it," someone suggested, "if he marries a rich broad."

"Ain't it funny, though," another said, "how few ballplayers manage to swing it?"

They were laughing, the uneasy laugh in the midst of tension. Mike waited, and then went on as if he hadn't stopped.

"But mostly it's your pride that's hurt, so back goes the lousy contract with nothing on it but a couple new finger prints. They hold it for a while, say three weeks, then back it comes, with all the same damn numbers on it. Pretty soon you start getting jittery, 'cause spring training begins and you've been reading 'bout trades and new prospects and all that hot-stove crap. You sit there sweating out an extra fifty bucks a month from them, a lousy three bills a year. But mostly you're thinking that they'll be putting the wood to it down there in the sunshine, and a couple of them kids are center fielders just like you, battling for your spot, ready to play ball for half the dough you're asking."

"Christ!"—he was interrupted again. "There's always somebody who'll play ball for less, ain't there?"

Mike continued rapidly now. "And then you get to thinking that maybe one of them is hot, red hot, and maybe the club'll like to dump you anyway. So you end up signing for the same stinking three hundred and fifty, because if you don't, you simply don't play—anyplace! And that's where they've got you in a goddamn vise!"

Orville had never heard this man talk so much in the two seasons he had known him. Nor had he ever known him to be bitter. It seemed as if he was speaking not only for himself, but for all of them. Orville worried that perhaps the article should not have been quite so strong.

He noticed that the card game had temporarily stopped. The dealer shuffled and reshuffled the cards, listening to Kutner as they all were, absorbed by what must have been their own comparable experiences.

"But I figured out something," the ballplayer went on, "because a man can't eat dirt all his life. A man's just gotta learn to stand up for himself. And if he's good, they'll goddamn well pay him for it!"

Orville was suddenly uneasy. The words were much too challenging, too defiant for his taste, for they poked into matters too basic to a man. He fidgeted nervously, unable to look squarely at any of them, as if all this were somehow directed at him.

His question was formed in his stomach.

"And suppose he isn't so damn good. What's he supposed to do then?"

Kutner did not hesitate.

"If he ain't, then I guess he oughta get his ass in a different job, or else he'll be taking the same kicking around forever. And that's for the birds, ain't it, Orville?"

The newspaperman cringed at the reply. He began to feel dizzy. He was fighting off an attack he could neither understand nor cope with.

Compulsively he resorted to baiting the ballplayer.

"Tell me something, Kutner," he said. "You figuring on going up to the majors?"

Kutner turned his head part way toward him.

"All ballplayers figure on something like that," he smiled. "You heard the boys. A man can't get rich on spikes."

From a far corner of the room, someone hollered, "Safe at home!" And they all laughed again.

Orville winced inwardly. The answer was not an answer for all their laughter, though he knew there was truth in it. For years he had heard these babies crowing about their prospects like they were sure bets, breathing big league ambitions, bolstering their cockiness by comparing their meager talents with the weakest players who had somehow made it. "Christ," they would mumble, "I outhit Saunders by thirty points back in Atlanta. Lookit him up there now in Philly." Or, "It don't figure . . . old 'cousin' Koenig is working with Boston and I never failed to murder his curve." The old pipe dream—there was always someone on top with whom a man could favorably compare himself. It could keep a stupid man going forever.

But he knew he had never heard Kutner pop off like this, and somehow, that gave the man the right to talk now.

"All ballplayers don't get there, Kutner!" Orville said. "There's only four hundred in the majors and seven or eight thousand down here in the minors. That's one out of twenty, Kutner!" He was demanding now. "So what about you?"

Suddenly he knew what the man would say. But for some reason, he wanted to hear him say it.

Kutner smiled. Orville knew they were all watching.

"I'll make it," he said simply; and there seemed to be no doubt about it.

At that point, Orville Jenkins hated him. He looked down at Kutner again, older than most of them, seeming even older than he actually was at twenty-seven or twenty-eight. His thinning hair and his heavy glasses seemed incongruous in the locker room with the younger, bigger men who at least looked like athletes even around a poker table. Where does this little squirt get off being so damn cocky? Why does this guy think he can play ball where Ruth played?

He didn't want to believe he could. Suddenly, his resentment boiled over.

"Not without a contract, you won't!" Orville snapped at him, his voice inadvertently pitched much too high. He felt them all turn to stare at him, fascinated by this strange show of hostility. He lowered his eyes and moved over toward the window to settle himself, trying to ferret through his confusion for a meaning that would bring comfort to him. His brain was swirling without reason or logic and it frightened him. He couldn't feel sure of anything.

Behind him he heard the game continue, listlessly now. He caught himself nervously scratching himself through a hole in his pants pocket and quickly withdrew his hand. They were thinking about him, he knew, and it bothered the hell out of him.

The late afternoon sun spread long shadows over the field before him. From the office window he watched the heavy, wire mat erasing a myriad of spike wounds as the groundskeepers dragged it over the infield. The tan and green colors were sharp and clear at this hour, and he thought that a well-kept baseball field is a beautiful and exciting thing.

Behind him, the business manager finished a phone conversation and leaned back in his chair.

"Well, Orville, that was Kutner," he said. "Finally managed to make contact."

"I gathered that." He was about to say "Clark," but thought better of it. Somehow, this young man didn't lend himself to quick familiarity. This was Orville's first invitation to the inner sanctums, and he would play it right. Besides, this was definitely a different type of business manager. Dark gray flannels, knit tie, good-looking young college flavor. Mellon spoke softly, smoothly, without the usual baseball bluster. He had a kind of class that Jenkins had heard about but never seen. The reporter found himself speaking better English in this man's presence. He liked the atmosphere.

"He's coming over?" Jenkins asked. He knew Kutner was; the phone conversation clearly indicated it.

Young Mellon nodded. "He said he'd be here in fifteen minutes. Please have a seat, Orville."

Jenkins sat in the leather chair in front of the desk. Mellon fumbled over the papers until he found what he wanted. Orville could see it was a contract, presumably Kutner's. Mellon appeared to study it briefly, lost for a moment in conjecture.

"We need this man badly, don't you think, Orville?" And he added: "Of course I haven't seen him play for a few years."

Jenkins smiled. The man was asking him for his opinion, and he found it most gratifying.

"He's been here at Houston for three years, two before the war. He was good then, first rate. Last year . . . ," and he shook his head to finish the thought.

Mellon tapped a pencil on the papers before him.

"He's not thirty yet; now, is he . . . ?"

This one didn't seem like a question to Jenkins. So he didn't answer. But he knew Kutner was older than his years, older than the record showed.

"The war ruined a lot of ballplayers"; and he finally added, "Clark."

Mellon nodded without looking up. "War has that definite tendency," he said. His voice was mild with the understatement. It made Jenkins feel foolish, and he reddened. "The question is," Clark went on, "what kind of an attitude does the man have? About baseball, and his future?"

Jenkins thought for a moment. You had to think carefully with this man. "Kutner has changed. He's older now. It's hard to say about him. I really don't know."

Mellon was thinking. "My problem here is a difficult one. I

have a salary limit and I've got to stay within it. Chicago purchased this club because we need a testing ground; we have to develop new kids to compensate for those war years. It's my uncle's policy that kids get preference. He's looking for talent first. A pennant down here is secondary."

Orville smiled. "That, of course, is not for publication."

Mellon ignored this, and went on. He seemed to be the kind who did his thinking out loud.

"Kutner can't be considered a kid. He's a veteran already. Almost anyone who played AA or AAA ball before the war is now considered a veteran." The words came out with a trace of sarcasm, clearly indicating what he thought of this. "That puts him in a less desirable spot when it comes to bargaining. The truth is that my uncle has a nineteen-year-old outfielder he wants to throw in here."

Orville looked up, surprised. Would they get rid of Kutner?

"I argued against it," Mellon went on, "and apparently I won."

Jenkins saw the dilemma. Clark Mellon could keep Kutner in lieu of trading him but only on Jim Mellon's terms.

"However," Mellon was saying, "this Mexican situation puts a monkey wrench in the works, now doesn't it?"

True enough. But Kutner, Orville guessed, wasn't going south. Nor was he going to take any salary cut. He wondered whether Mellon knew this. He offered it to him.

"I'll tell you one thing, Clark: I don't believe Kutner would play for you on these Chicago terms, Mexican or no Mexican."

There was a long silence that Orville didn't understand. Mellon was tapping his pencil again. Without actually seeing his eyes, Orville knew the man was looking at him. The tone of his last words lingered in his mind and he feared lest they sounded more like a threat than a sympathetic piece of advice.

Then the pencil stopped.

"Did you ever hear of a man named Durkin Fain?" Mellon asked.

"Sure. He was a scout up in Chicago. For your uncle, wasn't he?"

Mellon nodded. "One of the best. Just about the last thing he did for us was bring Kutner in."

Jenkins wondered what this man was getting at. He was beginning to feel uneasy. He volunteered a question, though the answer would not interest him.

"Where's he now?"

"He's coaching college ball, over in Indiana. He makes nothing a year and turns out good ballplayers."

There was a pause and Orville waited for what would follow.

"We lost Kutner once, years ago," Mellon said. "It was a mistake. A bad mistake. I don't want to lose him again."

The door opened behind him, interrupting the talk. Orville turned to see who it was.

"Oh, hello, Skipper," he said pleasantly.

"Hi, there, Jenkins." The manager carried his beefy ex-athlete's body heavily. He had been a number of years in the majors and Orville regarded him with considerable respect.

"How's the ball club after three sunny days out there?"

The skipper grunted. "Only thing I know is that they oughta be goddamned beat. I sure as hell am."

"You sure do drive 'em," Jenkins replied. "Run the winter out of their bones."

Mellon smiled. "They look good. We'll have a good club."

The skipper turned toward young Mellon. "What about Kutner, Clark? I thought I'd drop in to check. You signed him yet?"

Orville saw Mellon smile, as if he thought the question funny.

"Not yet. He's due here almost any minute. I finally got him to come and talk."

"He'll sign, then." The skipper's voice was rough-edged. "Why shouldn't he?"

Clark looked up at him, still smiling. Orville knew that there was something between the two of them he didn't understand. He hated things he didn't understand.

Clark said, "Rumor has it that the Mexican is here . . . and he's talked with him."

Orville nodded as though they'd been talking to him. "They were seen talking at the hotel, early this morning."

Clark shrugged. "Two and two is four, even in pesos, unless we can talk him out of it. Apparently there's a lot of money enticing these boys down there."

The skipper interjected. "You ain't gonna lose him, Clark," he began. "He don't wanna go to Mexico even for the big dough. Kutner wants to play ball in the major leagues, U.S.A.; that's what he wants to do. Tell him you got it straight from the old man in Chicago that if he has a good year he'll get a chance next season. Tell him we got our eye on him; promise him a goddamn bonus, even. You can promise guys like that anything; you can always forget words. And if he don't fall for that crap, then you just gotta threaten the sonofabitch! Threaten him with suspension and blackballs and whatever you can think of. Tell him you'll see to it he never plays ball again, anyplace. You can do it, Clark! And make it clear that if he goes to Mexico he's breaking the friggen law, and he's hurting both himself and baseball. Christ, if you pour it on thick enough, he'll end up happy to sign! It never fails." And he added as if in afterthought: "I'm sick of these punks who come back from the wars thinking they're worth more money. Goddammit, they're worth less!"

They were quiet after this. There seemed to be nothing more to say. Orville was impressed by this kind of solution. He would give a month's salary to watch Kutner face the music.

The skipper's massive body filled the doorway for a moment. "The boys tell me he works out at the high school," he said. "Runs for hours chasing fly balls."

Orville nodded eagerly. "Yeah. He's got some kid hitting fungos to him. I heard he even has a crowd watching him."

The skipper went on. "Eager beaver. You should know about them, Clark. They'd rather play ball than eat." He held the door open now. "Let me know," he said; and then nodding at Orville, "See ya."

Orville watched the door close and looked at his watch, wondering when Kutner would arrive. The thought of the coming conference excited him, and he speculated on the possibility of remaining in the office to witness it. But he discarded the thought quickly. He would have to be content to learn the details in the morning. For reasons he did not bother to fathom, this distressed him.

At his desk, Clark Mellon straightened out the random papers that cluttered it. Then he got up and walked to the window.

"Seems like I spent the best part of the day on the telephone, chasing after that fellow. You'd think he'd be sitting there waiting."

Reluctantly Orville got up to leave. As the skipper had done, he lingered in the doorway.

"Kutner's been waiting," he said, and he patted his chest to supplement his thought; "only he does it inside."

Orville Jenkins awoke early the following morning. He lay restlessly in bed waiting for the alarm to get him up, for there was no point in rising before it. His first waking thought was about the ballplayer and Clark Mellon, and he wondered about their meeting. He had tried to get hold of Mellon the evening before, but he had been unable to reach him. This had irritated him, piling layers of time on a feeling of suspense he could not understand.

Somehow, this had been on his mind all night, as though there was something more to the story than a minor salary dispute to be decided by conference and routine give-and-take. He could not free himself of the picture of the ballplayer, the back of the head and the faceless voice. The words had sniped at him at first, those sharp digs at his column. Orville had been only briefly annoyed. Yet what followed was something else again, something that shook him up. A man had spoken up with a kind of courage that made Orville uneasy. A player had put himself on record, quietly defying the authority of the men who owned his talent, owned him. Kutner had slapped at them, the giants, the big wheels. He had talked tough from a position of weakness and made it sound like a position of strength. In that locker room, a crummy, minor-league ballplayer, over the hill at that, had lectured to the children in the voice of a mature man.

But talking defiance was one thing; acting was another. Through the long, twisting hours into dawn, Orville cursed himself for not trying to stick around Mellon's office last evening when Kutner was due, instead of politely withdrawing. He knew that a whole piece of the story had been removed, and he'd never really know what happened at its climax.

But now he itched for the answer, aware of the terrible ambivalence of his hopes. He disliked the ballplayer, though he did not know exactly why. Was it because he was smaller than most, as Orville was? Or was it because he wore glasses, as Orville did? Or, more likely, because he was both these things and a damned good ballplayer besides? Was that it? Would he like Kutner better if he was just mediocre, or less than mediocre?

The whole question now was whether Kutner could get away with his rebellion. Orville felt a drop of sweat roll down his side onto the sheet. The simple truth was that he was afraid lest the man could. Then, Orville would have to justify a whole lifetime of cringing and bootlicking, of keeping his mind and thoughts constantly in line, of saying nothing except what was acceptable to the men who kept him around. He did all this, and more, only because he believed he had to. There was no other choice, no alternative for a man with few talents like himself struggling to be a success.

He hated the test Kutner had to face. He hated even more the man who was willing to face it; and in his heart, he knew he wanted him to lose.

The alarm refused to ring. He leaned over and flipped off the button. He washed and dressed hurriedly, hoping that the morning paper would be waiting for him at the door of his two-room apartment. It wasn't, and at once he decided that a glance at the sports page was more important than making coffee at home.

He went out into the chilly morning air of early spring and walked to the diner a few blocks away. He ordered coffee and borrowed the counterman's paper. Quickly, he turned to the sports page, not knowing exactly what he expected to find. He saw the five-line piece, finally, and he grunted his annoyance as he read it:

KUTNER SIGNS

> Last night, the final member of the Houston Steers' roster came into the fold after a conference with Clark Mellon, business manager of the Steers. Terms of the agreement were not disclosed.

He was annoyed at what the piece told him. Kutner signs. He was even more annoyed at what it did not. On whose terms? The news was not news at all. What in hell had happened in there?

An hour later, he turned into his office, tired from an aimless walk. He had tried to forget this business, to enjoy the early sunshine and the clear freshness of the day. He couldn't.

Yet why did it matter so much? It wasn't anything he could put in his column. He had another cup of coffee and fumbled aimlessly through some papers on his desk, filling time until 9:30, a respectable hour to call Clark Mellon.

At 9:30 he decided he'd wait ten more minutes, a token of his non-concern.

At 9:37 he called. The voice he heard was polite and distant.

"Well, Jenkins, how are you this fine Texas day?"

"Fine, sir. Good sleeping weather, isn't it?"

"Always is. Well, what does Orville say today?"

The mention of his column irritated him. He didn't exactly know how to ask this. "I've been thinking about your meeting with Kutner last night." And he blurted out: "How'd it come out?"

"Why, satisfactorily, Jenkins." But there was a pause. "Yes . . . I was going to call you, as a matter of fact."

"You were?"

"He agreed to terms. He started in by bringing up that Mexican offer and I jumped right on him." There was another silence. "He signed inside of an hour."

"On your terms?"

"Practically."

"I mean," Orville was pressing now, "he isn't getting *more* than last year?"

There was another pause on the line. Orville held his breath.

"Well, now, part of the deal is that I'm not supposed to reveal terms. But, just don't print this, Jenkins. No. He's not getting more than last year."

Orville felt the laughter rising inside him. He bit his lip to control it.

"The skipper was right," the voice went on smoothly. "The promises did it. Kutner wants to play ball in the big leagues."

Orville nodded into the phone. "Clark," he said almost obsequiously, "I'm guessing that it was your firmness that swayed him. It's not that Kutner isn't tough; it's just that you know how to handle these men."

He heard the quick, much-too-polite laugh.

"I hardly think so, Jenkins. Well, see you later."

"Yes, sir. Bye."

Orville hung up and leaned back in his chair, filled with the bittersweet taste of a peculiar victory. The ballplayer had crumbled, he thought. He had to face the big shots to prove his independence and he crumbled at the first threat to his security. The man didn't know his own strength, didn't know how much the club needed him. He fell for the phony promise of a sure shot at the majors and it all ended up with the status quo. The words were empty, spoken for comfort and out of a false courage before the fact. Orville grinned again. Kutner was just another two-o'clock hitter after all.

There was no one yet on the field when he arrived at the ball park, earlier than ever. Today would be Orville's reward, and he hurried his short legs toward the locker room. At the door, he suddenly stopped and altered his pace, ambling into the routine boisterousness as casually as he could, dimly aware that the fresh-paint smell was giving way to more typical locker-room odors. In the far corner, he saw the one he wanted. He was almost through dressing.

"Eager beaver," Orville grunted to himself, and he moved to the bench across from him to listen to the talk.

"The skipper's a killer out there, Mike. Run, run, run. You'd think this was a track team we was trainin' for."

"It's good for you, Clem. It's good for your arm!" said another.

"My arm, my ass! Trouble is I'm too friggen tired to hit when it finally comes my turn."

"Oh, so that's the reason! Now tell me, Clem; kin you hit when you ain't tired?"

They laughed. Orville thought he never saw a pitcher who didn't think he could someday be a hitter. Most of them kept it to themselves, however.

"I can hit that rock, Curly. Don't you ever think I can't. But this running! Christ, maybe I shoulda been a holdout like Kutner, here, and missed these cruddy running days."

"If I know Kutner, he ran."

"Didya, Mike? Whattaya been doing these days?"

Kutner smiled.

"I ran," he said.

Orville snickered to himself. You ran, Kutner. Boy, you did more than that. You crawled! And if he had had courage, he would have spoken the words aloud with the sneer he saved for his private dialogue. As a consolation to his pride, he snickered again, aloud this time but seconds too late for any effect. He looked at the ballplayer, trying to pry into that impassive, distant face. Their jabbering rode right over him.

"Did you know Curly played ball in Venezuela over the winter? Tell the boys about them Latins, Curly."

"The dames or the ballplayers?"

"They got women down there too?"

Curly grinned.

"Play ball in South America and you make plenty of money . . . and dames."

"What about Mexico?" Clem broke in. "What's the deal down there? I heard a lot of the big boys are skipping."

"Yeah. They're payin' big money."

"Ask Kutner. The Mexican was here talking to him."

"Yeah, Mike. They offer good dough?"

Kutner nodded. "Enough."

"I heard they double your check without batting an eye."

"They could triple mine without even flickin' an eyelash."

Curly leaned toward Kutner.

"How come you didn't grab it, Mike?"

Kutner shrugged as he buttoned his shirt.

"I guess I like it here," he said quietly.

"Well, I hope you made 'em pay you, Mike. Seems like them bastards in Chicago could raise a few salaries without bleeding."

The others looked at the center fielder, wondering if he would comment. Ballplayers generally respected the privacy of others' salaries.

Kutner removed his glove from the bag and worked the leather neatly with his fist. He seemed lost in gazing at the flexibility of the pocket.

Orville waited. For an answer, apparently, there had to be a question.

"Well, what about it, Kutner?" he asked, anticipating his moment of triumph. "What about your contract?"

Kutner looked over toward him, a slight smile on his lips. There was no trace of shame or regret in his eyes; only a faraway look into the future.

"I did O.K.," he said distantly. "I got what I wanted." And there was no doubt but that he meant what he said.

Orville sighed and nodded to himself. Sure . . . my God, sure! The ballplayer really believed it! How could it be otherwise? What could you expect in this kind of a battle? Orville was watching a man protect the thing most important to him, his struggle to make something of himself. Everything he did was geared toward it; every thought and action was a means to an end, even if you had to kid yourself a little about the availability of that end. The other day's bravado was a sham, strictly for effect, a crutch. He thought now with satisfaction that Kutner was like himself, that Kutner played the game like all the rest of them. When the time came, in his own way, he knuckled under; yet none of the basic rules were broken and even the dream remained intact.

Orville Jenkins was relieved. He thought he would do a nice, friendly story about Mike Kutner.

He heard the sudden silence around him and he raised his head to it. He saw the skipper moving heavily down the row of benches toward his private room in the back. The players held their conversations until he had passed.

"Hello, Jenkins," the skipper said, trying to smile as he approached. "How's tricks today?"

Orville smiled his friendliest. Who was buttering up whom? he thought. It occurred to him briefly that maybe he'd been underrating himself.

The manager turned and walked over to the bench where Kutner sat, lacing his spikes. He stood over him, waiting for the ballplayer to look up. Orville tensed at the strange silence around them. It was as if others were waiting too.

Finally, Kutner finished and looked slowly up at the big figure looming over him. Orville strained to see some change of expression in the ballplayer's face but there was none.

"Well, if it ain't little old Kutner," the skipper said finally. His voice seemed ugly to Orville, unnecessarily so. After all, the guy had signed. "Long time no see, eh? I see you're still totin' them goddamn extra pair of eyes."

The ballplayer stood up in his new pair of spikes, looking much taller than he was. He took off his glasses and wiped them clean. Then he returned them to his face and looked back at the manager.

"Hello, Phipps," he said quietly. He picked up his glove and made his way out of the locker room.

# 8 *The Negro*

On the players' bench, Ben Franks sat wedged in amongst the hot, tired bodies, listening to the sullen obscenities that reflected their mood. The dugout suddenly seemed like a small, overcrowded house with a huge picture-window looking out over the diamond. Quiet, he stewed in his own sweat, waiting for the turn at bat that would permit him to leave; and he thought that this was a helluva place to feel so damn alone.

He tried to concentrate on the ball game, nursing a weird feeling that he hadn't been in it. Everything was strange. Strange park. Strange city. Strange ballplayers. It made the day seem unreal, almost dreamlike. (What the hell, man! You slept last night in a crummy flea bag in Scranton, Pennsylvania, and here you are like a bird, suddenly, in Kansas City, hustling your ass with Minneapolis in a nifty triple A circuit. Man, that's something; so get with it!)

Up at the plate, the hitter was Kutner, waving his bat at the pitcher like he would knock the guy's head off. Ben leaned back and suppressed a routine desire to holler encouragement, for he sensed this was not wanted from him. Not now, especially not for Kutner. For today Ben had moved in cold and taken over center field as though he were the greatest prospect since Tris Speaker. The manager had announced it in the locker room, apologizing for something he had no control over.

"This is Franks, men. He'll play center field for us. Kutner moves to left."

Orders from Chicago, Ben knew. "Move the big nigger in there and see what he can do!" It seemed like a damn-fool way to run a ball club.

The silence that followed had crushed him. They had looked at him as if he had engineered the deal himself. He had sneaked a first glance at this Kutner and saw the man barely nod to the manager, the muscle on his jaw twitching nervously. Ben had swallowed heavily, and it sounded like thunder to him.

So he sat back on the bench now, quiet and alone, contemplating his coming time at bat for he followed the next hitter. The prospects of belting one excited him, as always. He knew he would have to talk with his bat and talk big. This was not his ball club just because he wore the uniform. He tried to forget everything else.

Even as he saw Kutner lift a simple pop foul, his stomach fluttered anticipating trouble. He waited until the catcher had settled under it before going to the bat rack. He grabbed three bats and started out of the dugout toward the batter's circle, suddenly hating the baseball tradition that required him to be there. He saw Kutner coming toward him, his eyes lowered to the ground, sputtering his anger and frustration between his teeth.

"Sonofabitch!"

Ben grumbled to himself as he heard. Listen to the man cussing himself. That ain't nothing to what they gonna be callin' me! He spat through his broken tooth and moved nervously into the batter's circle.

The voices greeted him again.

"Well, well. Look who's here!"

"Shine, boy?"

He tried to shut them out of his consciousness, to close his brain to their viciousness. But he was too vulnerable there, a kneeling duck, trapped by a white circle of lime and an old article in the rule book.

"Nigger! shine! boogie! coon! slave!"

They used all the words on him. There was a sudden harshness to their yelling, now more agitated and severe than before, as though they were building up to something. It seemed like more than a razzing job to get his goat. He'd played ball for four years in the Negro leagues and they could jockey with the best of them. But this was more, much more. This was the hoarse, rasping voice of hate, and it struck close to home.

He had guessed it would be something like this when he had signed. This was white men's baseball. Up in Chicago Jim Mellon had told him as much: "You'll have to swallow plenty, boy. This is still a new thing. You'll just have to learn how to control yourself!"

He was getting plenty of practice.

"Hey, porter, take my bags."

"Yeah, where's your red cap?"

"Ya big ape! Go on back to the zoo!"

He thought wryly that back in the dugout he was lonely and wanted out. Now he was worried and wanted back in. O.K., big Ben. Take it easy. Remember this is where you want to be. What did you expect, cookies and tea between innings?

"Watch out, nigger. The chucker's got a real hard one."

"He's gonna stick it in yer ear, black boy."

"Look here, nigger!"

"Hey, boy, here!"

In front of him, he saw the pitcher step off the mound, suddenly distracted by the spectators. Mechanically, Ben turned to see them, the faces behind the jeering voices.

Someone was dangling a handmade noose from a long pole.

Big joke. He heard their mocking calls and their savage laughter, and a slight chill ran through him. Then he saw them on his own bench, peering over the dugout like kids at a ten-cent peep show, and they were laughing too. Sure . . . great big gag. He wiped the sweat off his hands on the rosin bag and turned back to the game.

"Come on!" he roared at the hitter. "Ride one!"

He wanted them to know: Ben Franks was here to play ball.

He watched the feeble grounder and the simple play at first and he moved in to hit. It was his moment now, and he would make it good. He saw only the pitcher and a beautiful vision of a drive riding over the big fence in right. He knew this chucker was duck soup for him, that he could pick out the throw he liked and blast it. The thing to do was to be loose up there, to think only of hitting . . . only of hitting.

The pitcher had more respect for him than the jockeys, or, at least, a different kind, and he kept the ball away from him. Ben fouled off one, then another, and the count worked up to three and two. He got set for the big one, and watched the curve ball sweep down and away. He held his swing for the obviously bad pitch, but even as he did, he heard the umpire's call, the much-too-hasty grunt meant to cut him down.

"Stee-rike three!"

He turned like a cat at a sudden noise, his whole body alive with protest. This wasn't jockeying any more. A man can't hit a pitch like that, no matter what. In the stands they saw his contorted face, and they hooted with joy at this unexpected treat.

("You'll have to swallow plenty, boy. You'll just have to learn control!")

He bit his lip at the fury rushing through him. Control, Ben. Control. Don't throw your bat. Don't argue. Don't!

He moved back from the umpire, and as he did, he saw the stupid smile through the fat mask.

It was time for him to get out of there.

He dropped his bat and jogged back to the outfield, fighting back his rage. He picked up his glove and pounded the pocket viciously.

The sonsofbitches.

His mind was knotted with his anger. He knew it was the goddamn jockeys who had called that pitch, not the umpire's eyesight. The ump was riding on their catcalls as he waited for the pitch, ready to holler "strike three" before he even saw it. The guy was playing it safe; he'd call them with the crowd whenever possible.

So he stood out there in the field, balancing his pride and hopes and ambitions against this monster of hate and pressure. He tried to believe he could live with this kind of thing and play ball despite it. He knew he was plenty good at bat, that he could hit with the best of them. But it was the other factors that tore at the roots of his confidence—the fans on him, the umps against him, his teammates cool toward him. He thought of Jackie Robinson up there breaking in with Brooklyn and he let his mind speculate over what it might be like in the big leagues. Pretty rough, he knew. People are people whatever the circuit. There's good folk and there's bad. The bad ones will put the spike in your leg and the hard knee in your groin, and the good ones will sit back while it happens and just be damn sorry that it does. Sure, a man would have to be pretty terrific to stick, not just good enough. Pretty damn terrific. He wondered whether he'd ever be that.

Then, as if out of nowhere, he heard the crack of the bat. His body tensed, waiting for his eye to focus on the drive soaring out toward him. He turned with a jerk to take off for it, terrified that he hadn't even seen it hit! At once his concentration returned to the game, and somehow, through his reverie, he had recorded that there was a man on. He panicked at his unreadiness. He drove his legs desperately over the turf, wondering how hard it was hit, and as he ran, he sensed suddenly he was misjudging it. He tried to shift his direction, but his big body seemed unwieldy. At the last moment, he twisted his arm behind him in a wild, clumsy maneuver. The best he could do was to get a piece of his glove on the ball.

He turned quickly to pick it up, and couldn't. It was as if the ball were alive, eluding him. Out of the corner of his eye, he saw Kutner, standing there a few feet away, and he almost laughed through his exasperation. He grabbed at it again, and whirled to throw.

"Home," he heard.

He threw desperately, with all his power, and before he let it go, he knew he would throw it away.

The savage roaring of the crowd blasted in his ears. Ben stood there for a moment, looking at the players around home plate.

"Shit!" he heard Kutner snarl with disgust.

"Shit. . . ." he nodded.

He walked back to his position, torturing himself with a recount of his actions. In those few moments, he had been all wrong as a ballplayer. In fact, he'd been no ballplayer at all. He had let his concentration drift from the game. A ballplayer should be thinking. A ballplayer should always be thinking.

He set himself for the next hitter, who popped out to third, and the next, his teeth clenched with concentration on every pitch. He begged for the ball to be hit to him. He prayed for the chance to redeem himself with a great catch this time, or a great throw. To me, goddammit! To me! Hit that sonofabitchin' thing out here again. And he felt he would burn up at the terrible waiting that is baseball.

Then he saw the pitch, the swing, and the ball floating out into left center like an answer to his plea. He cut loose after it, thinking only that he was happy that there were two men on, that with two outs they'd be running, and that the game would be over if he failed to make the catch. He took off for it with everything he had. Then, near the end of his dash, he heard the hurried cry a few yards away:

"I got it! I got it!"

He had all but forgotten that Kutner was out there in left field.

Ben's big body was charging like a locomotive and he didn't want to stop. He saw the ball in its downward flight and he knew he could get there in time. This should be his catch. Somehow or other he felt that they owed it to him.

"No!" he cried. "Mine! Mine!"

But at the same moment, Ben heard him again, repeating his call. It was too late; the decision would have to be made by instinct, without corroboration by the other. There was too much of Ben's will in his race for that ball; the commitment had been made even before the ball was hit, and he could not control it. His body drove for the catch, but as it did, Kutner's body crossed into his line of vision. Ben automatically swerved violently, throwing himself to the ground to avoid a crash. He rolled over twice with the momentum of his fall, and when he stopped, he turned to see Kutner standing over him, his face red with anger.

A few feet behind him, Ben saw the white ball, slowly trickling to a stop. He realized then how far he had moved into left field.

Slowly he got to his feet, listening to the hooting and laughter of the crowd. The game was over and the crowd had won it. He stuffed his glove into his hip pocket and began the terrible walk into the clubhouse.

In the locker room, the players sat on the benches taking too much time to undress. Ben fingered the laces of his shoes, wanting to take his shower and get out of there. He remembered he hadn't eaten since this morning, at a stopover in

Chicago. Christ! What a day! But he felt the rest of them half-eyeing him, as if they were defying him to be first after what he had done. Furtively, he stopped unlacing, resigned to taking the scorn they were throwing at him without so much as opening their mouths. Somehow, he had hoped there would be quick respite for him, that they'd offer him some polly-annish word of encouragement to prop him up. And when the manager came in, Ben looked up toward him and winced as the man threw his little cap at the corner in a ludicrous, adolescent gesture that passed for rage. Like the others, he could say nothing but merely moped in the special chair reserved for him.

Goddamn you all! Ben was ready to explode. Say it! Go ahead and say it!

Then he wondered what he wanted them to say. There was too much against him to package into a few choice words of profanity. He had walked in there a few hours before, hated for as good a reason as any white man could have dreamed up to hate a Negro.

Ben Franks was labeled to go up *because* he was black.

He knew it. They all knew it. Up in Chicago, Jim Mellon had his eyes on Brooklyn, shifting from the gate receipts to Robinson's ability and back to the gate receipts. The black man was being accepted and the ball club was making a fat dollar for its "crusade." So Jim Mellon had to get himself a black man.

Ben looked down at the color of his arms. Coal black. Sure. Mellon's boy would have to be black. With kinky hair and big feet. He remembered Mellon suggesting slyly that Robinson seemed like the wrong kind of black boy to bring up. Too smart, too aggressive, too tricky. His feet were too small. The public might not like too much of that. But a big, lumbering, quiet boy who can blast that long ball. The crowds would really go for that.

Big and dumb, Ben grunted. But not too dumb. He hated Mellon for that, and he hated himself now because he hadn't proved the old bastard wrong. Ben was big, yes, and he lumbered on the base paths without grace or too much speed. Therefore, it followed that he must be dumb. Jesus, he thought now, they hadn't even told him the signals before the game, as though he wasn't expected to play that kind of baseball!

The whole deal had a peculiar flavor to it. It seemed too arbitrary, too simple. He felt he was being judged by a special set of standards that applied only to him. Back in Scranton, just a few weeks ago, a foolish young pitcher had grooved one with the bases crowded, and Ben had laid his power into it. The ball had soared over the lights in deep right center, out of the park and into the huge parking lot, some 560 feet from home plate. It created a big stir. No ball had ever been hit that far in Scranton. He was told that Jim Mellon had hopped a plane the next night and flown to Scranton to watch him play. Then he went out to the parking area after the game to see where the ball had landed. They had even sought out the man whose windshield had been smashed by the blow, and they paid him ten bucks to drive to the spot where his car had been parked.

Apparently this had been enough to sell old man Mellon on him. It was crazy. He knew he was good enough. But he also knew he was no better than dozens of others, black or white. But he alone had belted one 560 feet. You're a freak, Ben, he told himself. A 560-foot publicity stunt. You're gonna be Chicago's symbol of tolerance and democracy, and you'll be paid for your pigment, your yardage, and your docility.

He sat there now, brooding, unable to undress until the last man had showered, as though this were a kind of self-inflicted punishment, a token of his guilt. There was something sickening about all this. He was being used to exploit the breaking color line in baseball by a man who was simply trying a new angle for an extra buck. Ben would be fed nickels and the familiar pot of sugar about how thrilled he should be to be playing white man's baseball, to be a hero to his people. And he'd go up the ladder to the top, hated most by the men he was told to walk on, like Kutner here.

He took off his shirt and hung it neatly on the hanger. MINNEAPOLIS it read, bridging across the zipper down the middle. He told himself to be proud. What the hell, he was doing fine. The world was a crazy place and it wasn't up to him to explain it. Things had moved fast for him since April, faster during these four months than for most people in a lifetime. He was going up and that's what counted. Forget today, Ben. Tomorrow will be better. Everything's gonna be O.K.

But it wasn't that simple. There was a tense pressure in AAA baseball that was strange to him. They played to win with a new kind of concentration, for these were the eager boys close to the top, knocking at the big doors. They looked for likely targets and knew a million ways to knock a man down. That he should become such a target did not stagger him. It was a way of winning he knew all about.

But a bad beginning can hound a man; the breaks can turn against him, developing a reputation that makes him out a complete bust. After a week, Ben found his confidence severely shaken, especially since he had done nothing to prove himself. Those first three days in Kansas City had been a nightmare. After that first game, they never gave him a chance to climb out of the hole he had dug for himself. The pitchers had given him nothing to hit at. At the risk of walking him once or twice a game, they dusted him off with their high hard ones, and he spent half his time at the plate thinking about protecting himself. He was not going to make the big leagues on a record number of bases on balls. If he belted a few, at least some of the fans would welcome him in Minneapolis. He wanted that. He needed the crowds behind him.

He also needed his teammates, but some of them made it rough on him. He came to feel a weird kind of pressure as though they were making him a slave to his new reputation. Quietly, he was needled in a hundred different ways with irritating pricks at his nerves that left him raw and edgy. His bats would disappear from the rack just before game time, and he would have to borrow someone's stick he didn't feel comfortable with. In batting practice, he'd occasionally be fed bad pitches so he couldn't get loose and swing away freely. At night, he'd get strange phone calls in his hotel room, interrupting his sleep. He even received a letter threatening him if he didn't go back "where he belonged."

Yet he knew who they were. He could tell by the way they looked at him. A couple of drawling punks so full of hatred they reeked of it. He tried not to care. He told himself it didn't matter; he wasn't here to win a popularity contest. He kept to himself.

One afternoon he arrived early at the ball park with a pair of new bats and a dried turkey bone to rub them down with. He was thankful for the quiet of the locker room, and sitting on the bench in front of his locker, he went to work on his bats lovingly. From across the room, he saw Kutner and Meade come in. They nodded and went to the table to play cards. Ben nodded back, relieved that they did not choose to talk to him.

For some time he rubbed, deriving pleasure from the work for it lent itself to the kind of daydreams he most enjoyed, the pictures of the fat barrel of the bat laid powerfully to the ball and that long, wonderful ride up and out before his eyes.

"Aren't those bats already treated, Franks?"

Ben looked up toward Kutner.

"Yeah . . . I guess so. But not like this. Seal up the grain real hard and the wood won't chip on you."

Kutner was watching him.

"See the difference?" Ben said. "Rubbed this side; not this."

They examined the barrel, and nodded.

Ben smiled, encouraged. "Josh Gibson, he showed me. He had some sticks, they last for five, maybe six years. Bone-rubbed the hell out of them." Ben chuckled. "I think he went out and found his own tree."

"You play ball with Gibson?"

The question made him feel good.

"Yeah. Two years."

Kutner shook his head. "I never saw such a hitter. Played one lousy semipro game against him. That guy hit one by me so hard I could've been playing infield. I never had a chance to move for it."

Franks nodded and they were silent again. Ben heard the cards shuffling above him as he worked. He thought of Gibson, the greatest of all Negro catchers, and he wondered what Josh'd be thinking about him, going up like this. It seemed crazy, for Josh had been ten times the ballplayer Ben was. Ben let his mind picture Gibson in the majors, jogging his squat body around the bases while they scrambled for the ball deep in the bleachers. He knew how much Gibson wanted to play there. Too late. They were too late for Josh Gibson. And damn lucky for them white-boy catchers like Cochrane and Dickey. Old Josh would've showed 'em how.

That's a waste, ain't it, Ben thought. A lousy waste. He remembered Josh with that little picture he carried around which showed him shaking hands with Babe Ruth. That was as close as they let him come to the major leagues.

"Say, Franks. You ever hit against this guy Satchel Paige?"

It did not escape Ben that they must have been thinking along the same lines as he was. It made him smile.

"No hitting, just swinging," he said.

"Really rough, eh?"

Ben nodded.

"He threw 'em and they looked like peas hopping in the wind."

"They say he's mighty quick."

"He has several speeds. And the plate is all corners, no middle."

It was quiet again for a moment. Ben sat there containing his laughter. He felt he could see right into Kutner's mind and it amused him. The man was thinking that black men were coming up, wondering if there was a mess of them who might beat him out.

"I suppose they'll bring Paige up, if he's not too old," Kutner said.

"They'll have to pay him some, 'cause that boy don't pitch for peanuts any more." Meade and Kutner listened over their cards. "Why, Satch has a private plane. Did you know that? Flies to work, he does. I heard one day he pitched in three different states all in one damn day! He works the first three innings of a double-header in Charleston, South Carolina. He hops his plane and hustles down to work the last three in Savannah, Georgia. Then he takes his time and has a good feed. That night, he goes for nine in Jacksonville."

Kutner and Meade laughed.

"He must've been tired," Meade said.

"Maybe. But he left a trail of goose eggs across a good slice of the country. And he was ready to work again the next day, I'll bet."

"What's it like in the Negro leagues, Franks? Anything like this?"

Ben looked around at the pleasant locker room, at the half-dozen showers with hot water. He thought of the well-planned AAA schedule, the almost leisurely three-day stopovers, the high-class Pullman rides, the first-rate hotels, the five-bucks-a-day meal money, the beautiful well-trimmed diamonds; and he thought back to the all-night bus rides, the double-headers followed by night games in another town, the flea bags they ate and slept in, the sand-lot ball parks, some of them where they didn't have lockers and you rode all night in your sweaty suit. You got paid by the week, and not much either, and they'd keep you working as many exhibition games as they could book.

"Not much like this," he answered finally. "But they sure play a lot of ball."

Kutner persisted. "How would you rate it? What class?"

Ben thought for a moment. "I don't know. Some of them clubs were pretty damn good."

"As good as this?"

He didn't like the questioning now. He had a feeling that maybe he'd talked enough.

"I don't know," he repeated. "I guess I ain't been around long enough to say."

He looked up at them as he replied, wondering what they were thinking of him. He hadn't intended to talk at all, and here he'd been spinning out the story of his career. And especially, why in front of these two? His arrival had pushed them out of their regular spots and shuffled them around the outfield. Meade had been the left fielder; he was an older guy and apparently a buddy of Kutner's for Ben saw them together frequently. In some ways he would have found it easier if these two had hated him. Then he could hate them back. But it was clear that they didn't. For all the stolid expression in Kutner's face, Ben saw no hatred. Resentment maybe, but no hatred.

For the most part, Kutner had kept away from him. Until this moment, there had been few words between them, even after his blunder in the outfield that first game. Ben had found it rough to shake it off; it was so much more than just another error in another ball game.

But in his way, Kutner exploited the situation. Ben saw it happening and shrugged it off. At first, it seemed almost ludicrous. He had been with the club less than a week when a crucial fly ball looped out to left center field, a short easy run for him. He moved in for the catch that would end the inning when suddenly he heard Kutner's yell: "I got it!" He stopped quickly and watched the other tear in front of him, making the catch on a dead run.

On the way back to the dugout, neither of them said anything.

Then it happened again the following night, this time with a runner on third base, tagging up for a dash home after the catch. The fly ball was clearly Ben's, but Kutner claimed it, moving over toward center field as though his throwing arm was needed to make the play. Ben stood by, helplessly, and found no relief in the fact that the run scored.

He knew how plays like that looked to everyone. They put a stigma on a man. A ballplayer doesn't go up holding another guy's glove.

His ear became tuned to all kinds of talk, a word here and there, a line in the newspapers, a stranger's voice over a glass of beer. "This guy Franks ain't much; Kutner takes the show from him." Kutner was playing ball like a demon. He was all over the place. He'd back up Ben on a simple can of corn, scurrying across the outfield as if there was a chance that Ben might let the ball get away. Ben hated it. He'd hear him charging toward him, yelling advice when none was needed, always at his elbow on every play.

The treatment would have to stop.

One afternoon after the game, he waited for Kutner until the locker room had emptied.

"Let's have a talk, Kutner," he said. "Got something on my mind."

Kutner nodded.

"O.K. Let's have it."

"I want you to get off my back, little man. You're giving me too much trouble."

Kutner shrugged. "Your trouble ain't my fault."

"Some of it is, man. You can turn it off. I'm here to play ball, not to play games with you out there in the gardens. You can't stop me, Kutner. You'll be wasting your time trying. It may be a lousy deal for you and that's t.s., but it all adds up for me. They brought me up here, see, and I don't aim to step aside for you."

Kutner looked up at him.

"And what the hell am I supposed to do? Pick my goddamn nose? I been in pro ball for ten years and I don't like to get pushed around."

"I ain't pushin' nobody."

"That's not what's written in my book. I was due to go up next spring. Me. Mike Kutner. I was due to go up because I've fought for it and deserve it. Then you come along and I get shoved over. Sonofabitch. I never played anything but center field in my life and you shove my ass over."

"You blame me for that?"

"O.K. O.K. All I know is you're the bastard who's stealing my pie, Franks, and I'm the kid to protect it. That should be clear enough." He started to walk away.

Ben grabbed his arm. He didn't want to leave things like this. He didn't want a perpetual fight with this little man.

"Wait a minute!" he snapped. "You talk about what's fair! You got some idea this is a picnic for me?" Then he said aloud to a white man the words that had been going around in circles in his head for days. "Even without you bastards on my hump this is no picnic. Every goddamn chucker thinks he's throwing balls at my head like I'm a Little Black Sambo at a carnival. Yeah, that's it. Three balls for a dime. Win a kewpie doll if you can stick it in his ear! And they try to cut me down on the bases with them sharp spikes like I was hamburger; and the polite folk in the stands will look at the gashes and say, now ain't that too damn bad. And all the time the friggen holler-guys, on and off the field, night after night, calling me a black sonofabitch because they mean it. That ain't no way to become a ballplayer, Kutner. No way at all. It's like getting up to bat with two strikes on you; you ain't even when you start!"

He looked at Kutner, trying to find a measure of understanding. He saw the man's indecision. Then Kutner shook his head slowly and pulled off his glasses.

"See these stinking things?" he said quietly. "I got troubles of my own."

The bite had left his voice. He looked almost sadly at Ben for a moment, holding his glasses in his hand. Then he turned and left.

It had never occurred to Ben that Kutner's glasses made any difference. But he saw it now. There was more than one way for the odds to stack up against you. He'd heard about the trouble guys with specs had, though he never figured it himself. He remembered one kid going into the Negro leagues back home who wore them. Some man loaned him fifty bucks to get himself a pair of those lenses you wear right on your eyeballs so no one could tell he needed them.

Yeah, Kutner had troubles of his own. And he was the kind who would fight all the harder because of them.

And so it happened.

Kutner kept working on him, crowding him, backing him up, showing his greater knowledge of the hitters by conspicuously advising him to move as each one stepped up to bat. It seemed to Ben that Kutner was spending half his time in center field and the other half calling and beckoning to him from left.

But Ben ignored him. Things began to go better for him. Late one game, he homered with two on to put them ahead, and he jogged out to his position sensing the elation that rides with a turn in the tide. He'd be O.K. now, he felt. He'd blast another and they'd get off his back. When a man's producing, there ain't a thing they can do but love him.

But a tight ball game is a fickle thing, and a late rally snuffed out the lead from his hit. He stood out there waiting, feeling the power of his old confidence and wishing for the ball to be hit to him. And when it came, a savage drive through the infield, he legged it rapidly, prepared to scoop it up on the run and cut down the runner moving around third with the big tally. He knew the runner was fast—he was prepared, this time, he'd been thinking—and had the jump on him. Though a long shot, this was the tying run and a long throw home was the correct play. But as he stabbed for it, he heard the sharp call from behind him.

"Third!"

At once his mind reacted, automatically. He whirled to throw to third, figuring the runner had cut back or stumbled. It could happen. But this time it hadn't. He watched his throw hop beautifully into third base, and he choked on the truth he saw too late: The runner was crossing the plate standing up.

He looked back at Kutner and barked at him.

"What the hell did you do that for?" He fought back his rage.

Even as he said it he knew, and all he could do was stand there helplessly watching Kutner turn from him without bothering to answer. He stood there smoldering against a background of derisive yells from the bleachers. Control, boy . . . control! Sonofabitch. You'll control your ass right out of organized baseball.

He walked back to his position chewing on his anger, and he waited. He didn't know what he was waiting for, though he had to believe there was a way to prove himself once and for all.

He waited until the ninth. From center field, he watched a base hit and a walk with two outs threaten their one-run lead again. Then it came, the long fly ball to deep left center. Ben got a good start on it and pumped hard, determined to put it in his pocket for the final out. He saw Kutner sprinting over from left, still a long way from it.

At once, Ben called for it. "Mine! Mine!"

Kutner kept coming, moving rapidly toward the point where the ball would drop. Suddenly, Mike hollered:

"I got it! I got it!"

Ben drove his body harder.

"Mine, Kutner. Mine!"

Kutner waved his glove at him as he ran.

"Stay away! Stay away!"

They were converging rapidly now. Ben felt the fury rising in him.

"Get away, you bastard. Get away!" His voice boomed out across the thirty feet between them, and he wondered what was in Kutner's mind. Would the little man dare keep coming? Would he still try for it? Would he? *Would he?*

He measured his stride for the end flight of the ball and gritted his teeth for the catch and whatever else might follow. He saw the ball sinking rapidly toward his outstretched glove and then, with terrible suddenness, the body crashing into him. Ben fell heavily over him, and somersaulted awkwardly on the soft turf. He was conscious mainly of the ball securely wrapped in the webbing of his glove.

He got up to the screaming of the crowd and went to the body prostrate on the ground.

"You O.K., man?" Ben knelt beside him.

Kutner moaned and rolled slowly over on his back, gasping for breath.

"Yeah, I'll be O.K.," he said. "Just leave me be."

Ben saw the bruised face and the twisted metal frame of

Mike's glasses. He pulled them off as gently as he could and turned aside to straighten them out. He twisted them carefully until they were properly fixed, and as he worked, he was proud of the steadiness of his hands, as though he almost did not expect this of himself.

The infielders came rushing out and stormed into him, shattering his mood with their hot faces spitting rage into his.

"You sonofabitch. What the hell you think you're doin'?"

"Goddammit, nigger, you trying to ruin this man?"

They pushed him violently, plucking at his uniform as if they wanted to strip him of it. He held one hand behind his back to protect the glasses and tried to ward them off with the other. There was nothing he could say.

There were more of them now. In the stands they probably think I'm being congratulated, Ben thought crazily. He stood there taking their shoving and their angry abuse. They could kill me, probably. Crowd around and kill me. Nobody'd know.

And then he saw the little man scrambling among them, pulling them off with a fury of his own.

"Stop it!" Kutner cried. "Pete! Lefty! Fer Chrissakes, lay off him!"

They saw who it was and they stopped, and suddenly Ben was free. The whole thing hadn't lasted thirty seconds; yet a sea of threatening faces had hemmed him in. They stood around him still, not yet ready to make peace, waiting for what Kutner would say. Kutner stood there breathing heavily.

"Leave him alone," he mumbled. "It was my goddamn fault."

They started to protest, and stopped. Kutner stared at them with his naked eyes. His whole face seemed naked.

"You heard me!" he said. "Come on, let's go in."

Then they broke up, quiet in their confusion and the baldness of their violence. Ben saw the hate drain from their faces and he stood there nodding his head as if in approval. He was shaking.

"Here, Mike." He handed Kutner his glasses. "It's lucky them things didn't smash, ain't it?"

Kutner looked up at him, red-eyed and pale.

"That's O.K.," he said quietly. "It's happened before. They bend, but they won't break."

He looked squarely at Ben, and smiled slightly. Then he put them back on and walked in with him.

# 9 *The Sister*

Marian leaned over the big kitchen sink, scrubbing the baby bottles in the hot soapy water, and she wondered how many thousands of times she had done this exact thing. Remember the first times—when was it, three babies and seven years ago? You worked the long thin brush into the wet soapy bottle, in and out, in and out, like a piston; and Walt stood over you, his arm around your shoulder, and suddenly you both became embarrassed and broke out laughing. Good Lord, you haven't brought that silly thought to mind in years! She raised her glance to the window before her to look out into the black winter night, but she saw only her own reflection made clear by the bright light overhead.

It brought her no pleasure. Her image seemed colorless and worn. Her hair was messy, and without make-up her naked face appeared surprisingly harsh. She had never kidded herself into believing she was really attractive; yet somehow this reflection emphasized the lines she liked the least: the deep-set eyes too close together, the long, thin nose that case a shadow, this time over her lips. She tried to move her position to change the angle of light, hoping for a more flattering look at herself. But she was distracted by the view of her sister-in-law behind her, sitting at the kitchen table, staring into a cup of coffee.

Marian watched the beautiful girl and unconsciously made a dozen comparisons. Laura looked wonderful. Her hair was soft and wavy, even with a simple home permanent. Her skin was fresh-looking, though Marian had noticed she'd been using more cosmetics this year. The lithe figure could look lovely even in the cheapest clothes. Marian subtracted the years she'd been bearing and raising children; it would make them even, give or take a year. She shook her head sadly; she seemed so much more than seven years older. Then her candor forced an admission. God, when did I ever look like that!

But mostly it was Laura's freedom that Marian envied. Without the burden of babies, a woman could stay attractive almost indefinitely. Besides, there was variety and excitement in Laura's life. Marian had tasted it during the summer six months before when she and her husband had driven the 180 miles to Louisville. They had turned a buying trip for Walt into a holiday for them both, deliberately timing it for the Minneapolis-Louisville series so they could see Mike play. Laura had played the gracious hostess, composed and lovely, and had taken them to the huge stadium all lighted up and bright green below, all noise and movement around them. Marian felt the excitement of the crowd, and later she thrilled at the shouting and applause for her brother who played so well. After the game, they ate thick steaks together at a fine restaurant, and they laughed and talked until almost three in the morning. This was the way Mike and Laura lived. Clean hotels, good food; no dirty dishes, no diapers, no squalling fighting kids. This was really being alive.

The contrast cut into her all the more deeply on her return to Austin. She and Walt drove up to the old Kutner home and she thought coldly, this is the house I've lived in all my life. No other except for a day or two. It shouldn't be this way. It should be possible to get out; if not to the big, clean hotels, at least to a home of our own. She squinted her eyes down the endless row of houses, all so much alike for the years had blended their differences under a thick layer of coal soot.

The sight suggested the smell, and the dismal tang of the area somehow brought her thoughts back to her children. The car slowed down at the entrance to the narrow driveway, and she looked up at the kids' bedroom, trying not to hear the bedlam of their voices. The quick, wonderful vacation was over; the housewife drudgery would begin again. When Walt stopped the car, she sat for a moment staring at her hands, not yet ready to get out and face her own family. It wasn't right to think like this. She loved them, she loved them all very much. Yet somehow her routine seemed so endless that she could not help but question it.

She felt Walter's hand tenderly on hers. "We're home, honey."

"Home," she repeated, hoping it didn't sound bitter. She tried to smile for him, knowing he didn't want it this way either. Walt tried so hard for them. Recently he'd taken all his savings, something over three thousand dollars, and bought a hardware store. In time, perhaps, there would be more savings which would go for a home of their own, someplace away from the perpetual smell of the mines, up in the hills where the homes were sunny and white and the coal dust in the smoky valley below was only seen in the distance and not tasted.

This was the best that could happen to her, Marian knew, and perhaps it was better than most lives. Except when she stacked it up against the life of Laura Kutner.

She finished the bottles and went to the stove for a cup of hot coffee. At the table, Laura was staring distantly into her cup, and they sat in silence. Marian wanted to talk but Laura seemed deep in private thoughts. After a while, Marian fumbled for an opening word:

"I guess Mike should be getting back soon."

Laura nodded, clearing her throat. "From a day of pumping gas and wiping windshields." The words were a sudden reminder to Marian. Laura's eyes left the coffee cup cradled in her hands and sought the end of the kitchen table. Marian followed the line of her vision, resting finally on the long white envelope alone in front of the seat Mike was accustomed to using.

Their eyes met for a moment. Then Laura reached over for the envelope. Without opening it, she studied its face as if that had some special significance of its own.

" 'Chicago Lions Baseball Club, Incorporated . . . ,' " she read slowly, letting the sound of it roll off her tongue. "It's postmarked February 3rd, 1949. That's two days ago, isn't it? You'd think they'd at least send the thing airmail."

Marian saw that Laura was as nervous as a child waiting to see his first report card. The envelope seemed to grow huge in her hands.

"This is a rough moment each year," Laura went on, "watching Mike wait for the letter. You can almost feel the knots in his stomach when he finally gets it."

She laughed nervously and hurriedly put the letter back.

Marian shook her head. "The other night Mike was telling me how wonderful it was going to be for you two, up there in the big cities."

The words hung in the air. Laura got up for the pot and poured a warm-up for them both. She sat down and watched the bubbles in her cup disappear one by one.

"I'm glad he's so certain."

"Well . . . but aren't you?" Marian leaned across the table. "That boy is good, honey. He's been good from way back!"

Laura tried to smile. "I'm sure . . . but I don't know. Does it really matter so much?" Her eyes seemed to ask for an answer that would curb her doubts.

Marian almost smiled. How the mighty had fallen! She reached over and patted Laura's hand. It was a peculiar moment of fulfillment for Marian, and she felt the strength rising inside her. She would enjoy propping up Laura.

"With Mike, it matters," she began. "I can tell you something. He's always been the best. When he was only eleven or so, he played with kids older than him. They used to bully him a little, especially after he started wearing glasses. I remember once their ball sailed into the swamp. It was the only ball they had, and someone had to fetch it. They decided they'd have a race, and the last kid to finish would have to go. But first, just for fun, they tied a couple of tin cans to Mike's ankles, tin cans loaded with dirt and stones. Poor little Mike, he hated to lose, even with an excuse like that. And he couldn't just laugh it off like some other kid might. So you know what he did, Laura? He told them he'd go in and get the ball for them. Forget about the race. But they got angry. 'No,' they said. 'You gotta race!' "

She warmed to her story, leaning over the kitchen table, telling it eagerly to this girl from another world.

"And so they did, and believe me, it was something. At first, they all ran slowly, just fast enough to keep a little ahead of him, all the time laughing at the cans dragging behind him. But then, twenty yards before the end, Mike gritted his teeth and started to really run, cans and all. He had something extra left, and wouldn't you know? He finished before half of them!"

The story ended, Marian stared at her listener, trying to measure its effect. Laura sat quietly, as though she were expecting more. And when there was none, she looked up quizzically and shrugged her shoulders.

"He didn't win."

"Win! Isn't that asking *too* much?"

Marian was a little annoyed. Life gave some people so much, and yet they never seemed satisfied. Laura had lived winters in Austin since the end of the war, four years now, pretending she wasn't the beautiful big-city girl in a broken-down coal town. Yet she seemed completely out of place. Even her job in the best woman's shop in town seemed beneath her. Marian had watched her quiet brooding these past months, gathering God-knows-what dissatisfactions within her. Apparently she thought they were too trivial to speak of until now. It was hard to feel sorry for Laura, somehow. Marian felt like laughing at the position she found herself in. And she began to resent it.

Laura was shaking her head. "Those cans . . . ," she said slowly. "I guess, in a way, they're still tied to him. And beating some isn't enough. Now he has to beat them all."

Marian didn't understand. She heard the unmistakable sadness in Laura's voice and wondered at it. Was all this because of the letter? What was so terribly crucial about it? She had a feeling that Laura was dramatizing and, worse yet, doubting Mike. To Marian, this was ridiculous, for Mike had always seemed the sure thing. She pictured him now, almost thirty years old, still smaller than the men he played with, still conspicuous in glasses, still spirited and unchanged by all the years. Didn't he even look like a boy, the same as he always did?

Laura got up from the table with her cup and laid it in the sink. "I was thinking," she said finally. "I guess I kind of envy you, Marian. Your being a mother, I mean. Working for something like a home and a family. You and Walt seem so . . . so solid . . . the store and saving money and having kids and all. . . ."

Marian turned around to look at her, trying to make sense out of this strange confession. It occurred to her that Laura was simply trying to make her feel good. Like that two-thousand-dollar-a-week singer she heard crooning "The Best Things in Life Are Free." It didn't seem to follow.

Yet there was something honest in her tone. Marian stared

hard at Laura's face; it was true, the doubts were there, and the fear that goes with them. Marian felt a wave of confusion; the thought of Laura wanting to change places with her moved her strangely. She swallowed uneasily, suddenly aware that she really didn't understand this girl at all.

Outside, they heard the car door slam shut, the crunching of gravel underfoot. They regarded each other for a moment, waiting in silence for the back door to open, unable to exchange one last word or even a glance to give some final meaning to their conversation. Their eyes fell away, and the door burst open.

"Hi, ladies!" Walt lumbered in. "What's cooking?" Walt was a big man and—you could almost tell at a glance—an amiable and a clumsy one.

Behind him, Mike moved slowly into the room. Marian saw his brief smile at Laura as he hung his soiled gas-station jacket behind the door. This was his usual greeting to his wife, Marian knew—the price of a shy man living in a crowded house. Laura had learned to accept it.

"What's cooking?" Walt repeated. He came toward his wife in his neatly pressed suit, and he squeezed her hand. Compared with Mike, his dress was formal, even elegant. Somehow it seemed a strange comparison, Marian thought, as if it should be the other way around.

"Lamb stew," she said, somehow pleased with Walt and suddenly happy, "left over from the early shift. It wasn't bad." She went to the stove to serve them.

When she turned back to the table with the loaded plates, she noted the letter again, lying face down on the table. She glanced at Laura wondering whether it would be opened here, before all of them.

"You're terribly dirty, Mike," Laura said quickly. "Look at your hands!"

He shrugged his shoulders. "Cars—oil and grease." He examined the blackness under his nails and shook his head. "It's really in there, ain't it?" After a moment, he added quietly: "It comes out in the spring, honey." Then he reached for his fork and began to eat.

It was quiet again, except for the sound of silverware on dishes. The evening had a strange atmosphere, Marian thought. Or was *she* dramatizing now? The sound of soft slippers shuffling in the doorway broke into her consciousness and she turned to face it.

"Hello, Pop," she said. "I thought you went to bed."

"Your mother wants tea," Joe said. "She can't sleep so good."

Marian got up from the table and filled the kettle. "I'll fix some."

"Hi, Pop," Walt said. "Have a seat." He drew a chair up to the table.

Marian smiled at the old man in the undershirt as he sat. He was tired, and it made him seem older than his sixty-odd years. His few hairs lay sloppily across his shiny white scalp, and he smoothed them out in front of the ladies. His hands went to his eyes to clear the sleep from them. He looked over at Marian.

"Better make for two," he said, and he turned back to the table. For a moment, he watched his son eat. His stare was so intent that it made Mike look up from his plate and smile. Joe nodded. "So. . . . You worked late tonight, eh, Mike? How's the job?"

The question was meant to dig at Mike. This was Joe's habit, Marian knew, to question the menial jobs Mike worked at through the winters. Road-gang worker, Christmas postman, lumber-yard delivery man, now gas-station attendant. The fact that he managed to stay clear of the mines only further irritated Joe.

"I helped Walt after I quit at the station," Mike said simply.

He returned to his food without any show of annoyance or irritation.

Walt reached over and slapped Mike's back. "A good man, Pop." He spoke with his mouth full of lamb stew. "You know, he's got ideas. One day last month he says to me, 'Walt, you should put a sporting goods department in here. There ain't a store in this town that's got a decent sporting goods department. Why a man has to go twenty miles to buy a fishing rod!' And you know, he's right, too."

Marian grew uncomfortable. This was not a new topic. Her husband too often got carried away by his enthusiasms, conveniently forgetting what subjects he had already covered all too thoroughly. She looked over at Mike, occupied solely with his eating. What a kid, she thought; you couldn't budge him.

"It's a good idea, Pop. I actually think it would make out. But I'd need someone to help me. Can't run a bigger store all by myself."

This was an old wound that her husband, with all good intentions, was salting, and the direction of the conversation made her wince. She tried to catch Walt's eye but failed.

Then she saw Joe's old hand move up from the pocket of his robe. His eye had caught the letter, the long white letter lying on the table. Absent-mindedly he reached across and picked it up, holding it close to read the address. She watched his face come alive, shedding its last sleepiness as if a pail of cold water had doused him. He turned it over to see that it was still unopened.

The room fell quiet for a moment, disturbed only by the faint murmuring of the kettle just beginning to boil.

"I'm really only learning the hardware business, Pop." Silence was a vacuum and Walt abhorred it.

Joe turned toward his son. "It's for you, Mike. A letter!"

Mike took it, recognizing at once the nature of its contents.

He looked quickly, severely, at Laura, as if to ask, "Why didn't you tell me this was here?" He pushed his plate forward to clear away the room he needed to open it and inserted his knife into the slot of the envelope. Marian could see the several printed pages as he unfolded them; she chose to read only the expression on her brother's face. Mike glanced at it briefly, then folded it back in the envelope. He turned to Laura, trying to smile. Walt kept on talking.

"I tell you, Pop, a man has to know about sporting goods. You just can't tackle a department like that without knowing what people need."

Laura laid her hand on Mike's arm. They looked at each other for a moment and he shrugged briefly. He laid the envelope on the table, pulled his plate back to him, and began eating again. The whole thing took only a few seconds, but to Marian at least, it had seemed much longer.

"You see, they're what you call luxury items, Pop. It's different with that kind of thing. You have to promote them."

Joe wasn't listening. He looked over at Mike and reached for the letter. He unfolded the contract slowly, carefully, and squinted over the complicated print, turning the pages in a confused search for information.

Mike dipped a big slice of bread in his stew. "It's on the first page, Pop. Everything you'd want to know. Back to Minneapolis, at six hundred dollars a month." His voice was low but with an edge of anger. Joe glanced quickly at his son, too intent on these details to be embarrassed.

"Same as last year, eh?"

Marian had stopped watching.

"The same," Mike said. "And if you're interested, Pop, I'm sending it back. Same old business."

" 'Same old business' is right!" Joe's voice was suddenly sharp. But he had begun something here he quickly chose to abandon. Marian slid her hand quietly over his. He wrapped his gnarled black fingers around hers and said nothing more. For a moment the room was held by his silence.

She groped for a word to begin again in a new direction, sick of their tired, old battles. Why did it always have to be this way? Why couldn't Pop leave Mike alone?

But Walt beat her to it. "As I look at it," he began again, "I need a man I can trust in there . . . a man who knows about these things. With the right man, we could make a lot of money." And then, with a big grin, he slapped Mike's shoulder again. "A man like your son, Pop, whenever he decides to quit playing ball!"

Marian shuddered. My great big wonderful husband. I've told you a thousand times, you talk too much. This house just doesn't have enough room for you. Oh, damn!

She looked quickly over at Mike, who sat nibbling at his bread, eating just to occupy his hands. She heard Walt's foolish cough and turned slowly to him. The small room was full of those waves now, bouncing furiously off the father and the son. Walt looked back at her with his big frank mobile face, finally aware of tension. He wore one of those what-did-I-do looks, and she shook her head at him. I'll tell you what you did. A man was down and you stepped on him. Oh, I know; you didn't even see him. But it hurts anyway. My God, it's time we had a home of our own!

Only for a moment, Joe had nothing to say. Then his voice spoke out, quiet and controlled as though he were imitating his gentle wife.

"Mike. You hear that? You got a chance to make money. It don't happen many times, Son." He leaned forward in his chair, carefully pointing his finger for emphasis. "You oughta think hard this time, Mike. Think hard."

Marian felt Joe's hand press tightly over hers in his effort to control himself. He was talking about Mike's career, yet trying not to mention it, avoiding the word "baseball" as though he knew the speaking of it would trigger a whole lifetime of battles. She saw Mike look up from his plate; his face seemed drawn, and the lines ran deep around his mouth. From where Marian sat, his forehead appeared unusually high, exposing his oncoming baldness. In that moment, he looked a little like the father. It startled her, for she had always thought of him as her little brother, as the kid banging his fist all day into that baseball glove.

"O.K., Pop," Mike said finally. "I'll think hard about it." The words came out sounding like a big concession to his father's will.

At once, Joe realized his moderation had been costly to him. He had lost his attack. He became flustered; his face reddened conspicuously as he looked for a way to continue.

But Mike didn't give him a chance. He got up from the table with a sudden movement and turned to his wife. His hand came down gently on her soft brown hair and she looked up at him, trying to smile. At once he withdrew it, spreading the fingers of both hands out straight. He turned them over slowly before him; the contrast of her silky hair to the ingrained dirt of his hands was written all over his face. He backed away to the door, looking at her. They communicated their fears in a brief glance, trying vainly, by silence, to cover their need for intimacy. Marian blushed at being there and lowered her head as one would pull down a shade.

She heard Mike's footsteps on the stairs. Behind her now, the kettle was hissing in her ear, reminding her of tea and Edna. She rose to pour it into the pot, thankful that the simple chore distracted her from this sorrow she did not understand.

Later that night, she lay in bed waiting for Walt, half-listening to the radio idling on the table beside her. Sometimes it took a dreadfully long time to get into that bathroom and poor Walt was always the last. She felt tired and depressed, and as she frequently did in such moods, she began to wonder how other people lived. She'd seen movies about large families whose members had to crowd in with their parents. Especially since the war. They got along fine, though. And when they'd had a bad day and fought over something (it always turned out to be a trifle of some sort), someone always bought a box of chocolates for someone else and they ended up by embracing.

It would be nice to be part of such a scene. For as long as she could remember, there had been fights, but no chocolates. Their troubles seemed to lie too deep for that.

When Walt finally returned and began to undress, she heard loud, emotional voices in the small bedroom behind her. For a moment it didn't seem extraordinary. The walls were thin, people had disagreements. Then she realized that it had never happened before with Mike and Laura in that room. She looked over at her husband and she saw that he shared her surprise, then her sadness.

For whatever it's worth, she thought, at least they should have it in private. And she turned up the radio to cover the sound.

With the midnight music flooding the room, she welcomed her husband to bed. They held each other for a few moments, while the voices grew louder through the thin walls.

She whispered into his shoulder. "Walt, Laura wants kids, a house and all." She shook him slightly. "Walt."

"Sure. Why not? What else should she want?"

"But the big hotels they live in, the nice restaurants, that whole life! And Laura looking like she was twenty-five. . . ."

There was no answer except for her husband's heavy breathing.

"Walt," she whispered, "I love you." She felt his sleepy kiss against her ear, and finally when there was silence in the next room, she reached over to turn off the radio.

"I love you," she whispered again. And she realized she hadn't used those words for a long time.

# 10 *The Commissioner*

The hotel dining room was huge. The long rows of tables stretched into the mirrored walls, down and back an endless number of times. Above the trim, decorous, potted palm trees, the giant windows let in the white light of morning, but they were set too high for anyone within to see the streets or even the adjacent buildings, as though everything must be kept cleanly anonymous and impersonal. The gray-haired man in the worsted suit looked up from his morning paper toward the mirrors and studied himself in the infinity of reflections. He thought, perhaps, he had indulged himself when he chose the light, checked pattern instead of a more sedate shade. He raised his glance to a reflection of his still wavy hair, and considered a possible clash of tone with the suit. No, he liked the way he looked. Even the tie was colorful, and he liked it. He frequently argued that color need not be confined to women's clothes. He knew he was a good-looking man, tall and properly slender, and he always recognized a responsibility to dress himself in a way that did not minimize these attributes.

He moved his hand to his tie as if to adjust the knot but actually to enjoy the sight of so many hands in unified movement. At once, he felt silly, as though he were being watched, and he turned again to his newspaper.

He glanced at the unfamiliar type of the headlines, for this was a city more or less strange to him, and he sought the more familiar areas of the sports pages. He had not slept well, for no particular reason he could put his finger on, nor did he anticipate eating well. Of all the meals a man had to eat away from home, he speculated that breakfast was the worst. Breakfast, he felt, should be a simple meal; just the thought of a breakfast menu irritated him. Breakfast should be eaten in the pantry, or even in the kitchen itself a few feet from the bubbling coffee pot. Breakfasts should have a routine sameness.

Now as he waited for his food, he studied the paper for some reference to his arrival in town, wondering what the press of Chicago had to say about him, if anything. When he found no mention of his name (he was adept at scanning a page for it), he felt both relief and disappointment, though more pointedly the latter. An occasional public notice served to compensate him for the frustrations of his job. Commissioner, they called him. The Commissioner of baseball. The title carried prestige, he would admit. A man doesn't work for bread alone. And then, in the mirror, he saw a myriad of waitresses with trays moving toward him with tired steps from the distant kitchen, and he knew that under those metal domes, his toast and eggs would be soggy and cool and the coffee too long in the serving pitcher.

He propped the skillfully folded paper against the sugar bowl and divided his attention between the food and a more thorough examination of the sporting pages. Over the rim of his coffee cup, his eye rested on a five-line piece reporting the sale by Jim Mellon of a Chicago "farm hand" named Sam Moore—from Grand Rapids down to Macon, Georgia. The Commissioner had heard about a number of minor-league transactions at a meeting two days before but had paid little attention to them. He did not know this Moore, nor did he care about the sale. However, he found himself picturing the man sitting at his breakfast table with his wife and maybe a couple of kids, picking up the same newspaper and reading the same piece of news, and he felt certain, somehow, that this would be the way Moore would hear of his transfer. It was the kind of thing that happened too frequently, and he felt a familiar revulsion for the callous tactic. It was bad enough that the player was not consulted prior to the sale.

It did not escape him that this was all a speculation on his part, an artificially generated resentment; for there were no real facts to go by. However, since the story came out of Jim Mellon's office, there was the logic of past experience to back it up. Nor did his negative interpretation of the article surprise him, for this was his mood preparatory to every meeting he had with Mellon.

The Commissioner pushed away his distasteful cup of lukewarm coffee and looked up for the waitress.

"Hot this time, if you please," he said, unable to hide the accumulation of irritations. "Really hot. The only way to drink coffee is to drink it hot!"

The words lashed out at her, but her years as a waitress were a thick shield, and she smiled at him with a kind of tired tolerance.

"Yes sir!" she snapped, almost in mockery. "Really hot!" And she withdrew in exaggerated haste.

The Commissioner was immediately aware of his unbecoming conduct. It was not typical of him. He had used the waitress as a scapegoat. He would apologize.

Yet the source of his aggravation remained like a thorn in his side. Every time he returned to Chicago, old man Mellon successfully undermined what the Commissioner was most concerned with: the power and, what was more important, the dignity of his office.

"Commissioner."

He heard the title echoing distantly in his consciousness, as if it were whispered by his alter ego to be weighed and measured for its value.

"Commissioner . . . ," he heard again, this time closer. Yes, he was the Commissioner. His mind repeated the word for the ring of pleasure it gave him; the title was impressive enough. But what did the position amount to, really, after five years? The money? Sixty-five thousand dollars a year was a lot. Every time he deposited his monthly check he thought quickly of his very first reaction to the sum; he had asked himself simply, And what does the Commissioner do for all that salary? The private joke became a serious question. But long ago he quit trying to answer it.

"Commissioner."

And suddenly he was startled to see a young man standing beside him, waiting for his attention.

"I didn't mean to intrude, sir. . . ."

He looked up into the lean, dark face, the spectacles, the thin hair above the dark, receding hairline. There was something familiar about the face, and he ferreted in his memory for the key to this recognition. A road secretary? Which office? A business manager? Where?

"That's all right, young man. What is it?" He was anxious to pin it down.

"Commissioner. I heard you were here. I came to . . . well, you see. . . . I think I'm getting a rotten deal. . . ."

The voice was thick with a halting shyness, but behind that a suppressed anger. He felt his curiosity rising.

"Yes?"

"They're waiving me out of the League, and I know I'm wanted."

"Wait a minute, son. Who are you?"

"Kutner, sir. Mike Kutner. I'm with Chicago."

"Oh, sure! I've seen you play in Minneapolis. First rate. Sit down."

"Thanks."

"Now, start at the beginning. Let's get the facts straight. I always have to know the facts."

"Yes, sir. Like I said, I'm signed with Chicago. I went down to spring training with them."

"And you did pretty well, too."

"Well, I expected to stick. I've had some good years in the American Association. Hit over .320 my last two years. Chicago was weak out in center field and I figured I was in. But Mr. Mellon must've thought I didn't measure up, because he goes out and buys Hank Dreiser for straight cash."

"At a fat sum, as I recall."

"Yeah. A hundred Gs." He practically spit the number.

"Dreiser is quite a ballplayer," the Commissioner said.

"No doubt. But that don't do me no good. In less than no time, Mr. Mellon figures I'd serve him best back there in the minors."

The Commissioner looked again at the intense face, wondering how old Kutner actually was. It was apparent this man was no young chicken. He had never seen him this close, or out of uniform, for that matter. A man can look younger in uniform.

"I've had it, sir." The voice was biting now, and loaded with emotion. "I've been playing organized ball since 1938. That's thirteen years, counting the war. I've been AA and AAA since 1941. When I was subject to be drafted by another club, Chicago finally gave me a contract and optioned me right back to the minors. Yes sir, three times. That's the limit, Commissioner. So this year I figured they had to use me or ask for waivers."

That was the rule, the Commissioner thought. After three years with a major-league contract, you could not send a man to a lower league without first asking the other clubs if they wanted to buy him. If they didn't then you could waive him out of the League. Yes, that was the rule.

"Well, about a week ago, we were coming north from training, and I heard that my name was no longer on the roster of the club. Rumor had it that I was sold outright back to Minneapolis. But when I talked to Mr. Mellon, he denied it. 'Rumors,' he said. 'Don't believe that stuff.' But I figured something was up. When we reached Chicago for an exhibition game, I picked up the score card and noticed my name was not even on the roster. I am not that stupid, Mr. Commissioner. Evidently they'd been trying to get waivers on me figuring they'd be able to sneak me back to the minors. But since I was still with the club, I figured my waivers had evidently been held up someplace."

The man paused in his recital. Thus far the Commissioner was impressed, interested. If he was any judge of character, Kutner was telling his story straight.

"But yesterday Mr. Mellon sends me a note saying I am to report at once to Minneapolis. Nothing else. Just report. Just that.

"I'm thirty-one years old, Commissioner, and my life has been in this game. Like you say, I'm a good ballplayer. Thirteen years in the minors, sir, and I've yet to play a major-league ball game! I don't think I should have to go back to Minneapolis!"

The Commissioner looked up at the waitress as his hot coffee was placed before him, but he did not touch it. He wanted it, all right. But he felt so intensely the pull of this man's sincerity that any desire on his part for food at this moment might indicate that he was taking the interview lightly. He kept his fingers away from the cup and made the only comment possible.

"But Jim Mellon *did* get waivers through. Apparently no one offered to buy your contract."

After five years as Commissioner, he knew better than that. Whatever truth there was on the surface of the statement, there was but little justification for his using the stock reply. He heard Kutner's quick sigh.

"But that's not so, Commissioner. That just ain't so! I went back to my room and sent out a mess of telegrams, to every big-league manager I thought could use me. I did it on my own. By evening, I had an answer."

"From whom?"

"From Bill Bostwick in Philly. I called right away and told him I'd been waived out of the League and was being sold to Minneapolis. He said: 'Gee, I didn't know that. We could use you. Sit tight, Mike. Pack a bag and be ready to come to Philly tomorrow. I'm pretty sure I can work a deal for you.' Then I got a phone call from St. Louis, and they wanted me too. I figured I was in, Commissioner. So I sat in my hotel room and waited. Last night Mr. Bostwick called and told me I might as well go back to Minneapolis, that there was nothing he could do about it."

The words trailed off and stopped as if there was nothing more to say. The Commissioner waited for a moment, embarrassed by the silence. He watched Kutner clench and unclench his powerful right fist. The Commissioner looked at his own hands, white and soft by comparison. There was no power in him to make such a fist.

"And St. Louis?" he asked. "Did you hear from them?"

"I called them. Same answer. Go back to Minneapolis."

The Commissioner nodded. St. Louis could really use this man, he thought.

"So I called Mr. Mellon, sir. I called him and told him to let me go. I wanted to play ball in the majors and there are clubs who could use me. He asked me who. I told him and he said: 'Nonsense. They're just giving you a lot of talk. Nobody wants you.' So I told him I'd buy my own contract for the ten-grand waiver price, I was so sure I could make a deal!"

"What'd Mellon say to that?"

"He said no. Just plain no. He said he had too much invested in me to let me go."

The Commissioner tapped his cup with a spoon. "Well, he's got a point there, son. You have to admit that."

There was a pause for a moment and it baffled him. He raised his head for the reaction, if there was to be one.

There was.

"Mellon has invested a lot of blood, sweat, and tears, Commissioner . . . but they're mine!" The words came low through his clenched teeth.

The Commissioner understood. He began to wonder what he could do. His eyes rested uneasily on the coffee pot again, and he wondered how much it had cooled. What the devil *could* he do? He was Commissioner of baseball and he wasn't sure.

"I hesitated coming to see you like this, sir. I didn't want to do it. A man can be blackballed right out of baseball if it gets around he's a guy who squawks. They got a special treatment for him. But the talk is that you're a good man, Commissioner, and *for* the ballplayers. . . ."

The young man left off and sat back in his chair as if exhausted by his plea. The Commissioner was moved. He felt drawn to this man. In a vague way there was something of himself involved, an earlier self. He saw the undaunted, naive drive to the top, and the buffeting of almost inexplicable forces through the years. A good man deserves a break, he thought. A good man even *needs* a break.

But the chill that shot through him was a warning, and in his mind, his no-longer undaunted, naive mind, he balanced the limitations of his position against the pull of his sentimental sense of justice. He looked over at Kutner and their eyes met, almost for the first time. He saw what suddenly he was most afraid to see, the look of trust and faith that goes with respect for a man.

The Commissioner reached finally for the pot of coffee. He tried to believe it was still hot enough, and he poured himself a cup. He sipped it slowly, thoughtfully, fully aware that the other was watching him and waiting. When he spoke, finally, it was as if he had found courage in the cup before him.

"Let me check your story, Kutner. If what you say is true, we'll have you smelling those Shibe Park daisies by opening day. Just you leave it to me!"

Kutner stood up, grinning broadly, almost on the brink of laughter, and extended his hand in gratitude. The Commissioner clasped it, sensing a greater warmth than he had found in a handshake in some time.

"Call me tonight around six," he said. "I'll have news for you."

The Commissioner was moved. He watched the young man walking away, following the rhythmic stride down the line of mirrors. He saw the athlete now in that walk, in the spring of those powerful legs. The shoulders were hidden in the ill-fitting suit, and he tried to X-ray through the heavy fabric for a sense of the graceful, sloping lines he remembered on the ball field. The last thing he saw was the neck bronzed by the hot Southern sun as the ballplayer disappeared in the lobby.

The Commissioner was moved. ("You're a good man and *for* the ballplayers.") He repeated the words as he had heard them, trying to recapture the rich sincerity of the man. What is it to be "for the ballplayers"? What, then, does one have to be against? The Commissioner had never really looked at professional baseball that way, as a basic conflict of interests. If this man's story was true, and it seemed certain that it was, then Kutner was victim of a gross injustice. The Commissioner could still taste the restrained desperation of Kutner's plea, as though the man could not believe such a thing was happening to him.

The Commissioner did not wish to believe it could happen.

He rose abruptly from the table and made his way to the lobby, acutely conscious of an impulse to imitate Kutner's walk.

("You're a good man, Commissioner.")

He nodded at the still-fresh sound of it. For a good man, he told himself, there are responsibilities.

The Commissioner watched the old man clean his fingernails with a letter opener and waited for comment. Mellon seemed oblivious to his presence.

"Jim," he began again, "a man who gives his life to baseball has a special right to play in the major leagues, if he's good enough."

Again there was silence for a while. Jim Mellon spoke, finally, without looking up.

"What do you mean, 'good enough'?"

"Mike Kutner is good enough."

"Not for my club."

"There'd be a lot of baseball men who'd argue that with you."

"They don't win pennants, Commissioner. I don't like the type of ballplayer. Too much cute stuff. Not enough power for an outfielder."

"He'd hit .300 for you, and then some."

"Maybe . . . then, maybe not. But I'd rather play a .260 hitter who can blast that long ball."

The Commissioner chose not to pursue it. This was a famous Mellon prejudice. It was not for him to argue the point. It was true Mellon won pennants, but not with .260 hitters.

"There are other clubs who'd use him, Jim." He was wary now. "He'd fit in well."

"I asked waivers on this man." The answer came back impatiently. "No one claimed him." The old man could lie with a straight face, it seemed. The Commissioner was not surprised.

"What's on your mind, Commissioner?" He looked up now, searching for motivation.

"He came to see me, Jim. He claimed you were giving him a rotten deal."

Mellon grunted. "They all do when they don't make it, don't they?"

The Commissioner resisted a smile. "Maybe. He told me he spoke with Bostwick in Philly and Bill said he wanted him. Even told him he'd try to get him."

"And so he did, Commissioner. And so he did."

Here was an admission that he had lied, and Mellon made it sound like a challenge.

"I, too, spoke with Bostwick, Jim."

Mellon grinned sheepishly, showing his tobacco-tarnished teeth. "Seems like just about everybody spoke with Mr. Bostwick," he said.

The Commissioner bit his lip. Big joke. Kick a man around and laugh at the footprints you leave on him.

"Look, Jim. I promised the man I'd get this matter straightened out for him. I promised that if his story held up I'd get him set in Philly." He spoke in intimate tones, as if they were a couple of old cronies ironing out some trivial matter.

The old man set him straight.

"You shouldn't have done that, Commissioner."

The Commissioner bit his lip again. There was a new urgency in his voice now.

"Philadelphia wanted Kutner, Jim . . . wanted him badly. Bill told me he could've used him for the past five years, too. But he couldn't get him. He said to me on the phone: 'Let's be frank, Commissioner. Jim Mellon tells me he needs that man out in Minneapolis. I gotta respect that, you know what I mean? I've gone begging many times. I gotta scratch his back, too, once in a while.'" He paused now to reach for his handkerchief, letting the words sink in. "A little gentlemen's agreement, eh, Jim?"

The old man spoke slowly. "I got a fine club in Minneapolis, Commissioner. We're pennant contenders every year. We draw big. Kutner is good out there. The people like him. He's worth money to me in Minneapolis. A lot more than a lousy ten grand."

"So Bill told me. He said you offered him for sale at forty thousand."

The old man laughed. "I'll bet that's more'n he paid for his entire outfield."

"Forty grand seems like a lot of dough for an outfielder who can't hit that long ball, Jim."

Mellon ignored the sarcasm. "I'm more concerned about the finances of Minneapolis than I am of Kutner or of Philadelphia!"

The Commissioner nodded, and he let his voice rise slightly with his own challenge: "You're also more concerned about your finances than you are about the rules of professional baseball!"

Jim Mellon made no effort to hide his smile. He shrugged his shoulders and returned to cleaning his fingernails.

"You heard Bill Bostwick, Commissioner," he said finally. "He doesn't want him any more. That's the way it works."

"But the rules!" he insisted. "You simply can't bypass the rules that way!"

"Oh, come now, Commissioner. Let's face it. It's done every day. No reason for you to get so hopped up about it."

He hated that tone. He hated the way the old man kept calling him "Commissioner" with every phrase, as if he had nothing but contempt for the office. The word was ugly when he spoke it.

"You go too far, Jim." He began a new thought. "Your

whole organization goes too far. You tie up ballplayers like they were real estate. The rules limit you to forty, but you buy up ball clubs that net you control over four or five hundred of them. You hold in reserve not only the players you need, but you cold-storage those you think you might need in the next five years. Old Jim Mellon's big, happy family. . . ."

Mellon seemed interested.

"The farm system," he nodded with a smile. "It wins pennants."

"Sure. You buy up talent to win pennants to make big money to buy more players to win more pennants."

"That's bad?"

He could almost taste the old man's contempt. Mellon was being tolerant, as if the Commissioner were a child to be humored and encouraged and finally educated.

"It's bad for the players—like Kutner. It's bad for the other clubs—like Philly."

"But it's damn good for me!" Mellon laughed. "Like I said, it wins pennants."

"And it's bad for baseball!" The Commissioner's voice was louder than he wished.

"That's the sour grapes department, Commissioner. Everybody wants to win pennants and they all got farm organizations. It's a good system. Anyone can win in it. That's America, Commissioner, free enterprise and all that. But, then, maybe you got some suggestions in mind?"

"I've stated them: a freer interchange of ballplayers, especially to the clubs that need them most."

"You wouldn't attack the reserve clause, would you? Even the ballplayers don't do that. Take away the reserve clause and the players become free agents. It'd be like anarchy. The rich clubs would gobble up all the good ones."

The Commissioner almost rose from his chair.

"Who's got them now, Jim?" he shouted. "The poor clubs?"

He waited for an answer, but there was none. What could the other say? Flushed with this bit of triumph, he went on.

"I'm not arguing the reserve clause, or the rest of the rules. I'm arguing simply that you violate them—if not in fact, then in spirit. You even make believe they weren't written. And you, the big owners, are the men who wrote them!"

He was getting much too aroused, the Commissioner told himself. This was not the way to make his point.

"I'll tell you something, Jim," he started again, moderately. "Baseball gets a good sock in the nose every once in a while, and men like you start bleeding all over yourself. Like in '46 when the millionaire Mexican came North to the training camps with his pockets full. He offered the players good money for their talents and they quickly forgot all the glory in working for you. You cried all over the place, ready to call out the marines to invade Mexico City. American baseball was being betrayed for fifty pieces of Mexican silver! But actually you were frightened. Yes, scared to death of losing the one thing that held your one-sided system together, the dependence of the ballplayers on you!"

The Commissioner wanted to see Mellon's face now, up there at the window watching the city below him. He saw only the back of the bald head and the wrinkled neck.

"You weren't so cocky then, Jim. The ballplayers got together and won a few concessions for themselves—a five-grand minimum, and the start of a decent pension plan. You almost had a strike on your hands to boot! And you weren't so cocky when the players back from Mexico fought the suspensions we slapped on them. They challenged the reserve clause, and they challenged us! And were you violating the rules during the weeks when Congress was investigating monopoly practices in baseball? Was it 'done every day' then, Jim? Or did you wait until they quit, until the big litigations against us bogged down in the courts, or settled out of court?"

Those had been the early years of the Commissioner's term, and he had hated the disputes, for they had compromised his devotion to the game. He could not speak of them dispassionately. This was a sport they were supposed to be running; a great, wonderful game developing youth and character. He believed in that, and his past confirmed it. Most recently, he had been an officer of a large corporation; he resigned from his position to devote himself to the administration of baseball. He enjoyed rolling his memory back to his earliest days on a ball field. It was by the local railroad station in a small California town. He could still picture the community excitement at the Sunday games wth neighboring towns. It was spirited and honest. He could recall how they had gathered at the telegraph office for a disjointed account of a world series game coming over the ticker from 3,000 miles away. He liked to believe his memories and reactions were representative of all baseball fans.

He looked over now to the back of that wrinkled neck, at the man who destroyed this sentiment, and thought of the bronzed neck of the ballplayer who was his victim. ("Mellon has invested a lot of blood, sweat, and tears, Commissioner . . . but they're all mine!")

"You're winning now, Jim," he said finally, "and you're cocky again. So you've started pushing the pendulum back, and the players are feeling the squeeze. That's a rotten way to run a sport! You can't shove ballplayers around and expect baseball to support you. I tell you, Jim, I spoke with Kutner and you're cutting the heart out of that man. If he kicks up a fuss, it'll make trouble for you!"

He heard Mellon's comment, a half-laugh, half-grunt from the window.

"Hunh!"

It was a kind of derisive sneer at the warning. As if some lousy bush leaguer would dare to make trouble for Jim Mellon! The Commissioner let himself smolder at this contempt for a man's dignity and found fuel in the mounting emotions so long dammed up. His voice rose with his anger.

"Dammit! Kutner belongs in the majors, Jim! You can't just pass off a man's right to what he deserves with a couple of sneaky phone calls. The man belongs in the majors and the rules are written to see that he gets a chance! And that's the way it's gonna be!

"You're going to take this phone right now and call Bill Bostwick and tell him you've changed your mind, you hear? You tell him he can purchase Kutner at the regular waiver price. You're not going to violate the waiver rule. No, sir, not while I'm the Commissioner!"

He was up from his chair holding the phone in his hand, stretching the length of the cord toward Jim Mellon's back. The words had poured out, crude and unplanned. He had surprised himself by the sound of his own passion and by his show of strength. This is the way to handle him, he knew.

("Just leave it to me, Kutner . . . leave it to me!")

The old man stood there impassively, picking at his ear with a bony finger yellowed by the touch of ten thousand cigars. The silence was broken only by the impatient, demanding hum of the receiver.

The Commissioner looked at the instrument, conscious of the sudden power of his grip upon it.

"Come on, Jim," he roared. "Call him! Goddammit, I'm going to wait right here till you do!" And he prodded the mouthpiece harshly at the old man's arm.

The old man was annoyed. He turned to the Commissioner and brushed slowly past the outstretched telephone into the large swivel chair at his desk. A fresh cigar parted his mouth and he lit up carefully, billowing a cloud of smoke toward the Commissioner. Too deliberately, he tapped the thin edge of ash into the reclining nude statue he'd had made into an ash tray.

Jim Mellon looked at the buzzing receiver a few inches from his face, too close to be ignored, and he took it finally from the Commissioner. Gingerly, he balanced it in his hand, as though he didn't know what to do with it. He heard the sudden crackling change of tone within it, and he looked up at the Commissioner hovering over him.

"You must be kidding!" he said, sounding almost incredulous, and he replaced the receiver back on the hook.

The Commissioner was stunned. He stared at the instrument, trying to urge it off the hook by the power of suggestion. He was frozen by this quiet dismissal of his demands. But the phone lay there, black and silent and dead.

The old man was quick to say more.

"Talking that way won't get you anywhere, Commissioner. You should've learned that by now. When you get interested in the players, you gotta learn just how far to go. I can tell you, Commissioner, the owners might not like it!"

It didn't matter what Mellon said any longer. The Commissioner pulled out his handkerchief and wiped his face, perspiring from the aftermath of his rage. He felt that he had been somehow led on and deceived by his own build-up, that his reason and emotion had combined against him in a weird kind of treachery.

"At the moment," he said bitterly, trying to save face, "I happen to be mostly concerned for the players."

He did not see Mellon's grim smile, for he watched the smoking red ash as it rested against the statue.

"Well, that's too damn bad, Commissioner." Mellon's voice was rigid and cutting. "You've been forgetting another rule that comes closer to home. The rule that the Commissioner is elected by twelve of the sixteen owners—and none of the players. I'll tell you, Commissioner, you get paid your fat sixty-five thousand dollars a year to keep peace in this business, and I got strong feelings that twelve of the boys ain't gonna see it your way!

"So I'll tell *you* how it's gonna be!" The old man was waving his cigar at him. "Jim Mellon owns that man, so Jim Mellon decides what's to be done with him. That's the only rule that counts, goddammit! You can forget about the others. He goes where I send him. And that's back to Minneapolis!"

There was a crude finality to the words that seemed incontestable. What chance did he have now? The Commissioner thought suddenly of batting against Bob Feller in the heavy haze of twilight. If a man had courage, he could stand up there and take his cuts. But the odds were he wouldn't get much wood on the ball.

He heard the old man bearing down again in a savage postscript.

"And you can tell him for me, Commissioner, if he don't report in two days, I'll get him suspended!"

The Commissioner thought of Kutner's six-o'clock call. ("Just leave it to me, Kutner . . . leave it to me!")

He loaded his cigarette holder and lit up carefully, wondering if he had ever really believed he could fulfill that pledge, even in that inspired moment when it was made. He saw Jim Mellon fingering his gold watch, and he thought with irony that to support his position, all he had were the rules of the National Baseball Players' Association. And he was no less than its commissioner! The fact that he couldn't laugh out loud annoyed him.

When he took office, the Commissioner had wanted to believe his job would be an ennobling one. He had seen himself as the czar for the protection of baseball, the purifier of the almost pure. He would keep the game honest and clean, free of the corrupting touch of gamblers and racketeers. He would be the final arbitrator of disputes within the baseball world.

For baseball must remain a game and the baseball world a big family, whose house he would keep in order.

It seemed, now, that Mike Kutner would have to become an obedient son.

"Commissioner . . . ," he heard. The voice was firm and too damn paternal. "I think you oughta reconsider a few things. Baseball is going through a rough time with a lot of these frustrated malcontents kicking up since the war. A boy isn't worth a plugged nickel, so he screams 'injustice!' We've always had them—the clubhouse lawyers, the bushers who claim they're getting screwed. Now, you were a big man in business before, Commissioner. Baseball needs a big, respectable man at the top. That's why we chose you. I don't see where it's the Commissioner's problem when some little punk comes along squawking about the bum deal he thinks he's getting."

The words were a jumble of pious nonsense. The Commissioner bit his lip groping for a way through this maze of hypocrisy.

Behind him, the door opened and shut; he saw Jim Mellon nod to the new arrival, beckoning him to sit. The Commissioner discreetly swallowed the top of his anger and turned to see young Clark Mellon.

The old man smiled around his cigar. "You know my nephew, of course."

"Certainly." He moved his own lips into a smile. "How are you, Clark?"

"Fine, sir. Nice to see you again."

They shook hands politely from adjacent chairs, and returned to the electric silence of their interrupted clash. As if by design, the three of them reached for their individual smoking devices: the cigarette holder, the cigar, the pipe. For a moment, they watched the smoke filling the room, seeking escape from each other in a mutually fabricated smoke screen. The Commissioner looked over at young Mellon and wondered why he was there. He did not believe the argument should be continued in his presence.

But Mellon would not stop.

"I'll tell you something else." The old man's voice was charged with authority. "A little piece of advice. Don't ever get the idea you can push the owners around. I can tell you it won't work. It isn't the way to make friends with the boys who elect you. There are certain things they like to decide themselves about the way this business should be run."

The Commissioner crushed out his cigarette. This pointed reference to his lack of power was less for his ears than for the nephew. A lesson probably, in dynamic ownership. (This, my boy, is the way we make the Commissioner eat crow when he comes for lunch. And don't you forget it!)

The phone rang and Jim Mellon picked it up, settling back in conversation. The Commissioner began struggling for the words that would save him, but his mind twisted in a messy circle of anger, fear, and futility. He could not think in a straight line. He watched the old man in grinning conversation, listening to the pompous, boastful, much-too-confident dialogue of the powerful. He thought, suddenly, This is no place for me to be. Not now, anyway. Quietly, he rose from his chair and made for the doorway, trying to find a suitable parting word or gesture. What should it be? Thanks for the advice? He grunted to himself and merely waved at Clark, covering his face with what must have been an insipid smile. It was an abrupt and graceless exit.

In the elevator, he became aware of how his departure must have looked, and it embarrassed him. He turned his mind to the other meetings still ahead of him that day, trying to focus his concentration on routine duties. But the prospect of Kutner's phone call overcrowded his thoughts. There could be no escape.

He blew his nose as he left the building. He knew he had not left quite soon enough.

# 11 *The Wife*

She hurried up the ramp and turned into the grandstand, hoping to be on time. The green field lay shimmering under the brilliant lights, still naked and clean without spike marks. She was relieved to see the umpires huddled at home plate with the rival managers, the moment before game time. She made her way down the steps to the box reserved for the players' wives, conscious now of the shrill whistles of hungry men that her trim, appealing body was accustomed to draw. They were spectators, and it was a moment when they had nothing else to look at. They had paid their buck for an evening of fun, and fun is where you find it. The whistles mushroomed into catcalls as more of them looked up from the peanuts and score cards, following her swaying walk down the steps. Maybe I ought to have a number on my back so they could identify me, she thought. Number 13, Laura Kutner, wife of Mike Kutner, to be used occasionally on the off season.

God, you sure timed this wrong, she mumbled to herself. There were two or three drinks inside her for a bracer but no dinner to brace the drinks, and she took her time moving unsteadily down the steps. She saw the girls in the box looking toward her, turned by the wolf whistles and a stock pile of jealousies, and she knew they'd be saying she timed this deliberately.

To hell with them, the boys and the girls. Nuts to them. Big and small, nuts to all. And the middle-sized ones too.

Don't be bitter, Laura. Especially not tonight. For this is the night of expectancy, and hope, and climax. Tonight is more than a ball game, more than a pennant or a play-off, more than a whole season of games. Tonight is a lifetime being tested. A marriage stripped and put suddenly on the block. A man and a woman caught with all their eggs together in the same flimsy basket. Buy them, Mr. Clark Mellon! Buy them now . . . *now!* Buy the shiny white eggs before they turn rotten with too many passing years. Laura snickered, for the picture was all wrong. He didn't have to buy. He owned them already, owned them all outright.

Laura quickly scanned the row of boxes for a sight of him, the rich, suave, cultured Clark Mellon; the young, about-to-be Chicago baseball bigwig, condescending to visit his farm club for a look at the veteran Mike Kutner. But it was crowded. People were moving down the aisles, and she could not see him. To hell with it. It doesn't matter. Mike is what matters tonight. "Baseball Mike," king of the minors. It was up to Mike to show him how good he was, to make the impression. It was up to Clark Mellon to see his ability and bring him up to Chicago.

Why did it have to be this way? Why should a man's whole life be judged on a night or two, or even three? Wasn't the record good enough? But Mike had told her, over and over, he was not a "record" ballplayer. His value lay in abilities not altogether apparent in record books. But it was there for the big shots to see, Laura knew, if they would only look . . . all these things she knew, of course, and not only because he told her. But she questioned them repeatedly because she simply did not wish to believe; it made everything so tenuous, their lives so subject to the whims of arbitrary men.

Tonight they would put him through this test once again.

Up in Chicago, the mother club was having its worst year in a dozen; and conversely, Mike was having his best. They needed him, she told herself over and over. They needed her fast, steady, seasoned, smart, aggressive Mike. The fat was clearly in the fire; it made this night different from all the others.

She descended the last few steps to the box, suddenly regretting she had automatically chosen to sit there, with the other wives, just like for other games. Tonight was different; it was a time of crisis, and the game, or rather Mike's part in it, would be more than sufficient to compensate for her loneliness if she sat alone. She didn't need the girls tonight.

But the commitment was made, and it was not in her to turn away from them at the last moment. There they were, the chirping adolescents, the dear little crowd of sparkling cuties. Damn them and their brainless chatter and their petty jealousies! She could take them, she thought, if only they weren't so young!

"Hi, Laura."

"Hello, darling."

"Well, well . . . look who's here!" As if they just discovered her arrival.

"And in time for the first pitch!"

It was as if they were smiling at her with their voices, and she smiled back. It was true. She never came early to ball games and she stayed to the end only for some special reason. The truth was, the games themselves no longer interested her; she had seen too many of them through her ten years of marriage to Mike. But she had no desire to be considered different, and she never admitted her boredom, not even to Mike. She looked at them now, the high-breasted young twits, the newly married hopefuls, as eager as their husbands, talking loudly to each other about only themselves and the husbands who were but appendages of their big-time desires.

There, but for a war and a dozen empty years, go I, she thought.

The nearness of their jabbering dissolved into the roar of the crowd around her as the players scrambled out of the dugout and ran to their positions. As she turned to the field to watch, the sudden change of concentration made her dizzy and all too aware of the liquor-lined tensions within her. In a minute they'd play the national anthem (or did they skip it on Thursday nights?). Oh say can you see, Mr. Mellon, it's my dear husband Mike. There he goes, out to center field. Do you see the way he runs, even now before the game, strong and agile like a big cat? Look at the way he picks up his glove, tenderly working in the pocket with those strong fingers. Doesn't that show you something about a ballplayer, Mr. Mellon? And look at the way he stands there, smack in the middle of the outfield, like it was all his and no one could hit one by him. Did you ever watch his face through a pair of power glasses when he ran? Did you ever see the naked, animal determination that fairly screams "No, nothing gets by me. Nothing! Nothing!" Who else is like that, Mr. Big-shot Owner? Who? Watch him, Mister, wherever you are. Watch him! It's time you saw, after all these years. My God, it's time!

She watched the pitcher set himself for the opening pitch and a momentary wave of trembling rushed through her. She bit her lips harshly for control until the pain itself stopped her. She offered up her feeble plea, audible only to herself:

"Have a great night, Mike. Please. Have a great night!"

It did not escape her that she had felt nothing like this for years. She rode her memory back to the almost-obscured moments of their early romance, and even before, when Mike was only another man on spikes to watch from a distance. Laura was a girl of great beauty, or so everyone said, and hence one for whom life would be rich and wonderful. Or so everyone said. The world lays out a plush carpet for a beautiful woman, Laura. All you have to do is walk down the aisle and the prince awaits you, holding out a pot of gold. But apparently she didn't know a plush carpet when she saw one, and the princes she met were old and fat and sloppy with money and the taking of it. So it turned out that the early years of her artificially inseminated hopes were unfulfilling. She floundered through the maze of unsuitable suitors, trying to believe that all she had to do was sit back and wait for the solid-gold one to appear and then nod her head at the right moment. The result was a siege of emptiness, and the prospect of the future began to frighten her.

At the ball park, she enjoyed being lost in the spirited, impersonal crowds. She was there only for escape, ostensibly to watch that clown in right field, and to forget the day and the endless petty problems of a life without direction. But one night she recognized in another the stern qualities of strength and survival she lacked in herself. She saw a man in full control command all his abilities inning after inning, performing with a remarkable consistency. Here was someone who knew where he was going. He had everything she lacked, and she returned to watch him, over and over, hoping that some of it might someday rub off on her.

She had reached out for him, this twenty-one-year-old beauty, already tired and afraid. She sought his strength for herself, wanting to be a part of his irrepressible will to succeed. And when he seemed distant and inaccessible, she interpreted his moods as an indication of his independence, and she wanted him even more. What she did not understand in the beginning were the reasons for his reticence. Here was a boy who excluded from his life anything foreign to his ambitions. To him, Laura was the much-too-beautiful interloper, a potential distraction, a deterrent to his clear and simple ambition. Actually, desire pulled at him more than he admitted, even to himself, but in his fears, he wanted none of it, and he kept away. It was only when she could convince him, however unwittingly, that she had identified herself with his aspirations, that he felt ready to give her some small piece of himself. It was a start and she clung to it, begging for more.

Behind her, the sudden blast of the crowd scattered her memories, drawing her back to the game. She saw the runners taking off, and in the distance, Mike's sprint for the liner sinking in front of him. His body lunged forward with a desperate yet graceful dive, and he skidded on his belly with his glove outstretched before him. The ball smacked into it, burrowing deep into the soft leather pocket. For a moment he just lay there, as if he had extended himself too far. Laura watched him, knowing he had learned to dramatize these diving catches. Years ago he would have rolled with the catch and jumped right up. Now she speculated whether he was prepared to admit this piece of crowd-teasing artifice for what it was, even to himself. As he pulled himself up, ready to jog back to the screaming embrace of the crowd, she knew there'd be heavy grass stains on his white shirt, across the letters. Yet when she saw the stains she was startled. She felt the sudden impact of her memories.

Ten long years back Mike had courted her, but he had taken his miserable time about it. It had been a terrible summer for Laura, despite the excitement of love's beginnings. She ached through those endless, unfulfilled months, nursing an ever-growing desire for him that sometimes twisted her insides until she was sick. She knew he wanted her, and she supposed he had love for her in his way, but he kept his thoughts and hands to himself, as though he reserved both for use on the ball field only. She would go to the games and feast on the sight of him as he worked through the evening. He was graceful and strong and tireless. His movements, sharp and sometimes startlingly sudden, sent chills through her for the sensuality she found in them. She learned to watch him through a pair of high-powered binoculars, studying his intensity as he stood at the plate, fiercely waving the shiny white bat as he waited. And all the time she wondered what this poised and dynamic man would be like inside her.

Then one night toward the end of that summer, the change occurred. From the stands she saw a low liner send Mike on a quick dash toward the infield. She followed him with her glasses as he hurled himself through the air for the catch, inches above the ground. He skidded face down on the soft turf as if it had been greased for him, and she could see the jubilant smile on his face as his glove swallowed up the ball. That catch had been a climax to a wonderful night for him, and after the game he met her, glowing with some secret triumph but too shy to talk about it. Later, she learned that the manager had told him they would send him up next season. She sat with him as he ate the rare steak and drank the cold beer. There was something different about him, and the way he looked at her made her voice catch in her throat. He took her by the hand and walked her as if aimlessly until they came back to the ball park. He found an open gate and led her up the winding ramps and onto the field, now dark and vast and vacant, the shadowy silhouette of the grandstand towering over them. His arm reached around her, pressing her close as they made their way across the diamond. She felt his heart beating hard against her shoulder, and she shivered anxiously through her expectations. The soft grass of the outfield was underfoot when they finally stopped. She stood there waiting, trembling and waiting, feeling his nervousness through the touch of their hands. Suddenly, she heard his awkward sigh. His hands were firm on her arms as he pulled her to him. In a second, he was crushing her in an overpowering embrace, his lips hard upon her face, clumsily searching for her mouth. They kissed for a long time, moving their bodies only to bind them together. Gradually, then, he sank to the cool grass, pulling her down with him. "Oh Laura . . . oh Laura," she heard him mumble through his fumbling attempt to unbutton her dress. "Laura . . . Laura." He hurried in a kind of frantic desperation as though he were in pain, seeking some quick relief. Eagerly she helped him, and they loved, finally, through the terrible, nervous moments of his doubts.

The following night she saw his clean uniform shirt and she remembered the green stains on the letters after that belly catch. She thought of the same grass stains on her dress, and she scanned the brilliantly illuminated outfield through her glasses for the spot of their love-making. When she picked out a harshly disturbed area of turf, she wondered if they had done this—torn up the grass, leaving the scars of their passion.

Embarrassed, she looked around at the thousands in the stands. There, smack in the middle of the outfield, the night before, only two hours after the game. Had the hundreds of light bulbs even had a chance to cool?

And for the first time that summer she began laughing out of the joy and the humor of living, the full round rich laugh of a beautiful young girl who had finally found her man.

"Gee, Laura, that old man of yours can still go fetch 'em!"

"Magnificent catch, that was. No doubt about it!"

Their voices jarred her out of tender memories. She felt injured by them for they returned her suddenly to the harsh mood of the present. She quickly disregarded their reluctant praise and craned her neck to look for more vital reactions. Did you see that, Mr. Mellon? Did you see that burst of speed? Could you doubt even for a moment that he'd get his hands on it? Wherever you are . . . did you?

The crowd was applauding Mike as he finished his jog to the dugout a few yards in front of them. The girls, who never applauded, greeted him with appreciative squeals, trying only to catch his eye and dignify their wifedom by getting some special response from the momentarily celebrated husband. But Mike always remained aloof. He tipped his cap to the whole crowd impersonally, as if out of tradition and not affection, a reluctant token for their accolades.

"Gee, he never smiles, does he, Laura?"

"Not even to you, his dearly beloved."

Laura nodded as their words knifed into her. Oh, you catty little twirps. You're so quick to see these things, aren't you? And God, how you rush to spill them all over me. Wait, just wait till the years eat away at you, and those big, strong AAA husbands of yours are still dragging your fannies through the minor-league towns, further and further from that little piece of glory you're so sure is just up the street. The road is bumpy, my dear little friends, and longer than you think.

But they were right about Mike, so right. These last years he had played ball without a smile. When she came to watch him, he was oblivious to her presence though he passed right by her box seat nine different times a game. Not a smile or even a glance from him. It was embarrassing to her, sitting there with the girls. She learned to look away at the right moment, to peer into a Coke, to find a cigarette in her bag. God knows what had happened to him over the years to sour him like this. He used to be a spirited kid, playing with a fiery kind of enthusiasm that was wonderful to watch. He would make a difficult catch like this one and you would laugh for the simple beauty of it. But now the chip on his shoulder was too plain to see. He moved like an animal stalking his prey, fast and hungry and relentless. The quiet confidence was still there but it had a sullen edge to it.

He was tired. That's what it was, she knew. He was tired

from the endless drudgery of trying to scale the peaks, of always being promised (You belong up there, Mike. Sure, next season you'll have a crack at it) and then always getting the door slammed in his face as he reached for the top. (Next year, Mike. Have another good year at Minneapolis and there's a spot for you in Chicago, next year.) God, how they lied! She chased her memory rapidly through the storehouse of deceits and double talk, shaking her head now, depressed by it, swallowing her tears through the teasing remnants of her fading whisky jag.

Tired. Yes, she was tired too. The marriage born of love and hope was losing both. What kind of marriage had it been anyway? They had lived these ten years in cheap rooming houses, in the cold, drab mustiness of old hotels. Room to room, town to town—fortifying their resistance to their dismal life with a daily inoculation of hope. Next year . . . always next year. A man has to allow himself time to make the top. It doesn't happen quickly, even to the best of talent. It takes time, time. But how many years can you keep on kidding yourself, filling your empty days with a few well-chosen rationalizations and enough booze to help you believe them? Inescapably she would fancy herself in other settings, married to any of a dozen suitors way back in the days of her lush, young beauty, conveniently trying to forget now what made her reject them then. She would sit before the dressing tables of a myriad of hotel rooms, searching fretfully in the mirrors for telltale lines of her passing youth. She was only thirty, and the lines were faint in the still-fresh skin. But it seemed like a tired and empty thirty, and she allowed herself the luxury of too much self-pity. (You made a mistake, she would tell herself: why didn't you marry Carl Fleming? The man had a million and he worshiped you. Or Ernest Mills, the banker's son. He was young, too.) And off she would go into a misty flight of fantasy, covering herself with jewels and fancy clothes and nonsense in the always-wonderful world of wealth she would never have.

But always she would return to the realities of her marriage as Mrs. Michael Kutner, wife of a baseball player and consequently of baseball itself. In her better moments, she refused to interpret her life as an error. There had been excitement in the beginning, she had been alive with the drama of the life ahead of them. Baseball was fascinating to her, less as a game than as a vehicle for her husband's success, a stage for his talents. She would inevitably follow the games through self-seeking eyes, watching for the moments that distinguished her Mike from others, caring less for the victory of the team than the triumph of her man. She could see this in the other wives, of course, however much they tried to cover it with pious platitudes about team play. It was her man against all the rest of them, and every day was another test.

And when he fell into a slump—that terrible, intangible disease of a ballplayer—the world was an angry sordid place, concentrating all its evil pressures upon him to keep him down. Laura would watch him suffer, unable to help him, knowing that these days of his failure ate away relentlessly at those September totals. She would suffer with him. She would go to the games to pull him out of it by the sheer force of her will, mumbling prayers and collecting superstitions on every pitch, every time at bat, every game, until they crowded all else out of her mind. One week she swore she'd not change her dress until he snapped out of it. She defied custom and feminine vanity for so long that even the other girls stopped digging at her. During those weeks, living was a nightmare, for his love for her seemed to dwindle with his batting average. They lay in bed without words, with this monster hanging over them, picking their marriage to pieces.

"Love me," she would plead with him. "Come to me, darling." And she would reach over to caress him, seeking to arouse his passion, to have him love and forget and fill the quiet, restful night asleep in her arms.

But he was like a lost little boy held in agonizing suspense until he makes his way safely back home. Home was the big base hit, the sharp ring of bat against ball. Home was his confidence, his belief in himself.

"Don't, Laura, don't." He'd turn away from her, twisting through the long dark hours in pain at his complete impotence. She would hear him mumbling into his pillow: "Christ . . . Goddammit . . . Goddammit." And there was nothing she could do to be a wife to him.

When finally he came out of it and the world was rosy with hope and promise of fulfillment again, it seemed to her that a piece of their marriage had been chewed away somehow, never to be restored. She fought against this conviction, shoring up her hopes with each of his new triumphs on the ball field. And she tried to be patient.

But patience and hope are worn thin by time, and the years passed them by as if they were standing still. They frittered away winters in a series of random jobs, unable to avoid sponging off Joe and Edna. They idled through the cold, grim months in a kind of dismal hibernation, trying to believe that each winter would be their last in Austin, Kentucky. The home, the children—these were yet to come. How could she raise a family in a different town almost every season, with no home in the winter except a room in his parents' house?

At length, it became inevitably clear that baseball was no longer the bed partner of her choice. She wanted a man and his love, and for weeks she struggled to work up the courage to tell him.

"Mike . . . listen to me." It was late one night at Joe and Edna's, their fourth winter in Austin. She could feel the thoughts rise up to choke her before she even started. "I have to tell you this." (How could she find the right words?) "And . . . and . . . I know how you feel about it."

She remembered how he had looked at her, somehow already aware. He lowered his eyes to a studied manipulation of his powerful hands, guilty even before the accusation.

"What?"

"Mike . . . darling. . . ." It was the pleading in her voice that gave her away. "I think it's time. . . ." Now, Laura, *now!* Say it! "I think it's time you got out of baseball."

He reacted as if an electric shock had coursed through him. Whatever the extent of the guilt he felt at the course of their marriage, it had not reached that far. He jumped to his feet and stared at her, for the moment speechless. She turned her eyes from him and tried to light a trembling cigarette.

"Quit! *You* want me to quit?" He was standing over her, his voice huskier than she had ever heard it.

What do you say now, Laura? Exactly what did you expect?

Silence was on his side, and he used it. It was up to her to break down the barrier.

"Mike, it's just that there seems to be no end to it any more. Maybe . . . we're not getting anyplace."

She had completely lost her original decisiveness. Alone, many times, she had thought it out so carefully, so logically.

"I thought . . . it might be best if you gave it up while we're still young." And then with determination: "We could have kids, Mike."

When he didn't respond, she knew she had to pursue it all the way, to spell it out for him. "We could do it, Mike! Right here in Austin, even. Get into the store with Walter, why don't you? He needs you, Mike. I want you to . . . your pop wants you to. . . ."

His head jerked up and he glared at her, and his voice rose

to fill the tiny bedroom: "Don't be nuts, Laura. I'm a ballplayer . . . a ballplayer!"

He shouted it at her, as though he could overpower her logic with a single word.

"You're a ballplayer," she mimicked him. "So what! I'm a wife, but sometimes it's hard to realize. You make me feel like being a wife is a job of some kind, and that most of the time I'm unemployed! I want to be a real wife, Mike. I want to have a home of our own, with kids, lots of them. You know what that means to a girl? Just about everything, that's all. And you want them, too! I know you do!"

She had watched him one quiet evening that winter, sitting in the parlor with Marian's youngest baby crawling at his feet. The baby had played in front of him, trying to fit a peg into a hole. Mike had watched him through the long moments of the struggle, his eyes glued on the baby. The little hand would doggedly move the peg to the hole and repeatedly fail because of the angle of entrance. Each time his limited coordination defeated him, but he would try again, unaware that there was such a thing as failure. Mike was moved, Laura knew. She saw him caught up by the suspense involved in the tremendous effort. Finally the baby had succeeded. The peg had rested firmly in the hole and he had looked up, smiling at his triumph. Mike had sighed and then swept the boy into his arms, his eyes turned away from the others.

"We'll have kids later," he said now, almost distantly. His tone angered her. He made it sound as though he were wearied of some age-old argument they'd had a dozen times before. Yet they hadn't.

"Sure, when you're a major-league star!" she said. "No, Mike. I'm getting older, like you. It's not easy after a woman passes thirty."

He looked at her hard, trying to control himself.

"Don't say that. We're not old!"

"The years go too fast for us, Mike. You're sacrificing us both to your ambitions."

"I'll make it, Laura. Then everything will be worth it. You'll see."

"You're thirty-one, Mike! How long do you suppose they'll keep you around? You'll have too short a time up there anyway."

"I'll be good for years. My legs are stronger now than ever . . ."

"What do they care about your legs! They'll push you around again, just like always. They'll put in some big kid the first time you get a blister, and you'll sit the nine innings chewing your heart out. Don't you see, Mike? They run your life! It's not yours any more. God, it never was."

He shook his head, refusing to accept this. "I'm good, Laura," he insisted. "They can't keep me down."

"You're good. Sure—so what! What's so important about that?" She felt her voice rising with exasperation. "Lots of guys are good and don't make out. They don't ever make out. Not only in baseball, Mike . . . in everything. Show me where there are guarantees. I've never seen any. Don't you see? You have to be *more* than good. You have to be lucky; you have to be a bootlicker, or part your hair the way some dumb manager likes it. You're none of them, Mike. You're just good, and that's not enough!"

"You're wrong, Laura." His voice was subdued. "You've got to be wrong."

"Don't try to prove it to me, Mike! Just quit! Quit now and let's have a normal life together."

She reached out for him, touching his arm softly, hoping to communicate the urgency of her thoughts to him. For a moment, he stood there letting her. Then he jerked his arm away roughly and turned aside.

"No! I won't quit. Why the hell should I? You don't quit when you're young. You quit this game when you can't play any more. I'm gonna make the top, Laura. They can't keep me down forever. I'm gonna sit your fanny in a big-league box, and we're gonna live that big-league life like I promised."

She cringed at this repetition of his stale pledge. For the first time she really hated the sound of it. Out of her bitterness she struck at him blindly.

"Oh Jesus, don't be so sure," she mumbled, "don't be so damned sure!"

The harsh words were out before she knew it and there was nothing she could do to pull them back. It was a part of her thinking she had never wanted to voice, knowing the words would tear at what he considered to be the foundations of their marriage. She had hoped to convince him without indicating any doubt as to his eventual triumph, only that it just wasn't worth the struggle any longer. Now she knew she had lost. She saw Mike turn away from her, retreating into some silent place of his pride. You're a fool, Laura, she told herself. When you dare to question his success, you do so much more than that. You insult the man himself, for the man is the ballplayer and the ballplayer is the man, and you cannot separate them. My God, you should have learned that!

"Mike, darling . . . ," she said quietly moving to him. "I'm sorry. I didn't mean what I said. Really. You know I didn't mean that." It sounded feeble, the small voice from the bottom of the hole she had dug for herself.

"Sure, sure."

"No, Mike. Please. Listen to me!" She didn't know what she would ask him to listen to.

He retreated from her and slumped into a chair.

"Mike . . . ," she pleaded.

"Stop it, Laura!" he cried out suddenly. "Stop it!" And then his voice shook with his body, and he tried to bury himself in his big hands. "I know. I know!" he mumbled. "Everything you said. It's true!"

She went to him, trying to swallow her tears, knowing how much he hated them.

"Mike . . . oh, Mike."

She fell on her knees at his feet.

He let her caress him now, and her hand reached up to stroke his hair. For a long time she did not talk.

"I've known it for years, Laura," he said finally. "God, how many times I've thought of you! I knew it was wrong, the way we were living. I even thought of quitting. . . . Yes, I have. Quitting!" he looked up from his hands and showed the torment in his face. "But I can't . . . Laura, I can't. I can't quit! You've got to understand this. I have to win. I have to get there. I'd be a failure if I didn't. I'd never be able to do anything else. This is my life, Laura. Please, darling . . . please."

His weakness became their strength. She buried her head in his lap and kissed the hand against her face.

"It's all right, darling," she said finally. "It's all right. You'll make it, Mike. We'll make it together."

He lifted her off the floor and into his arms and brought her face up to his. Their kiss was born of renewed love and understanding and shared weakness. They held each other for a long time.

The thread of her memory seemed endless in its unwinding. Somehow, it stopped here, on this kiss, and she wrenched her concentration back to the present. You're here . . . at the ball park . . . in the box. . . .

"Mike!" She said it aloud, this time unabashed by the heads that turned to peer oddly at her. She saw him edging off third base, just a few yards in front of her, and it suddenly occurred to her that she didn't even know how he'd gotten there. Did he hit a triple? The thought excited her, bringing home again the full measure of what this night might mean. She looked at the scoreboard for the game situation, sensing she had lost track of time. The score was tied at one-all, still early in the game. There were two outs and nothing on the hitter. Then she saw that Sam Carter was at bat. At once, her mind registered that Sam followed Mike in the order, that Mike *must* have tripled! She sat forward in her seat now, conscious that her attention to the game was a moment late for the excitement of his hit. She wondered at her own inward concentration.

She watched Mike move slowly down the line as the pitcher got set to throw. His body was relaxed; yet she could see his heavy breathing, she supposed from his chase around the bases. The pitcher had his sign, and was beginning his pumping wind-up. Laura found herself counting at the first movement of his swinging arms. A-thousand-and-one, a-thousand-and-two, a-thousand-and-three. . . . She knew he'd be counting too. How long is a pitcher's wind-up? He had instructed her. Will he give you three seconds? If the game situation is right, that's all the time needed to steal home. Watch him as he winds up. Is his motion easy to cut short if he sees you're running on him? A lefty is easier to run on than a right-hander, for the lefty has so much of his back to you as he starts to throw. But it doesn't matter too much. Home is really the easiest base to steal.

If she hadn't counted too rapidly, there'd be time for Mike to make it. Besides, the pitcher was a southpaw. She saw Mike make the brief movement toward home, as though he were feinting; but actually he was timing his start. There was something in that move that told her he would be running. She wondered if there was anyone else in that ball park who knew this. Clark Mellon . . . do you? Do you know Mike is going to steal home and break this tie? She laughed nervously through her excitement, and moved even further to the front of her seat.

The lefty was composed and confident for he had blown the first strike by the hitter. Mike idled off third this time, making only a token move toward home. Laura knew what Mike was thinking. If he was going to steal, this pitch had to be a ball. You don't rush in on a hitter with two strikes. The pitch came in, fast-breaking stuff down by his knees. It was a ball!

Laura laughed again, knowing this would be it. She felt suddenly guilty at her laughter, as though she were betraying the secret, like a kibitzer registering surprise while looking over the shoulder of a poker player. This piece of nonsense amused her; nonetheless she tried to keep a straight face.

Here we go, she breathed quickly now. Mike was edging off the base, further . . . further. He was almost fifteen feet down the line. The pitcher squinted for his signal and began his pumping motion. Mike started cautiously, as if he were faking again, then abruptly broke for home in a sudden spurt. For a quick second the pitcher did not see him, and it was all the time the runner needed. The throw was hurried and on the first-base side. Mike threw his body into a slide along the outside of the plate. The catcher dove for him, but too late for that elusive body. The umpire spread his arms wide hollering into the excited roar of the crowd.

"Safe!"

Laura sat back now, proud of her diagnosis to the point of feeling a share in the cheers for her husband. She felt the tingling of pride under her scalp and the pleasing goose flesh over her skin. God, it was wonderful to be a winner, even if just for a moment!

She stood up now as Mike returned to the bench, applauding like a school girl along with the thousands around her. She sought his eyes as he moved toward her, begging for this chance to show him. Look at me, Mike . . . look at me, please. Just this once. Look at the joy running through me. Oh, look, Mike, *look!*

There was a fleeting moment before he turned into the dugout when she knew he saw her. His face was smudged with the dust of his slide and there was dust on his glasses. But she saw that his sternness had softened, and a slight smile parted his lips. She wasn't certain, for the lights above them glared on the surface of his glasses, but she thought he winked at her, a tiny flick of the eye. She wanted to rush down on the field and hug him for all the love and hope there was in her.

"Take it easy, Laura," she heard behind her. "You're jumping out of your skin."

Skin . . . skin . . . so what? It's mine, isn't it. I can jump out of it if I want to. Maybe I can wiggle out of it, like a snake. She felt young again. She turned to them, still radiating excitement.

"Wasn't that something, girls? Wasn't that just something?"

She saw the envy in their unconcern. They would sit tight, with their Cokes and cigarettes, waiting for the inning that might be theirs.

"It was exciting, darling, but was it smart baseball? After all, it's early in the game and Sam was up. He can hit, too!"

She realized that it was Mrs. Sam Carter talking, sitting through the very same torment trying to believe it was *her* husband whom Mellon had come down to scout, realizing that a chance to drive Mike across was a better deal than batting with no one on and two out. The girl could not resist a dig at Laura. And Laura understood.

"Really, though, Laura, you have to admit that Mike tries to be too flashy sometimes."

This was another voice, and Laura turned quickly to parry the thrust.

"Maybe he got a signal to steal. Did it ever occur to you that the manager told him to?"

She knew this was most unlikely, and the words came out sounding like an angry child's. But hell, she was on top. She could afford to make her own brand of nonsense. God, how the competition spread over them all till they snapped at each other for that single, glittering brass ring. She pictured their kids beating each other with their fathers' batting averages.

"Well, Laura. All I can say is that it's lucky for the team he made it safely."

She wanted to say that Mike always made it safely but thought better of it. She did not have to blow Mike's trumpet for these cats. There was only one man in the ball park she wanted to know all these things.

The ring of the batted ball turned them back to the game. Sam had lashed out a single to left. Laura watched the wife sigh at this waste of a critical run-batted-in, for the hit was a dull anticlimax to Mike's steal. Laura found this amusing and chuckled inwardly.

"That was a good hit, honey," she said. "Perhaps you were right after all." And she added: "Now maybe Sam can steal, too."

She was a little annoyed at the meanness so obvious in her own words. Why rub it in? She felt ashamed despite her jubilation.

You need a drink, Laura. It's time to pull your triple-A fanny out of this den of hungry wolves to clear your head with a little pure ninety-proof head-clearer. Mike's at his best. You've seen more than enough tonight.

It was all she needed. Disregarding the thought of the rest of the game, she rose from her seat to leave.

"Where are you going? To the little girls' room?"

That silly expression, "the little girls' room." Lord!

"No. I'm leaving."

"So soon?" They were amazed.

"Why not? Don't I always?"

"Yes, but. . . ."

Laura began to enjoy this. She stood there, waiting, compelling them to complete the thought.

"Yes, but what, honey?" she asked.

Say it. Say it. Go ahead, you queens of the third base line. Go ahead and speak the magic name, Clark Mellon. This night it's different, isn't it! That's "but what." All night long you've been sitting here, protecting those big-league fantasies that your husbands are on trial but never mentioning the big boss's name. No, you pretend it's a kind of secret or something. But deep down inside, you know it isn't true.

It's Mike he's here for. Mike! So now that I'm going, you can't stand it, because maybe Mike will bobble a few and end up the goat, and I won't be here for your gloating if he does. Or maybe you just can't stand the thought of anyone not sweating through it. I'm sorry, ladies, but I've had it . . . too many times in too many years. I can tell you straight that Mike won't give you an inch. The truth is that you bring me down, ladies. All year long you bring me down.

She smiled at this defiance within her, and watched their eyes turn away.

"Good night, all," she said. "Touch all the bases." And she stepped lively up the long walk to the ramp.

Outside the smoky stadium, she breathed deeply of the clear night air, feeling an exhilaration she had not known for too long a time. It was as though a turning point had been reached and life would be a joy after all. She hailed a cab with a lilt in her voice, and the driver smiled when she got in.

"Where to, Miss Beautiful?"

She laughed at this nimble flattery.

"*Mrs.* Beautiful," she emphasized. "Take me to the Hotel Croydon, please."

"Croydon . . . yes ma'am." He beat the first light at the corner by a shade.

"Mighty fine game tonight," he said to her. "I like to listen to the tight ones."

"A great game . . . a great game."

"The announcer sure had a field day when that Kutner stole home. He was screaming!"

"So was I. It was wonderful!"

"That guy is terrific, lady. I saw him play last week. He's a ballplayer, that Kutner."

"He's a ballplayer," she answered, and the happiness suddenly swelled up inside her until it almost made her weep. "Yes, he's a ballplayer."

What's happening to you, Laura? There's something pounding in your heart as if the world is just beginning for you. The feeling of promise and hope. A few hours ago you never would have dreamed it. You watched him get up from his nap and dress to go to the ball park, nervous and fidgety for the night that confronted him. It could not be otherwise, for you had long since put this man on trial, both for his marriage and his career. Through those moments, you tasted your guilt, and his, and the drab room was covered by that sickening pall of hopelessness that somehow swallowed you up before every one of these critical games. After all these years, how could it be different? He kissed you as he left, and you tried to smile as he bid you, "Watch me go tonight, sweetheart!" The same old business, the same old business. . . .

Yet, back there in that stadium something thrilling happened. A man played baseball for his life. It was your life, too, he played for. And another man watched and would make the judgment that would change your world.

The cab swung around the corner and stopped.

"Hotel Croydon, ma'am."

"Hail the Hotel Croydon!" Laura said. "Hail twice the Hotel Croydon bar. Here, Mister, buy your kid a new baseball."

"Thanks, lady. You're sure feeling mighty keen, eh?"

Laura laughed. "I'll be keener still in ten minutes."

"You meeting someone? Your husband?"

"A man named Ballantine . . . from Scotland. In five or six innings, we'll be joined by husband."

"Enjoy!"

"Thanks, Mister. So long."

"So long. Happy days."

Laura skipped into the plush room. Happy days . . . happy months . . . happy years.

"Hello, Max!" she called. "On-the-rocks, please."

She promised herself she'd drink the first one as a toast to the cabbie. Happy days to you, Mr. Cabbie. No. The first for Mike. Mike, the big-leaguer-to-be, the man most likely to succeed. My man Mike . . . my wonderful Mike. . . .

She stared at the glass as she spoke his name with special tenderness. The whisky was cold and the clinking ice cubes sounded her joy. She drank with pleasure swirling through her and ordered again.

"To you, Mr. Cabbie; a toast to you and those happy days."

She raised her glass to the familiar mirrored wall before her, already feeling the creeping numbness over her face. She laughed as she brought the glass to her lips. But she choked on the first swallow. Her eye had sent a message to the brain, to be duly recorded and relayed to all appropriate senses. The message was a shock, and it knocked the breath out of her.

For there, at the opposite end of the bar, sat the debonair Clark Mellon himself, not so debonair, but more in disarray . . . and obviously at home with the alcohol-gaiety around him. What in hell is he doing here!

Mirror, mirror on the wall, who's the biggest fool of all? Laura glared back into it, begging to be wrong. It's not him. It can't be! (Look, sister: the angle of incidence is equal to the angle of reflection, and there ain't a thing you can do about it.) You're not wrong, Laura. It's him. Drunk or sober, you're right. Sure, you're right. You're always right when you don't want to be.

She swung around in her seat to see him straight, and she had to crane her neck over the line-up between them. Oh, God, you've been trying to spot that bastard all night. After that catch, after every hit, after that steal! And look where he is!

But did he see them? She hurried to guess that maybe he just got here too; maybe he did see them, maybe he made up his mind about Mike and left when she did. It could be . . . could be . . . and through this trembling confusion she mustered the courage to find out. It was like some big, crazy joke she was playing on herself, for all the time she really knew.

"Max . . . oh, Max!" she called to the bartender. "Max, how long has that dark blue suit been here? Down at the end of the bar, with the white teeth on?"

Max looked. "You should know him, Laura. That's young Mellon down from Chicago."

"I know him."

"Harvard man. Real hoity-toity."

"Max . . ." There was desperation in her voice. "How long?"

"Coupla hours, maybe longer. Say, five or six drinks, taking it slow."

Sure, and six would get you five he came in looped to start with. All the world's a party for some guys, and they leave you out in the cold to shiver. She thought of Mike out there, driving himself for the benefit of this man's judgment. And look at him, just look at the baseball magnate, titillating himself with a horny leer down a low-cut dress, just like any two-bit traveling salesman away from his baggy wife.

Laugh. Laugh. Big joke. Big damn joke.

And she slumped over the bar in tears.

She clenched her teeth to keep from crying aloud. It was the first time she had ever done this, but she did not care. After a while, she felt a hand on her shoulder, gentle and comforting, and a quiet voice was close to her ear.

"Laura . . . Laura."

It was Max.

"Let me help you," he said. And he led her to the door of the ladies' room. "Have a good cry, kiddo. You'll be all right in a few minutes."

"Thanks, Max. I'll be O.K.," she muttered. Sure, sure. Happy days. And she crumbled on the couch, unleashing all the despair that was in her.

"Feeling better?" Max smiled at her.

"Like an empty shell. You're a nice guy, Max."

He waved away the compliment with a bottle of Scotch. "Here, pour something down, Laura. On the house."

"Thanks."

She fondled the glass in her hands and brought its coolness to her cheeks. In the mirror she saw herself again and shuddered.

"The shell looks pretty battered, doesn't it, Max?"

"Well, I guess sometimes you need a good cry. Things don't seem so rough afterwards."

The whisky burned a path down to her stomach, and she sat waiting for the glow it would bring her. But there was nothing left within her to light up. A dozen feet from her she heard a man's laughter. It was easy for her to believe it was Clark Mellon's. It was inane and giddy, as though he were being tickled. It clashed violently with her mood and brought her down again. Max was wrong. Things are just as rough afterwards. There's nothing changed by tears.

What are you going to do now, Laura? You can't keep on going like this . . . you'll hit bottom in no time. And what're you going to tell Mike when you get around to deciding? What's he going to do? For you, this is the clincher, isn't it? But for Mike?

"Max, please . . . another shot."

"Take it easy, Laura," he said gently.

Poor Mike. ("I'll play ball until they throw me out.") Hail to baseball, the national pastime! Jesus, they're throwing you out now, Mike. My poor, goddamn Mike. What in hell are you waiting for?

She looked over at Clark Mellon, as if to find the answer. He was laughing again. Why was everyone laughing tonight? Sorry, no answer. The man is busy laughing and can't be bothered. Who is Mike Kutner anyway that Mr. Mellon should stop laughing?

Laura stared at him, trying to pull him down from his liquored tower with her eyes. Eventually he saw her, and his laughter blew away for the flimsy thing it was. His attention was held for a moment by her stare, by her pretty face. Apparently he realized the face was familiar, and he made his way over to her.

"Hello . . . ," he said. "Say, you're what's-his-name . . . you're Kutner's wife, aren't you?"

Laura shuddered, and tried desperately to smile.

"Yes. How are you, Mr. Mellon?"

"Call me Clark. Lessee . . . you're Linda?"

"Laura."

"Sure. Laura. Tha's right. I remember now. Laura." He smiled. "You look very unhappy, Laura. Pretty girl like you shouldn't be unhappy. Have a drink with me. Bartender! Another drink here. Now tell me what's the trouble, Laura. Did you get stood up or something?"

"Yes. I guess I did . . . in a way."

"Well, that's too bad. Your husband do that to you?"

"No. He's playing ball tonight."

"Oh yeah. Game tonight. I forgot. Sure." He shook his head to clear it. "Your husband is a damn good ballplayer." He patted her hand, then tried to hold it for a moment.

Laura nodded and withdrew it. "I'm glad you think so," she mumbled, staggered by her own understatement. There was something so unreal about all this that it frightened her. She started to feel the shakes, and sought relief in her glass.

"We've had our eyes on him for years, Laura. Very promishing. . . ." His voice went thick again.

She felt sick to her stomach. Now your eye is on me, all over me. You're talking Mike but you're wondering how promising is Laura. She struggled for the courage she needed. It took her another five minutes of small talk to ask him:

"Why don't you bring him up, Clark?"

She tried to sound intimate, but the use of his first name somehow distressed her.

"We might." He spoke earnestly, reaching for her hand again. He smiled at her. "Would you like that?"

He made it sound like a special favor to her. Yet the words were a shot in the arm, sending shivers through her body. Her mind raced with a sudden thought: They're planning to do it! It still might be!

"Yes," and she smiled for the first time, controlling the trembling within her. "Yes, I would like that very much."

She felt his hand slide gently up and down her arm, and she wondered on what grounds this vital decision was to be made.

She drank again, no longer tasting. Her mind was a jumble of conflicting emotions, of terrible fears and hopes. She struggled for some measure of saneness to guide her, some way to get by this crisis unscathed. Through it all, there was only one dominant motivation in her mind.

"Mike has big league written all over him, Clark. Everyone says so. You should've seen him out there tonight. He tripled with two out and stole home." She was after him now. She would shame him for his absence. She would blow Mike's trumpet. She would plead and cajole. She would do anything. . . .

This was more, much more. This was the survival of their marriage. This was everything, and her heart beat wildly, pumping desperation through her.

"Well, that's fine," he said vaguely. "Damn fine ballplayer."

She looked at his dull, glassy eyes as he spoke. His concentration, what there was of it, had shifted more and more to the lines of her body. She sensed how ludicrous this was, to sit here for a half hour now, trying to fill this drunken lecher with the greatness of her husband, while he guzzled away, plotting to get her to bed with him. She saw the direction of the evening, but it did not stop her. She thought, through her gathering numbness, that she had to hurry now; it was getting late and Mike would be returning soon.

The bargain was taking form. Through the haze of stifling smoke and the endless flow of whisky, she worked his growing desire for her into an extravagant enthusiasm for Mike. She held herself from him, blowing hot and then cold, wrestling for the power he held over her head until he would speak the promise she sought from him. The magic words buzzed through her fuzzy mind: "Bring him up! Bring him up!" While the no-longer-suave Mr. Clark Mellon nodded his head and whispered sloppily "Bed . . . bed" back to her.

Laura, Laura, you're drunker than you think.

He got down from the bar stool grasping her hand and led her through the lobby to the elevator. She could not release her hand and after a while, she did not care. She stood with him as they went up to his floor, swaying against him with her eyes closed. She was conscious of the sudden stop and the sound of the squeaking gate. He led her out, his arm around her shoulder, and walked the long walk down the corridor to his room.

Oh, what's the use? What's the difference? The man's been screwing Mike for years. Your sweet, wonderful Mike. She cringed. And now he wants to screw you. Maybe this is the way it has to be . . . maybe. . . .

The door opened in front of her, and in the sudden light, she saw only the big bed. He led her toward it.

She was dizzy and tired and very weak all over.

"Bring him up!" she said once more. "You gotta bring him up!"

# 12 *The Junior Executive*

When Clark Mellon awoke, he was sprawled out, deep in the huge soft chair in the corner. He stared up through the faint light at the ceiling, aware of a weird rotation, first of the ceiling, then of the entire room. He closed his eyes tightly and tried to shake it off, but the whisky had taken over. He sat there trying to relax, to wait until the dizziness left him, anticipating that he would feel fine again. But his consciousness was sharp enough to warn him that he had more to fight than just the liquor, that there was a guilt-ridden depression building up inside of him, ready to greet his waking, sober mind. He delayed thinking of it, preferring the dizziness to the brooding.

Then he heard the long tired sigh of the woman on the bed and all the dirty pigeons came home to roost.

God, he thought. What did I do? He felt a quick current of panic shoot through him and he squirmed with his conscience. Strangely the movement brought relief, for he became suddenly aware of his twisted pants pulling against his leg. He was still dressed, more or less completely. Then he had not carried it off!

O.K., he thought sourly. What did I *almost* do?

His mind began to clear through his fuzziness and he tried to sort out the pieces. Back in the bar he had been drawn to a pretty, unhappy face. He had wanted to cut the never-ending dullness that was his life. So he'd played a little game for fun, going too far in its pursuit, not really believing he could win out until those last tired moments. But he had won. He would have traded his "victory" back for the dullness.

For this was no ordinary woman for Clark Mellon nor an ordinary set of circumstances. He had allowed drunken desire to ride roughshod over his normally reliable judgment about such things, conveniently ignoring what must have been the obvious nature of her interest in him. But he enjoyed flattering himself on the power of his charm, trying to believe that he was, in so many ways, an irresistible character. Too late, he had sensed the truth in her resignation. Despite all the drunken compulsiveness of his passion, he did not have it in him to go through with it. His ardor had shrunk with his deflated ego. This would have been something more than an act of seduction. Or, more accurately, something distastefully less. He felt dirtied by it, as though a party to some crude sale, to whoredom; but he was unable to properly measure which of them had been the whore. He had watched her sit on the end of the bed with her head lowered and her hands resting in her lap. This was her way of waiting for him, but something had urged him to move to the chair instead. There he must have passed out.

O.K., O.K. Stop judging it, he told himself. To hell with it. Forget it. You're still drunk and ill and stupid, so forget it. Just get your tail out of here. Anyplace at all . . . but out!

Clark Mellon, the bedroom scout. Line up, ladies, one at a time. Get your husbands a big-league job. Only AA and AAA wives eligible. The best lay wins.

Goddamn scout-on-the-bed.

His head was spinning again, and he let his mind go with

it. He knew he was overplaying his guilt, but the knowledge did not stop him. He even enjoyed it.

You're a helluva picture, Mr. Mellon. Look at you, sprawled out like a sloppy drunk making believe you're proud of an endless string of debaucheries. You're strictly a fizzle, useless and empty. Harvard University graduate, '38; Croydon Hotel fizzle, '51. Goddamn him again, uncle Sonofabitch Mellon. Goddamn his thirteen years of education. Sucked out everything decent you had in you with his tyranny. ("Keep your untrained mouth shut, son, and listen to the grown men who know this business. You'll be O.K.") Yes sir . . . yes sir. He dropped you, gagged, into a barrel of Jergens Lotion to slosh around in until you softened to death. Sure . . . that's what you're doing. You're getting to be like blubber.

And what do you think that woman thinks of you? Half-a-man. Feeble, flabby half-a-man. She has a real man. Hard, tough, full of guts. Probably never even heard of Jergens Lotion. Wonder what he's like in bed with her. Remember him? Remember him the first time, way back, down there in Mississippi? He told off that bastard Phipps. Like a little tiger, that Kutner. Who'd you ever tell off, Blubber? When's the last time you got tough with anyone, even yourself? You get paid for your charm, laddie, for being a stooge and a hatchet man for old Uncle James. That's the way to get ahead, that's the way.

Sure. You get ahead. Groomed to be a big executive and fill Jim Mellon's golden shoes. Harvard man in baseball. They like that. Even back in Cambridge, they like that. Every place but here in the Hotel Croydon, Minneapolis, Minnesota.

Come on, laddie. Got to get out of here. Drag your flabby tail out of this dump. Up!

He worked his way over to the bathroom, shaking with chills and cold sweat. He moved over to the sink and let a stream of cold water pour on his head. Vigorously, he rubbed his face and the back of his neck. He felt better now and steady enough on his feet. He straightened out his shirt and tie and put on his coat. Back in the bedroom, he moved quietly to the door, afraid that she would hear him and wake up. His eyes had become accustomed to the darkness and he glanced furtively at the bed as he passed. He saw the bare white sheet and the covers hanging over on the floor and it stopped him. He stood in the doorway snickering at himself. He had been sneaking out of an empty room, like a kid afraid of ghosts! He slammed the door behind him in disgust.

Then, almost as though he had just heard them, her last words rang in his ear.

"Bring him up. You gotta bring him up!"

And he thought that life must have real value for a man whose wife would do a thing like this for him.

It occurred to him now how much Mike Kutner had been victimized over the years. The man had not played a single big-league ball game! The thought somehow surprised him, for he always had assumed that Kutner would make the grade. From the beginning when Durkin Fain had told him the real qualities that make a fine ballplayer and how this man measured up—God, what a long time ago!—through the long list of Kutner's successful seasons. Somehow, they had never used him. His mind was vague with random memories. There was always some special reason, some deal cooking, somebody else they preferred. He recalled that last play-off game a few years back when Kutner had crashed into a shortstop, breaking up a double play and allowing the winning run to cross. It had cost him a broken collarbone. When he was asked to report to spring training with Chicago the following season, they had forgotten last year's play-off and saw him only as an outfielder who was too slow to get his arm in shape. So they farmed him out to Minneapolis.

That was the trouble. Too many tough breaks for Kutner.

Too many rough deals. The man kept getting the foul end of the stick. It was time he got a break!

Then, through his fading drunkenness, he had the feeling he'd been over all this before. He was tired of the problem of another man's career. So Kutner had been screwed. So what? The same things had happened to many guys up and down the river, and nobody gave much of a damn. Not in this business. Some guys make it and some don't. It's all in the way the ball bounces. What the hell, he thought, Kutner has more to show for his life than I do.

Just as suddenly as he had thought of all this, he tried to dismiss it. He had problems of his own to think of.

But then, for a weird moment, he could not think of what they were.

He reached in his pocket for his cigarettes and remembered he had left them at the bar. His watch read 11:47. There'd still be time to get a fresh pack at the cigar stand in the lobby. He pushed the elevator bell and leaned against the wall to wait.

Mellon, you're weary. What a long day! This morning in Chicago seems farther away than you'd care to recall. What the devil are you doing in Minneapolis anyway?

"Take another look at Kutner," the old man told you. "Look him over carefully, boy. He's getting older, and we wanna be sure he'll be worth messing with if we choose to."

Old Uncle Mellon. He no more wants your word on Kutner than he wants your Aunt Lulu's. He's got his eye on that sixty-thousand-dollar-bonus kid, Red Schalk, down there in Texas, and he can't wait to bring him up. He sends Keller and Phipps to see Schalk, and little old Clark out here to Minneapolis. That's two against one, pretty rough odds for a yes man who's been trained to keep his mouth shut. What's a man expected to do in a spot like this? Do you continue to be a yes man? To play it cozy? Or do you stand up to him?

Merely asking the questions was enough to bolster him.

He felt a surge of power rush through him. He pushed away from the wall and stood squarely on his two feet, willing himself sober and master of himself. His fist closed hard and tight and he smashed it into his open hand. He felt better.

Suppose you rush back to Chicago with an A 1 report on Kutner. Suppose, just suppose, you insist that this is the man, that he's still fast and twice as clever, that he hits better than ever and he's still tops with the glove. Suppose you did. . . .

The elevator doors parted before him. He shook his head as though this were all too much for him to cope with. He knew he'd be forcing the old man's hand with that kind of a report. They needed a man out there in the gardens and this would be the spot to try him. Better the seasoned, tested veteran than the rookie. Let the rookie develop in Texas without pressures on him.

Sure. With a report like that they'd have to bring Kutner up.

Then he considered how much he'd be shoving himself out on the limb. Suppose Kutner didn't measure up. Suppose he was over the hill or couldn't hit big-league pitching and Jim Mellon was right about him, had always been right about him; and Clark was wrong. How would he look then? Was this the test he wanted with the old man? Was this really the time for it?

He crossed the lobby to the cigar stand and reached in his pocket for change.

"Luckies," he said.

The man nodded and handed him a pack. Behind him, the radio quietly reported the familiar noises of the ball park.

"Game still on?" Clark was amazed.

"Yeah . . . still tied up in the thirteenth. Columbus has two men on."

He opened the package and lit up, conscious of the hoarse, tired voice of the announcer. "And there's a drive, hit sharply to center. Kutner is moving in for it. . . ." His ear caught the sound of the name. His breath quickened, and he stayed to listen, suddenly taut and nervous. He leaned against the counter and watched the cigarette quivering in his hand. "He's going to try for the catch . . . lunges for it, just off his shoe-tops. No! He couldn't hold it! It bounced off his glove and gets away. There's one run in . . . and another. . . ."

The man behind the counter groaned and flipped off the radio switch, prepared to close shop. "That's a shame," he said. "A tough one to lose. I thought he'd grab it for sure."

Clark tried to smile as he shrugged his shoulders. "It happens," he said. "Sure. It happens to the best of them."

He passed through the revolving doors out into the street, dragging on his cigarette and contemplating the direction he would take. It was strange how different he felt now. Much different. The cool night air refreshed him and he breathed in deeply. Somehow the whole burden of the evening had dropped from his shoulders and he felt good again.

Clark Mellon had made his decision in the only way he was capable of making it.

"Why should I?" He shook his head. "Why the devil should I?"

Coffee, he said to himself. A cup of hot coffee and something to eat. He remembered he hadn't eaten since noon. He spotted the neon-lit diner a few blocks down and stepped out toward it. At once he began to consider what foods would sit well on a touchy stomach.

# 13 *The Mother*

There were too many people in the room for Edna. She told herself they were here out of respect, because they had love for her—and Joe. But she didn't want to see them now. She just didn't want to see anyone. She would stare at the big chair by the window and she would think that only four days ago Joe sat there; and now it was one of the visitors. Somehow, the sight of his chair occupied by another distressed her terribly, and she allowed the emotion to rise within her, until wet-eyed again, she bathed in her tears and quiet bitterness. It didn't seem right; Joe had died too quickly and too soon.

Marian watched her anguish and came to her.

"Come on, Mama," she said. "Let's go for a little walk. It's lovely out and you haven't left the house at all."

Edna nodded docilely and rose slowly from her chair. Together they left the house and the subdued, useless mumble of mourners and went into the bright sunlight of the September day. She clung to her daughter's arm as they strolled through the busy streets, unable to hide her grief in conversation.

"It was a nice burial, wasn't it?" Edna spoke sadly. It seemed a foolish thing to say, but she had to talk about it.

"Yes, Mama."

"Your father would have thought so. It was nice."

"Yes, it was."

"Many people . . . many friends were there. They are very nice."

"Yes, Mama. Everybody came."

Everybody? No, she thought. Everybody did not come. The one she wanted most did not come.

"No," she said finally. "Not everybody."

"Mike?"

Edna nodded. "The son did not come."

She choked saying those few words. Marian pretended she did not notice.

"He will come, Mama. He will come very soon."

Edna felt how ludicrous that was.

When? When he's good and ready to come? Too late. It's too late already. She struggled to control herself. Yet when she spoke, it was to excuse his absence. She repeated the words she said to his father.

"I suppose he couldn't get away. Yes. He will come."

She found it difficult to understand. What was so important that could keep a son away from a father's deathbed? She began to torture herself with sharp memories from twenty years back of quarrels and recriminations that had all but torn the family apart. She had suffered through them quietly, gently struggling for a compromise in their attitudes. And recently she had seen the beginnings of such a compromise through the long winters that brought them together. It was as though the antagonisms were tired and dying of age. Time had mellowed the father and the son. It didn't matter that neither had basically changed; what moved her most was their growing fondness for each other that had begun to fade out the past.

But only just begun. In the early spring of this year she had seen them plan a Sunday-morning fishing trip, proposed by the father as a farewell event before Mike left for training season and enthusiastically endorsed by the son. In the very early morning, as they ate the hot cakes and bacon and coffee she had prepared for them, she shared their laughter and high spirits. They had left with their borrowed gear slung over their shoulders, arm in arm, like a couple of old cronies on a weekend party.

Finally, she had thought, after all these years, Joe Kutner and his son went on that fishing trip. She had smiled over her hot coffee and watched the sun rise into the kitchen window, and she had found herself hoping ardently that the fish would be party to this great occasion.

Behind her, she had heard scuffling by the stove, and she turned to see Laura, still full of sleep, pouring a cup of coffee.

"Hello, Mama," she said. "Is it 'good morning' yet?"

"Gracious, child, what got you up?"

"Smell of bacon and cakes and coffee, maybe. And maybe the sight of your son with his pop. They're worth getting up for."

Edna smiled. Laura spoke from the heart. Always Laura was tender.

"There's only coffee left, Laura."

". . . and I'm too late for the others?"

Edna nodded. "They left almost an hour ago."

Laura stirred her coffee in deep thought.

"He was anxious to go, Mama. A simple thing like fishing with his old man. I think it meant a lot to him."

"It meant a lot to Joe."

Laura smiled and reached for Edna's hand.

"And to you, too, Mama."

But the men returned earlier than they were expected, silent and lacking jubilation. They smiled without their eyes as they greeted her, and they couldn't quite laugh as they laid a tiny little fish in the huge frying pan. Edna saw at once that in some way the trip hadn't been everything they'd wanted, that the old wounds were still too tender under the rough edges of their pride. Oh, the wounds would heal in time, she knew, for they both wanted it so.

And now, it could not be. Time had failed them, having suddenly run out without warning, leaving them all unfulfilled. This was what crushed her now. She had watched Joe suffer through his last hours, shocked by the terrible suddenness of the attack that he knew would kill him. He had wanted more time. He had asked for his son repeatedly, shouting through his pain that he was not yet ready to die.

When she and Marian returned from their walk, they saw Mike standing on the porch, waiting. She had not seen him these many months, and she broke into tears as he came to her. He held her gently and patted her arm, saying nothing, and led her back to the porch. The fact that her son was not in tears only added to her own.

When they were spent, she wiped her eyes, a little ashamed of another show of grief.

Finally, he spoke.

"I'm sorry, Mama."

"You couldn't come home, Mike? You couldn't come home sooner?"

She saw his expression of pain.

"I'm sorry. I just couldn't."

She waited patiently for his explanation.

"There was one more ball game, Mama. It was important to me. Terribly important."

"One more game?" she asked. "Your father collapsed four days ago!"

His fists beat hard against his thighs.

"I know," he said. "But it . . . it rained."

"It rained?"

"Yes, Mama. We were rained out two days. I . . . we didn't play that game till last night."

He stopped there. She saw his suffering and turned from him. She waited for the rest of it. For a long time he did not speak.

She had to ask him: "What was so important about this game, Mike?"

He shrugged hopelessly. His voice, at first eager to explain, became subdued.

"I was trying to win the batting crown, Mama. The highest batting average. This has been my best year, and I thought it would be a big thing if I won it. You see, I needed two hits. Just two hits."

Everything he said seemed almost sinful to Edna, this meaningless jargon about foolish awards. She heard the mounting guilt in his words, and she knew he thought this too.

"Well," she asked. "Did you get them?"

He looked over at her questioningly.

"Did I get them? Get what, Mama?"

"The two hits you needed."

He turned from her quickly.

"No . . . ," he whispered.

"You didn't even get one of them, did you?"

He shook his head.

"No. I lost the title."

Then, somehow, the words came out; even as she spoke them, she felt they were wrong:

"Your father should have timed it better for you."

She saw his eyes smarting at her sarcasm. Suddenly, she was overcome. She poured out her anger and her grief in a rising voice that became unrecognizable to her.

"What have you done, Mike! All you could manage was a few words on a telegram! A few cheap little words about how you hoped he would feel O.K.! Imagine that . . . how he would feel O.K.! My God, Mike! Your father had a heart attack coming home from the mines. He lay two days in the hospital, dying. And he wanted to see *you*, Mike! He wanted to tell you he loved you, that all his life he loved you, only all these years he didn't know how to show it. He didn't know a lot of things. He wasn't a smart man, maybe. But he wanted to apologize to you. Yes, your father would've apologized for all the bad years between you. But you weren't here! Why weren't you here, Mike? *Why!*"

She fought back her tears as hard as she could. It wasn't easy any more; she was tired and too accustomed to crying.

She saw him turn away now, strained and confused, wearing the torment of his irrevocable error on his face.

"I don't know what it is any more, Mama. Fifteen years. . . . I've been fighting this thing for fifteen years. Up there in Minneapolis all I could think of was the fifteen years and proving that I could be a success. I thought maybe this one little thing, this batting championship, would clinch it for me next year." He stopped now, and snarled at his own words in disgust: "Next year . . . oh, Christ!" His hand reached over for hers. "What's happened to me, Mama? What's happened?"

Edna didn't know what to say. She could speak only through the pain she felt.

"You shouldn't have let him die that way, Michael."

Michael. She hadn't used that name since he was a child—a quiet, little child in a house full of women. Little Michael, they had called him, until he'd reached the age of protest. "The name is Mike," he would shout, and they'd say, "O.K., Mike. Mike it is." And the girls would smile at each other for his determination.

She looked down now at the balding head in her lap and she stroked his neck to comfort him. Finally, he rose from the chair and wiped his glasses. He stood there looking at her sadly, and she thought through his silence of all the words that had been left unspoken over these years, and she balanced them against the many terrible, angry things that had been said. O.K., my son . . . you're sorry and full of grief and guilt. You've learned something of yourself and your family that was never quite a family for you. Perhaps it wasn't your fault. Poor Joe. It was his fault, but he never had a chance.

"Laura is inside, Mama," he said finally. "Won't you come in and talk to her? She came to see you, too."

"All right, Son. I'll be in after a moment or two."

Edna sat alone on the porch in the gathering twilight, watching the sun dip behind the houses across the street. The dim, solemn voices behind her were gradually drowned in the comforting squeak of the runners on the old floor as she began to rock. She began to relax, for the first time in these last terrible days. Let it be over, she thought, let it be over. In the hidden distance of an adjacent street, she heard the sound of children playing, their laughter echoing gently along the rows of houses. The mother of three smiled through her grief and nodded her head at her memories.

After a while, she got up and went back into the house.

# 14 *The Rookie*

The rookie walked into the batter's circle behind home plate and listened to the noise of the largest crowd he'd ever seen. He swung two bats over his head, stretching the muscles in his powerful arms and remembering the deafening crowd-sounds of his past. Dropping to one knee, he stroked his favorite piece of shiny ash and wiped the dirt from the tapered white barrel. He could not resist looking up at the towering stadium around him. For the fourth time today, he waited there for his turn at bat; each time he had tingled at the exultation that ran through him, repeating under his breath for his senses to enjoy, "You're in the big time, Mike; you're in the big time!" And he reveled in the excitement that beat against his insides and almost made him laugh.

But now a wave of savage noise rose from the stands and brought him back to the sticky afternoon of this crucial September ball game. He turned to watch Red Schalk fidgeting in the batter's box and then the pitch twisting at half speed to the plate. He saw the hitter's badly timed stride and watched the ball curve elusively by him, the bat remaining ineptly on his shoulder. He heard the umpire's elongated cry:

"Stee-rike one!"

Mike braced himself for the new roar of the crowd, multiplying the tension in this ninth-inning climax, and considered the game situation. There were two men out, and the tying and winning runs danced helplessly off second and first, itching to head for the plate. The game was going down to the wire; it was clearly up to Red Schalk.

The rookie joined the bellowing mob behind him, calling aloud his desperate hopes.

"Keep alive, Red. Keep alive!"

But within him, he knew he meant something else: keep alive for me . . . for *me*. Get on base and leave those runners sitting out there. Mike felt himself begging for the hero's job—a chance to hit that big blow and bust up the game. He transferred his body, his power, his timing, his coordination, and most of all, his will into Red's. This day was a personal climax, far more important to him than the game. It had to be his day; he knew damn well he had it coming to him.

"Mike!" he heard. "The rosin. Gimme the goddamn rosin!"

He looked up to see Red walking toward him from the plate. He picked up the rosin bag and went to meet him.

"Sonofabitch." Red was muttering under his breath.

"Take it easy, Red." Mike tried to steady him. The young outfielder, a veteran now, was taking it hard. "Get loose."

Red rubbed the rosin over his sweaty hands.

"Can't get 'em dry enough. . . ."

Scare-sweat, the rookie thought. The guy is scared up there. A chance to be a hero and the guy is scared.

"Take your time, Red."

"Sonofabitch, Mike, can't get loose."

"Take it easy." He noticed now the guy was shaking.

Mike went back to the batter's circle and spat his contempt. He'd give half his pay to be in this spot right now, but the redhead was blind with fear, frozen solid up there. And this was a bonus baby. Red Schalk, the new-type ballplayer. They had handed him sixty thousand dollars for being a high-school hero, for hitting .400 against seventeen-year-old pitchers. Sixty Gs for merely signing his name! Mike thought back to the brick wall black with coal dust and to Durkin Fain, and the two-hundred and fifty dollars he ended up swallowing. He'd been born in the wrong decade.

He grunted his disgust. "Com' on, Red." Then his tone became one of demand. "Get on that sack!"

Mike watched the pitcher lean into the shadows to pick up the catcher's sign, his intense concentration hidden under the lowered peak. The pitch spun in, an exact facsimile of the previous strike, and it tied the redhead in the same knot. Mike groaned helplessly, and bit harshly into the back of his hand.

Fooled him twice. The lousy redhead. Fooled the big-time major leaguer, overanxious in the clutch like an overgrown high-school kid. Red had never even waved his stick. Christ, you'd think a guy three years in this league would know how to get set.

He shivered as if an icy wind had passed through him, frantic now that everything vital to him seemed so far beyond his control. The batter was out of the box again, playing with the rosin bag.

"Mike. . . ." The voice was low and charged with fear. "I've got a pain in my gut. Can't work it out."

Mike looked up into the quivering face, amazed at its pallor, and he knew that the kid had given up on himself.

"I don't feel good, Mike," Red was saying. "I can't stand up there. . . ."

Mike thought of the drunks he had sobered up; this looked like the toughest job of all.

"Don't tell that to the skipper, Red," he said. "I got a feeling old Tracy wouldn't appreciate it."

So now the bottom was really falling out. This was supposed to be the hitter who would give Mike Kutner a crack at the big one. Mike felt himself sinking helplessly into the quicksand of the other man's fear. The towering double tiers that enclosed them seemed to loom higher, much higher.

"Com' on, Schalk," the umpire growled. "Let's get the game movin'."

Mike grabbed the hitter by the arm. What the hell could he say? "Get back in there and hit or you'll never hit again. Not in this league, anyway." His voice was harsh and charged with anger. "Be tough, Red. Be tough up there!" And he turned away, spitting out the taste of his words. Maybe the jerk oughta pray too.

Oh you bum, you cruddy bum! He muttered the words under his breath, and let his memory take him back four years to a Florida spring-training camp. There he had first come across Red Schalk, a pink-cheeked, nineteen-year-old kid out of Georgia. He remembered how they had babied him, trying to justify the ridiculous sixty-grand investment. He was Jim Mellon's fair-haired boy, the big prospect. He had heard later how they coddled Red all season, letting him nurse his Texas League .302 batting average to make it look like something. A year later, they had moved Schalk up to Chicago.

Mike had burned up at the move. He'd outhit Red by two dozen points, and in a tougher league. He was a dozen times the better glove-man. What about the promises they had made? Why not him? He had demanded an answer.

He remembered the present of a box of cigars and the soft, ingratiating smile of Clark Mellon. "Sure, Mike, you're a better ballplayer at the moment. But we're after the younger kids. By all rights you should be up there, and if it hadn't been for the war and those years you lost, I'm sure you would be. Sorry as hell, Mike, but that's the way she goes. A kid of nineteen has a much longer ride ahead of him."

Sure, the wrong damn decade. Now he was thirty-five, an old man of thirty-five, a rookie of thirty-five playing his first game in the majors. It did not escape him that he was here by a fluke. Chicago had been riddled with injuries driving down the stretch, and they'd decided to use Mike in this crucial

September series rather than some green youngster. At the last moment, Mellon had called him in Minneapolis.

It was weird, the way it happened. He was just about to go for a walk with Laura, a simple little morning walk that would take them away for a lingering breakfast in a pleasant family restaurant they enjoyed. He was sitting on the bed, watching her finish dressing. She was putting on a fall suit for the first time, and it crossed his mind that she was doing it to remind him that the summer was ending, and another winter coming on. The thought set off a depressing chain of emotions. It was then that the phone rang and he listened to the peremptory orders from Chicago. They came so suddenly that he became dizzy. Afterwards he had to lie back on the bed to ease the shock.

He had to hurry with Laura to catch the plane. Now he thought sourly, Two minutes later and I wouldn't have been there to receive the call.

They flew down to Chicago a few hours before game time and taxied directly to the ball park, with hardly time to catch a bite to eat. Sixteen years he had plugged away for this chance. When they finally found they needed him, they threw it in his face like an insult.

In the locker room before the game, he knew the others were watching him dress, but he didn't care. A thirty-five-year-old rookie was something of a freak. Those who knew him saw his determination and understood. To the others it was simply a matter of winning a pennant and the pile of dough that goes with it. But to Mike it was more, much more. He looked at them quickly, responding to their greetings. He knew that some must be thinking he was good, as good as almost any of them, and if the ball had bounced differently, it might have been Kutner up there all these years instead of them. But now he was thirty-five, and he could be called old. He saw those who did not know him look curiously across the room at the partially bald head, the dark leathery skin of his neck, the heavy, uneven walk; and he thought they'd be wondering how many years they had left for themselves. Respectfully, they had left him alone while he dressed.

Mike had waited to finish until they were all out. His uniform was clean and he liked its fresh, sterile smell. He laced his shoes tightly and put on his new cap. With pride he didn't bother to conceal, he walked over to the big mirror by the shower room and stood solidly before it. He looked at himself for a long moment, allowing the glow to penetrate. The excitement of it tickled the back of his neck, bringing goose pimples to his skin. He had never felt so wonderful.

"You're here, Mike . . . ," he said out loud. "You finally made it!" Then he clenched his fists as the emotion welled up within him. "You're here, goddammit, and you're not going back!"

Behind him, he heard the scuffle of heels on the concrete floor. He shifted his focus briefly to see an old man coming down the aisle. Finally, he turned from the mirror to get his glove, suddenly conscious that the man had stopped and was watching him for a longer time than Mike felt natural. But this was not the time to wonder and he closed his locker and got ready to leave for the diamond.

Then he heard him, and at once it began to make sense.

"Hello, Kutner."

Mike spun around to face him, drawn by a quality in the voice he somehow recognized. He saw the old man, older-looking than anyone he thought he knew, wrinkled and squint-eyed, yet erect and alert. He saw the smile as he moved toward the outstretched hand, and at once his memory bridged the gap.

"Hello, Mr. Fain," he said.

They shook hands warmly, and Mike met his piercing eyes.

"I was in Chicago for this Philly series, Kutner. I heard you were here. Just thought I'd drop back to say hello."

The words sounded trivial as he said them, too trivial for

the importance of the moment. But their hands remained clasped for a long moment, covering the silence between them, and he saw in Durkin Fain's searching look that he felt deeply about Mike Kutner's finally making it.

What do you see, old man? Don't compare me with the kid you went out on a limb for. You're looking at an aging athlete, tired, almost bald, as old in his profession as you are in yours. Remember what you said, Mr. Fain: "I'm gonna make you a major leaguer." That's what you told me.

Sure. Here I am.

But this ain't what you meant, Mr. Fain. This ain't the way you meant it to be. I shouldn't be a rookie, Mr. Fain. I sure as hell don't look like one.

He looked hard at the old scout again, suddenly tired of this feeble self-examination. He could see the other man now and the brutal thing that the years had done to him.

"I heard you've been coaching the college boys, Mr. Fain."

The old man smiled. "No more, son. Too old to do that well. I haven't been up to it the last year or two."

Mike didn't know what to say to him. He turned back to his locker and grabbed the fifty-cent cigar he'd bought at the terminal. He had planned to smoke it later, as a kind of celebration for himself.

"Here, Mr. Fain," he said. "Have a cigar for old time's sake."

Fain took it, and put it in his pocket.

"Thanks," he said briefly.

"Don't you smoke 'em any more?"

Durkin Fain nodded.

"This one . . . after the game."

Mike nodded. He tightened his belt and started to the door, stopped and looked back. It was all so brief, so incomplete. There was nothing said. After all these years, there was nothing to say. It seemed strange, for he had thought of the scout a thousand times.

Fain smiled at him.

"Have a good day, son," he said, and then he nodded. "It ain't never too late."

The umpire's voice brought him out of his reverie.

"Play ball!" he hollered.

Mike raised his eyes to Schalk at the plate and watched him feebly waving his bat through the air as if he were flagging a train. Red was now an empty shell, a skeleton of bones in a big-league uniform, faking through the motions of being a hitter. Look at him, Mike thought. Look at what they picked instead of me!

The years of resentment boiled up inside him at this sickening symbol of his frustration. His disgust rose to his throat, almost choking him, and he exploded with angry violence.

"Stand up there like a pro, you punk!" he hollered. "Get on that goddamn base!"

He looked out to the pitcher's mound, thinking how much he'd like to be the chucker for this one pitch. If that mug knew the insides of Schalk's guts he'd be laughing out loud. But the pitcher was fingering his own rosin bag, and Mike smiled in spite of himself; that one was probably scared too. The rookie felt like the only veteran in the ball park.

The pitcher looked for a sign, a studied smile on his face. He'll curve him again, Mike thought. Any decent curve will get him. Red can't see any more, just little colored spots in front of his eyes. Count him out, ump. Red Schalk, K.O.

The curve spun rapidly in. Red went through the motions, stepping like he knew what he was doing, as if to take his cut. The ball curved sharply away from the corner too far inside, but it never reached the catcher. It bounded off Red's leg.

"Take yer base!"

Red lay moaning in the dust, rubbing his thigh.

Well, kiss my butt, Mike thought as he went to him. That was a sharp-breaking pitch but Schalk could have stepped back.

"You O.K., Red?" Maybe the guy did pray at that.

"Yeah . . . yeah. I'm O.K.," he mumbled. "It's funny, Mike. I never even saw it." And he got up, loosening his leg on the way to first. There was applause from the stands.

Mike grinned. It's good you didn't. It's goddamn good you didn't. Then he turned back to the plate, his concentration quickly on the job at hand.

Behind him, the crowd's excitement rose at the bases-loaded climax. He swung the two bats like a windmill and listened to the wild stampede.

It's all yours now, there's nothing left to the day but you. Go back, Mike, go back ten thousand turns at bat. None of them matter, none of them. Just this one, Mike. Just this one, big, beautiful moment.

He heard the manager, Al Tracy, from the bench, an anticlimax to his own thoughts.

"It's up to you, Kutner. Show me something!"

I'll show you something, Tracy, you dumb bastard. He tossed away the extra stick and started to dig a foothold in the batter's box. This is the turn that counts. The other three meant little. The neat sacrifice bunt, the base on balls, and that long well-tagged fly ball the left fielder dragged down. They were all routine. This is the spot, Mike. Blast one. Bust up the game.

They were really down to the wire now. All around him a tremendous din, wild, persistent, racked his ears. He looked up through the tight joy in his heart to face the pitcher. He saw the three runners dance anxiously off their bases. From the bench they were hollering at him:

"Com' on, Mike. . . . Clobber one!"

The pitcher was getting his sign, this time without a smile.

Here we go, rookie. Tag one and you're a major leaguer for the rest of your natural-born life. This is judgment day, the final one.

For Mike, there were no doubts. As sure as he was standing in the batter's box, he knew he was going to come through. He could hardly keep the smile off his face. This is the spot he'd waited sixteen years for.

He watched the pitcher take a full, slow-swinging wind-up. He cocked his bat high over his shoulder and waited for the throw. It came at half speed, spinning toward the outside corner. He stepped toward the pitch and lashed viciously at the ball with full power. As he finished his pivot, he knew he had gotten only a slice of it. The ball skidded off into the upper grandstand behind him.

"Stee-rike one!"

He leaned over to pick up dirt, muttering profanities at himself. He was set. He saw it all the way. Yet he hadn't met it squarely. Was it because he was tired? Or too eager? Then he realized it had happened to him too many times over the past year. His memory flashed him pictures of powerful drives off just such a pitch, years ago. But now he didn't always get around in time. There was something missing; the thin edge of timing and coordination had dulled over the years. He kicked viciously at the dirt at his feet and sprayed it over the ground. He remembered the words as they came from Clark Mellon: Thirty-five and past your prime.

He heard the cries from the other bench now, beamed directly at him over the crowd noises.

"Hey, pop, how'd you break in here?"

He took a moment to adjust his cap, and looked squarely into their dugout. They were all on the front step, nervously bellowing at him. He knew most of them from the minors, from training camps in March, from exhibition games year after year. Christ, who's been around more than Mike Kutner! Look at them: Black, Donnelly, Simpson, Caulfield. Yeah, Charlie Caulfield, the clown. Lost-in-the-sun Caulfield, the club's fifth outfielder.

His voice was as sharp as ever.

"Well, well. If it ain't the great lover! I thought you'd been pensioned off, Kutner."

Mike hitched up his pants. Very funny, he thought. What the hell does he do on that ball club—floor shows on washed-out nights? The guy who laughed his way to the top. Seven years in the majors, the only full-fledged clown on spikes.

Goddamn.

"Hey, baldy, where's your cane?"

He stepped back in the box and dug in again. Frig 'em all, big and small. He would talk with his bat. He thought now he would like that same pitch once more, just to prove he could still ride it. But he knew damn well he wouldn't get it again.

"Hey, rookie. Let's see that fine head of skin."

Be set, Mike, and stay loose. This punk has nothing he can throw by you. The ducks are on the pond, Mike, yours to knock in. It's a picnic, man. A picnic!

He watched the arm swing up and around, the big stride toward the plate, and the little white ball spun bullet-speed toward him. It came in shoulder high but too tight, and Mike fell carefully away from it.

"Stee-rike two!"

No . . . no, dammit . . . *no!* He turned fiercely on the umpire, ready to begin his protest. Then he backed away, knowing that rage would serve only to defeat him. Swallow it, Mike. Eat it!

No anger, Mike. You can't hit in a rage; not in this league, anyway. Let the crowd do the bellowing. Not you. There's no way to measure the pitch any more; it went by too long ago. The pitch is dead, long live the goddamn ump!

He slid his hand down the length of the smooth barrel of the bat and began thinking two-strike thoughts. You gotta stay loose, Mike. It's just another human arm throwing baseballs at you. You hit guys faster than this down in Texas twelve years ago when you were a kid. Just protect that plate, and cut away. You'll put a dent in this new stick and hang it over the fireplace like it had antlers. "This is the bat, sonny. Ten years ago your daddy blasted one they'll never forget!"

Easy, Mike. No anger, no anger.

"Play ball!"

Mike stood a few feet from the plate, still trying to collect himself. It had been a terrible call, that strike, at a terrible time. It put him behind the pitcher, making it tough for him to cut loose. He had to guard the plate now, instead of making the guy come in there with it. He couldn't pick out the throw he liked. He thought it was the kind of call umps would never make on a star. But on a rookie. . . .

Mike turned, still feeling the drumming in his gut.

"Take it easy, ump. I got something riding on this pitch, so take it slow."

The ump lifted his mask and leaned toward him.

"You're pretty sassy for a rookie, buddy."

Sure, Mike thought. There it was.

"Yeah," he said, as sour as he could make it.

"Get up there and hit, buddy."

Behind him he heard the skipper again, yelling to him as if his words were worth a million.

"To hell with him, Kutner. You got the big one left!"

Mike cleared his throat and nodded. Sure, Tracy. Nothing to it.

And Tracy would say: Sorry you had to swallow a call like that, Kutner, but you still gotta produce. That's what you'll get paid for, and nothing else matters. The umpire could call another zombie against you and you're out, just as if you whiffed one; and the game is gone. An hour later, it don't matter that it wasn't your fault. You didn't produce. That's what mattered. It's just a big round zero in the papers tomorrow.

Then he heard the jockeys again.

"Hey, grampa, who does yer grandson play for?"

"Get out the rockin' chair. Here comes ole Kutner!"

Mike reached down to finger some dirt. He rubbed his hands dry and gripped tightly the narrow handle of his bat. Back in the batter's box, he dug his spikes in position. He faced the pitcher and started thinking baseball again.

Get set, he told himself. Be ready for anything. It's still up to you. He can't get it by you, he can't get it by you. . . .

"Baldy! Hey! B-a-l-d-e-e-e-e-e-e!"

The arm swung around, and Mike's eyes followed the movement of the pitcher's hand, picking up the small quirk in the pitcher's delivery that indicated a curve ball. He set himself and moved his body toward the pitch. The ball spun down the inside and started curving too soon. He pivoted with all his power and met the pitch out front with the fat part of the bat. A sharp crack rang out, beautiful and clear, and everyone in the park knew the ball had been really tagged.

Mike took off for first, watching it sail up and up into the sky, way above the stadium roof, soaring deep toward the left-field bleachers. He heard the tremendous ear-splitting roar of the fifty thousand; and his feet left the ground and he was floating on air. It was the big one! You've done it, Mike! You blasted one in the clutch, with the sacks loaded!

He rounded first base with tears in his eyes and a single all-embracing thought in his head: you've done it!

As he made his turn, he looked up again to follow the end flight of the ball, wanting to feast on the sight of it disappearing into the seats out there. Suddenly, his throat constricted. The ball . . . it wasn't falling right. The wind above the roof had caught it and was pulling it toward the foul line. He followed it down now, sinking deep into the bleachers, but at an angle he could not guess. He saw the foul pole, the tall white shaft, and he froze as the ball fell out of sight into a wild scramble of spectators.

He never heard the umpire's call. Short of second base, he stopped and turned slowly back toward home plate. From some place deep within him, his instincts had called it a foul ball.

He was right.

It took him a long time to walk back to the plate. He needed all the time he could get now. A sense of failure swept over him and he couldn't shake it off. For a moment, he thought he'd been feeling it all day. Luck was down on him just like always; the *real* luck, luck when you needed it. Then he realized what he was doing to himself, and he cursed his weakness. He looked toward his dugout as he walked and nodded toward the players shouting encouragement from the steps.

But the thought of trying again depressed him, as if he were suddenly very tired. He wondered how much drive he had left in him. For too long, he had pushed his body and his spirit. Now, it seemed to him ridiculously unfair that his entire effort was to be packed into one brief moment of time. One more pitch, maybe. It must be now. There's no more time. No more.

Maybe it was too much to ask of a man.

What do you say, Mike? Time is a string running out. You can't wind it back. How long is the string for you? There's a beautiful woman named Laura sitting back there, choking on her fears and probably crying her heart out right this minute. She'll sit this one out, loaded down with all your jockeys and umpires and foul balls. She's sitting out time. For her the string unravels under a box seat at a ball park, day after day, year after year. And all she can do is sit and watch.

Maybe it was too much to ask of a woman.

He felt the knocking of his heart against his ribs. He tried to breathe deeply again. He moved in toward the plate where the bat boy was holding his bat, waiting for him.

"Straighten it out, Mike," the kid said.

Sure, sure. Stop the wind and straighten it out.

He ran his hand along the end of the bat, subconsciously feeling for the dent. He wished he had more time.

"All right, Kutner," the umpire called to him. "Batter up!"

Mike played with his belt, trying to stall. His mind was cluttered with doubts and he had to shake them loose. Hitting is a state of mind, as important to coordination, timing, and power as a good pair of eyes. He was thinking of too many things now to be a hitter.

"You're through, baldy. Too bad. You shot yer wad on a foul ball!"

"Back to the mines, old-timer!"

He was about to step in and the yell backed him away. Back to the mines. The words rattled around in his head like loose marbles. Can you hear that, Pop? Wherever you are, can you hear that? Is that what you meant way back when you threw my glove in the furnace? Is that what you meant? Back to the mines?

"Com' on, Kutner. Get in there before they dig you under."

"Wrap him up and send him home. He's through!"

"This is it, four-eyes. Three strikes is dead!"

He seemed to feel their hot breath on his neck and the overloud voices blasting in his ear. The ump was at his side, impatiently fingering the ball-and-strike tabulator.

"Let's go, Kutner. Two strikes." The blue suit was insistent. "Play ball!"

Come on, Mike. You gotta get up there. You gotta get up there and hit.

("It ain't never too late, son.")

Christ, Mr. Fain . . . yes it is. I can feel it now. For the first time I can feel it. It doesn't really matter any more, does it? You must know this, Mr. Fain. What's in this pitch for you? It's only your pride that's at stake now and nothing more. There'll be no apologies to you, no rewards. It's too late for that. You're a has-been with a record of improper decisions. Your string has run out long ago.

They've beaten you, Mr. Fain. You did what was right but they threw you away. But I won't let them do it to me, goddammit. Not to me.

Suddenly, Mike leaned over and picked up a tiny pebble. He told himself that unless he put it in his pocket he wouldn't hit. For a moment he stood there, studying the pebble, debating what to do with it. It was the kind of foolish superstition he had always rejected. If you let yourself go, a million little things distracted you, threatened you, stripped you of your will to hit. He had seen guys who became slaves to their petty superstitions. Like Herman Cruller. This stopped him again; he hadn't thought of the guy in years. Herman the weak, Herman the softhearted. ("Never be like me, Mike. Be tough. And then learn to be tougher.")

He threw away the pebble and stepped up to the plate.

They were ready for him again.

"Yo, daddy. I heard you were in the war. Which one?"

He moved his bat around, trying to loosen the clothing on his shoulders. It didn't seem to set properly. He dug and redug his back foot into the corner of the box. He felt that something about his position was different, some minute arrangement of his feet or the balance of his body as he set himself. He watched the pitcher get his sign and his mind began an agonizing conjecture. Would he curve him again, half speed? Would he waste one, or make him cut at something bad? Would he try to throw one by him, a hard one under his chin, or low outside? It was hard not to guess. Don't guess, he told himself. That's suicide. You're still the hitter. Just be ready.

He cocked his bat over his shoulder and was conscious of the wet pull of his shirt against him. He made a quick movement of his body to release it. He thought of stepping out of the box again. Then he remembered the pebble and he wondered about his scorn of superstitions. He regretted not saving it.

Mike watched the pitcher nod to the man crouched behind him. The wind-up was calm and kept him waiting. It seemed endless.

O.K., Mike, guard that dish. No fear. Guard that dish. The ball spun lightly off the pitcher's fingers and fluttered toward the plate. He saw it start to break, a slow curve breaking toward the outside corner. It didn't look good to him, but it might be. In a split second he had to decide, his judgment shaken by his fear of the umpire. The delicate instrument of timing was shattered and the balance of his power upset. He stepped toward the pitch and started his swing, lashing at the ball with half a will, half a prayer.

He didn't come near it.

The game was over.

For a moment, he just stood there, wondering how sick he must have looked. He even tried to guess how far outside the plate the ball had passed. Then, the roar of the crowd rose from the stands like a wave, blasting into his ears the full consequence of his failure. It was too much for him.

No. It couldn't be. No!

"*No!*" he screamed. "*Goddammit!*" And he beat the plate brutally with his bat, refusing to accept it. He turned to face the pitcher's mound, swinging his bat as if ready to hit again, demanding that the game go on.

"Throw the goddamn ball!" he hollered savagely. "*Throw the goddamn ball!*"

But their entire team had gathered around the pitcher-hero, slapping at his back, clutching and tearing at his triumph. They lifted him to their shoulders to cart him off the field. Mike could only watch them, letting their spirited laughter bite into him, as if it were aimed at him. He hated them now—the lucky sonofabitchin' pitcher, the lousy jockeys. He stared at them furiously, trying to smear them with his hatred, hoping to provoke one more derisive catcall that might unleash his rage and goad him to attack them all. But they never saw him. Finally, he turned away from the plate for the long walk in.

He moved toward the bedlam of the stands now, and the screaming faces. A moment ago they were all yours, Mike. They were yelling for you. He looked into the dejection of his dugout and his naked failure came home to him. In a rage, he pulled his bat back, ready to fling it into the crowd, to scatter them and shut them up. But somehow he knew better. He held on.

In the stands behind the dugout, they were waiting for him, the harsh faces of the two-bit punks who wallow in the luxury of a last kick at the guy who is down.

"Kutner . . . you stink!"

"You're a bum."

"Ooh . . . what a bum!"

He bristled at their hoots and sneering laughter and wondered how he could get through that gantlet. He gripped his bat tightly as he approached them, trying not to hurry his walk.

"What a star! Where'd they pick you up?"

"Back to the minors, Kutner."

Their stale-beer spittle sprayed into his hot face. A rough hand reached over and stole his cap from his head.

"You won't need this no more."

"Naah. Back to the bush leagues!"

He stopped on the bottom step and looked up at them. They taunted him, waving his cap just out of reach. Inside him, suddenly, the dam burst—the dam of repression and control and patience. He flung himself toward the cap, over the dugout and into the stands. In a second he caught the terrified heckler and wrenched the cap from him. With his other hand, he started smashing at him in a wild silent fury.

At once the crowd dispersed, scrambling over each other and the seats like scared chickens. Out of danger themselves, they watched in terror. The ushers and cops came for him, four of them pulling him off, trying to hold him still, for his rage was only partly spent.

They carried him down the steps again, into the dim corridors below the stands, and stood him hard against the wall, just outside the locker room.

"Take it easy, rookie," a cop said, his hands tight on Mike's wrist.

Mike breathed heavily, and looked through the door at the ballplayers inside. He saw them, glum and silent on their stools, unlacing their shoes, quietly passing around smokes and beer. As he felt the heavy restraint of the cops, he saw Red Schalk amongst them, close to the door, and their eyes met. His arms were pinned to his side and he tried to wriggle loose.

"Shut the door!" he hollered suddenly. "*Shut the friggen door!*"

"Easy, rookie, easy," he heard again. "That ain't the way for a major leaguer to act."

The words knifed into him, twisting into his thoughts, and he lowered his eyes from the redhead's. He stared blankly at the floor, wanting to cry. There was a pain in his chest as though a ton of rocks were pressing on him.

It was time to stop struggling.

He heard the door of the locker room close, and looked up to see Durkin Fain standing in front of it. The old man turned to one of the guards and nodded.

"That's all right," he said. "He'll be O.K. now."

One at a time they released him, furtively, anticipating some renewed outburst. But Mike just stood there, without even moving his arms, oblivious to his freedom. Gradually, as he subsided, he began to cry. As the tears came, the muscles in his face did not move or alter his expression. It was as if he did not believe he was crying at all.

It's all right to cry. Nothing much matters. Go ahead and cry. The whole damn day is unreal anyway—a crazy, wild, sweating dream. The dream you never remember. What's happened? Why is everything so different?

You're all washed up, that's why. You're empty. There's nothing left in your guts to drive you.

Cry, Mike. You've finally blown off the lid. Cry. No one cares if you cry.

He stood against the wall, letting the tears come, a flood of anguish and bitterness and despair. When it was spent, he took off his glasses and brushed his uniform sleeve across his face. His chest was heaving, he was weak and tired. But somehow, in a way he did not understand, he felt very much relieved. He nodded at Durkin Fain and opened the door to the locker room. Together, they went in.

The players looked up from their quiet dressing and nodded at him. They had stripped and showered and for the most part, he knew, cleansed themselves of the transient pain of defeat. There would be another crucial game tomorrow. He sat in front of his locker, staring at his feet. The late afternoon sun pouring in the window glistened off the metal of his spikes. Like a jewel, he thought. He flexed the muscles of his feet, enjoying the snugness of his shoes. No other shoes could be so comfortable. Whenever he put on spikes, he wanted to run. His whole body was tired now, but not his feet. They never grew tired in spikes.

Behind him, he heard the door open and shut. By the sudden stillness around him, he could guess who it was, but he chose not to turn. He felt as if he might have been waiting for this.

"Where's Tracy? Where is he?"

Mike listened to the coarse, old voice, and he repeated the words to himself with imitated inflections. He couldn't answer the question. Tracy was probably taking his shower.

No one bothered to answer. The voice defied their silence and bellowed on.

"Tell him to use Hahn tomorrow! Tell him to shove his goddamn logic up his butt!"

And the door slammed shut again.

Tell him to use Hahn! Not Kutner. Hahn. Kutner was a mistake. He folds up like a scared kid. Strictly minor league stuff. Like I always said, goddammit; just like I've said for years.

Yeah. You're Jim Mellon. You're always right.

He leaned over now, ready to unlace his shoes, depressed by the fullness of his failure. Suddenly, he stopped and rose to his feet, to stand again on spikes, trying to recapture, if just for a moment, the joy of his love for baseball. Then he sat and took them off.

He heard his name called from behind and turned toward it. Durkin Fain laid his hand on Mike's shoulder.

His tone was almost apologetic. "I'm sorry, son."

Mike shrugged. "Don't be, Mr. Fain. A man makes his choice. He has to take his chances." And he remembered the words of his wife. "There are no guarantees, none that I know of."

Fain nodded. "By God, that's true." He shook his head. "But, still. . . ."

Mike began to strip. He did not want to talk about it now. "Right now," he said, trying to smile, "I'm gonna take me the goddamn longest shower in history."

He let the hot water soak into him. He was too exhausted to think, to take stock of what this afternoon had meant to him. He was dimly aware that at some point he would have to make a decision. But he let himself alone, simply showering for a while, holding his humiliation at a distance. He had never admitted he was capable of such complete failure. He had never imagined facing its sickening consequences.

Instinctively, he felt that he was different now, a different man. He had been slapped down hard, and it didn't matter any more that he had succeeded year after year all the way up to the end. What mattered was that the assumption of his inevitable final triumph had been shattered. He could not keep on pushing knowing this to be true.

He turned his face to the hot, stinging spray, wanting to wash away irrevocably the marks of his grief. He thought quickly of that crying jag, the almost childish breakdown, and felt shame. Deep within him, he guessed, he had been pitying himself with those tears. Perhaps he'd been saving them up, actually suspecting he would lose this bitter struggle in the end.

Now it was all over. He was through. The gate had slammed shut in front of him, and he himself decided it was for the last time. It was final. Complete. To add substance to his thought, he said the words out loud: "It's all over! It's all over!" And he smiled, for he could feel himself coming up, off the bottom.

Gradually he eased the temperature of the water to cold,

and he stood for a moment, stoically, under the fierce needles of icy water.

By the time he had finished dressing, the locker room had cleared out. He stood in front of his locker, reluctant to close it. He picked up his spikes and clapped them together, trying to remove the last cakes of dirt. Then, gingerly, he tied the laces together, and just to see how it felt, he hung them up on a hook.

Behind him he heard the old man, and he turned to see the look of apprehension on Durkin Fain's face.

Mike smiled and extended his hand. "I guess I'll say so long, Mr. Fain."

Durkin Fain grabbed his hand. He nodded, a smile forming on his lips.

"I think I'll have that cigar now, Mike."

Mike watched him light up, enjoying the way Fain handled a cigar. In all his life, he had never seen any smoker caress a cigar with the appreciation that lent such style and quality to smoking. This is Durkin Fain, Mike realized, the number one baseball scout of his time. A time long past. Fain, for whom scouting was an art. Fain, whose only rule of judgment was pure talent, whose only conformity was to his own set of high standards.

Mike said finally, "I'm proud that it was you, Mr. Fain. . . ."

The old man interrupted him with a smile.

"Thank you, son. You got a right to be proud for more than that. You ain't a failure, no matter what they say. I can tell you that. You ain't a failure."

Mike swallowed heavily.

"Goodbye, Mr. Fain. And thanks for the sixteen years."

From the locker-room door he turned again to look back.

He saw the old scout on the bench by a pile of dirty towels, lost in a cloud of smoke. Mike shut the door and turned into the shadowy corridors for the winding passage to the street.

The musty smell changed the direction of his thinking. Yes. Laura. Laura would be there by the players' entrance, he knew. Laura the beautiful. Laura the loyal. Laura the wife. "I love you, darling," he said out loud, just to hear the sound of it. Oh, I love you for everything that's happened to us. For all the lousy years. For sharing them as if there was something special in it for you.

And suddenly, he couldn't wait to see her.

He hurried up the last ramp, feeling a quickening anticipation, as though he'd been away for a long, long time. He wanted to take her in his arms, to tell her what had happened to him, to make her know, at last, that he was her husband and life was for the both of them.

Mr. Fain had said it. "It ain't too late, son. It ain't never too late."

He pushed through the big door and into the street, reaching for her with his eyes as he blinked in the sudden light. But she wasn't there. There was no one there.

He waited for a moment, scanning the streets for her, feeling a sudden panic. Then his eye picked out the neon-lit bar on the far corner, and he knew for sure that he would find her there.

He realized then how long she must have been waiting, how crushed she must have been by the game and what had followed. For Laura, he knew, this would be old hat . . . failure piled upon tired, never-ending failure. She would have prepared herself, as usual, for the wreck of a stubborn man chasing the rainbow with a tin can tied to his tail, over and over, round and round. The man who never gets dizzy, at least not in public.

No, Laura, no more. No more. I'm through with it. I'm free of it! I want *you* only, and we'll begin together this time. Just like you've wanted it for years, darling.

He tore across the street and into the cluttered haze of the bar. She was there, sitting in a lonely corner booth with her hands on a tall glass. He went to her with his gathering tears, bursting with the love and gratitude in his heart.

Everything is all right! Laura, darling, it's all right! Look at me, darling. It's all over. Look at the way I feel.

He saw her look up dejectedly as he came to her, ready to cry out of habit, out of the layer upon layer of frustration that had made up their lives. She almost began, but he pulled her up with his smile, and she found her way into his eager arms.

For a while, they were unable to control the wonderful laughter that poured out of them.

*Widely published author and former minor league player, Eliot Asinof has written extensively on baseball. His publications include his first book, the critically acclaimed* Man on Spikes, *and* Eight Men Out, *his reconstruction of the infamous Black Sox scandal in the 1919 World Series. Asinof lives in Ancramdale, New York, in the house he built with his son.*